HOPE TO DIE

DI SIMON FENCHURCH
BOOK 10

ED JAMES

Copyright © 2023 Ed James

The right of Ed James to be identified as the author of this work has been asserted in accordance with the Copyright, Designs and Patents Act 1988. All rights reserved.

No part of this publication may be reproduced, stored in or transmitted into any retrieval system, in any form, or by any means (electronic, mechanical, photocopying, recording or otherwise) without the prior written permission of the publisher. Any person who does any unauthorised act in relation to this publication may be liable to criminal prosecution and civil claims for damages.

This is a work of fiction. Names, characters, businesses, places, events and incidents are either the products of the author's imagination or used in a fictitious manner. Any resemblance to actual persons, living or dead, or actual events is purely coincidental.

Cover design copyright © Ed James

OTHER BOOKS BY ED JAMES

DI ROB MARSHALL SCOTTISH BORDERS MYSTERIES

Ed's first new police procedural series in six years, focusing on DI Rob Marshall, a criminal profiler turned detective. London-based, an old case brings him back home to the Scottish Borders and the dark past he fled as a teenager.

1. THE TURNING OF OUR BONES
2. WHERE THE BODIES LIE
3. A LONELY PLACE OF DYING
4. A SHADOW ON THE DOOR

Also available is FALSE START, a prequel novella starring DS Rakesh Siyal, is available for **free** to subscribers of Ed's newsletter or on Amazon. Sign up at https://geni.us/EJLCFS

POLICE SCOTLAND

Precinct novels featuring detectives covering Edinburgh and its surrounding counties, and further across Scotland: Scott Cullen, a rookie eager to climb the career ladder; Craig Hunter, an ex-squaddie struggling with PTSD; Brian Bain, the centre of his own universe and bane of everyone else's.

1. DEAD IN THE WATER
2. GHOST IN THE MACHINE
3. DEVIL IN THE DETAIL
4. FIRE IN THE BLOOD
5. STAB IN THE DARK
6. COPS & ROBBERS

7. LIARS & THIEVES
8. COWBOYS & INDIANS
9. THE MISSING
10. THE HUNTED
11. HEROES & VILLAINS
12. THE BLACK ISLE
13. THE COLD TRUTH
14. THE DEAD END

Note: Books 2-8 & 11 previously published as SCOTT CULLEN MYSTERIES, books 9-10 & 12 as CRAIG HUNTER POLICE THRILLERS and books 1 & 13-14 as CULLEN & BAIN SERIES.

DS VICKY DODDS SERIES

Gritty crime novels set in Dundee and Tayside, featuring a DS juggling being a cop and a single mother.

1. BLOOD & GUTS
2. TOOTH & CLAW
3. FLESH & BLOOD
4. SKIN & BONE
5. GUILT TRIP

DI SIMON FENCHURCH SERIES

Set in East London, will Fenchurch ever find what happened to his daughter, missing for the last ten years?

1. THE HOPE THAT KILLS
2. WORTH KILLING FOR
3. WHAT DOESN'T KILL YOU
4. IN FOR THE KILL
5. KILL WITH KINDNESS
6. KILL THE MESSENGER

7. DEAD MAN'S SHOES
8. A HILL TO DIE ON
9. THE LAST THING TO DIE
10. HOPE TO DIE (31 Dec '23)

Other Books

Other crime novels, with Lost Cause set in Scotland and Senseless set in southern England, and the other three set in Seattle, Washington.

- LOST CAUSE
- SENSELESS
- TELL ME LIES
- GONE IN SECONDS
- BEFORE SHE WAKES

DAY 1

Monday

1

The townhouse stood tall, its brown brick worn and cracked. Wrought iron railings embraced the steps leading up to the dark oak door. Narrow windows on either side of the entrance allowed prying eyes only a glimpse into the world within. Mist hung in the early morning air, mixing with cigarette smoke.

Harvey stood outside, adjusting his collar against the cold, took another drag from his cigarette, then did another scan of the park opposite. All through his life he'd heard of Greenwich Mean Time, where all time centred. And here it was, in the middle of a park. And it was so cold.

Harvey let the smoke out slowly, then snatched at another long drag, savouring the warmth filling his lungs. He shut his eyes and remembered the heat of the sun from any number of theatres of war. The cold got right into your *bones* here and this was the warmest part of the UK. Just like back home.

Another scan, slower this time. Taking his time assessing for any threats.

Nobody about, save for a schoolgirl walking up the bank towards the other park entrance at the top of the hill. Maybe a bit too early, but this was London – parents worked long hours, which meant an early start for their darlings.

He took that last drag, then pressed the butt against the wall and pocketed it. The smoke coiled out of his lungs, in total contrast to the first smoke he'd ever had, under the bleachers with his buddies. Coughing and spluttering, trying to act cool.

Harvey missed school. Way back in Boise. Those snow-capped mountains cradling the city. Best days of your life, for sure. He hadn't made any mistakes back then. Wasn't stuck in this shithole of a city just for the money.

He looked back at the house, sitting proud and wedged between smaller townhouses, and reassured himself how secure it was.

'Excuse me?'

Harvey swivelled around to face the sound, fingers itching to go to the handgun in his pocket.

The schoolgirl was smiling at him, head tilted to the side. Thirteen, fourteen. Haircut like some New York salon, though. He recognised the uniform – Leigh Academy in Blackheath, a few miles down the road. 'I know you, don't I?'

Harvey inspected her face more closely. She looked local, certainly sounded it. All these months living here, he'd learned to pick out the subtle differences in the London accents. 'Sorry, darlin'. I don't know you.'

'Aren't you famous?'

'Me?' Harvey smiled. 'No. I'm a nobody.'

'Come on. Everybody's *some*one to somebody. Aren't they?'

'Not me.' Harvey stared at her, hard. 'You don't know me, no.' A polite nod. 'Have a good day, y'hear.'

'Mind if I have a cigarette?'

'Don't have them on me.'

She winked at him. 'Smells like you do.'

'Ma'am, you're way too young to smoke.'

'Am I...?' She walked away, heading on up the hill.

Way too young to be out at this time. And way too young to smoke. He remembered reading this article about how the government was going to move the legal age of smoking up a year every year, so a whole generation would be split by one year group being able to legally buy smokes for their whole lives while another would never be able to even start.

Man, imagine being a day apart from your buddy?

As much as he loved his country, he hated government interfering in people's lives. And over here, that's all it did.

Harvey's earpiece chirruped with the tone earmarked for the client. He tapped it. 'Sir?'

'Harvey. It's Rusty. Rusty Rivers. Can you hear me?'

'I can, sir. And I know it's you.'

'Okay, okay.' Sounded like he was running the bath. Asshole was practically a mermaid. Or whatever the male equivalent was – a merman?

'What can I do for you, sir?'

'I think someone's in the house.'

Again.

Same as every night. Harvey could set his watch by it. When the comedown from his pills and powders kicked in around dawn. Not that the sun had risen again.

He checked the time – tonight was an hour early.

Curious…

'It's not quite time for my—'

'Do it. Now.'

'I assure you, sir, I would've—'

'I *heard* someone, Harvey. *Please.*'

'Sir, I've been out here for the last hour and nobody could've gotten into your home.'

Saying the words out loud even reassured himself.

Harvey had done this gig for over three years and knew every inch of that place. But he also knew of three different ways to get in there undetected by a standard security sweep.

That whole back garden was open and Rusty Rivers wouldn't spend the money on the camera system he recommended.

Sure, Harvey could understand the need for privacy, but when you were that paranoid, your privacy had to be eroded a little bit to give the right level of security. Everything was a balance between two competing forces.

And the things Rusty Rivers got up to in there...

Yeah, Harvey could see why privacy trumped everything else.

Best not to think about it.

'Could the noise be from your guest, sir?'

Rusty spat out a noise. 'He's snoring for England.'

'Sir, I assure you. Nobody could've gotten in there.' Harvey looked up the hill at the young girl, just as she turned to glance back at him. Wouldn't be first time someone had employed a distraction... 'I can do a sweep, sir.'

'Please. If you could? And... do you have your gun?'

'I do, sir.'

'Please, execute the search now.'

'On it, sir.' Harvey tapped the earpiece again, then let out a deep breath.

As much as he liked to reassure his client that he had it all under control, a seed of doubt was blossoming in his head.

Harvey climbed the steps and entered the front door. The ground-floor hallway was filled with the majesty of the oak staircase spiralling up into the heavens. The garish pink wallpaper wasn't something he would've chosen himself, but it sure gave off an impression.

He took the first door, into the living room. Luxury oozed from every piece of furniture. Deep maroon velvet sofas with golden trim and a crystal chandelier hanging above. Baroque paintings on the walls, framed in gold. The white marble fireplace held the remains of a fire, the ashes still glowing from last night.

Expensive. Everything was expensive. And Rusty wanted any guest to know precisely how much.

Harvey moved through the room, his boots soft on the plush carpeting. A glance under the sofas, behind the curtains cascading to the floor in rich shades of burgundy. A silver tray with half-empty glasses of red wine rested on a polished mahogany table, the surface still bearing traces of white powder.

Harvey took a closer look – sure looked like coke, but the slight brownness in the shade gave it away. And explained the paranoia attack from upstairs.

Chasing cocaine with ketamine would choke anyone's sanity. And Rusty was batshit mental to start with.

Harvey would clean that table later.

He moved into the kitchen. Gleaming white countertops and state-of-the-art appliances. Copper pans hung above the island in the middle, each reflecting a slightly distorted image of the room. None of them were ever used – the smeared plates in the dishwasher were the only things that saw action in here. His meals were all shipped in from one of many restaurants across London.

Harvey opened the drawers methodically, his eyes skimming over silver cutlery and checking there were no knives missing. Japanese and French blades that hadn't been used, so were still just about sharp enough to slice through bone. All intact.

The only door led into the larder. Harvey stepped inside, gaze darting around, ever vigilant. The air was cooler in here, a mix of earthiness and sweetness. Rows of shelves, stocked with fine wines, truffles, Belgian chocolates, preserves and jars filled with delicacies. Behind sacks of rice and pasta. None of it ever used, except by him. He felt the walls, ensuring the hidden exit hadn't been triggered.

Nope, still intact.

Harvey walked back through to the hallway and the familiar disdain gnawed at him. This job was a joke. A lucrative one, but a joke nonetheless. And not a funny one. Watching over a washed-up rocker, ensuring his deluded safety in a plush prison. A gilded cage was the cliché, but it was so true – hell, even the curtains were all lined with gold thread.

But was Harvey the reluctant jailor or just another prisoner?

Something rattled upstairs.

Hopefully Rivers, but...

Harvey ascended, one hand on the Beretta tucked away. Short, stubby and discreet. His thoughts spread like spiderwebs, bringing back the urgency from former missions which actually meant something. The spike of adrenaline he craved.

He stepped onto the landing and grimaced. The library door hung open. The walnut bookshelves reached the ceiling. Ladders attached to slide along and climb to get at the thousands of books. A mahogany desk sat in the centre, its surface polished to a shine. The smell of old leather mingled with the fading scent of the last cigar Rusty Rivers had smoked before retiring.

As Harvey scoured the room, the bitterness intensified. He could almost hear the whispered secrets and wisdom these books held, yet they hadn't been touched in years, certainly not since the current owner had acquired them. The whole thing was a curated image to project to people.

A whole floor devoted to books, virtually all of them unread.

Something creaked above his head.

Rivers upstairs, walking around. Pacing the floor, wearing a groove into the carpet.

Harvey wouldn't be rushed, though.

The bathroom door was carved from rich mahogany and embellished with a brass handle. Marble tiles on the floor, each one polished to perfection. A freestanding claw-foot bathtub, its enamel surface gleaming in pristine white, the feet seeming to have been dipped in liquid gold itself. Opposite, a large walk-in steam shower, the clear glass cabinet stretching from floor to ceiling. Multiple shower heads, obsidian tiles with flecks of gold, shimmering under the spotlights. A double sink occupied another wall, beneath a mirror stretching the full width, its edges framed with gold-leaf detailing. And a toilet. But not just any toilet: a state-of-the-art electronic bidet-toilet combination from Japan.

The floor was clear, though, so Harvey moved up to the next one. Each step on the staircase reminded him of the farce his life had become. Instead of the frontlines, he walked these decorated halls, working for a rich asshole.

Up to the third storey and the recording studio door was shut. Unusual...

He nudged it open with the Beretta. Dark inside, so he flicked on the lights. Soundproofed walls, padded with foam. Guitars, keyboards, drum kit and a vintage mixing desk strewn around in organised chaos. Three leather sofas bearing the scars of many a jam session.

Golden records adorned one wall, a testament to Rusty's glory days – to Harvey, they were just shiny bits of plastic, nothing anyone would ever listen to. Another two walls were filled with guitars and neatly coiled lengths of cables.

Harvey scanned over each piece of equipment in the room, ensuring nothing was out of place.

His own room was behind a hidden door recessed into the wall. A single bed and a rack of identical suits and some running gear. The stack of books on the table was just how he'd left it.

Nobody in there or the tiny en suite behind. The shower was still dry.

As he moved back through the studio, his pride threatened

to surge. But he suppressed the feelings – here, he was no hero, just a caretaker of a relic from a bygone era.

Harvey climbed up to the top floor, each step a reminder of his tethered existence.

Three bedrooms up here.

Rusty's guest was sleeping in the spare room. Not snoring now. He'd passed out from too much powder and had to be helped up to bed. Hopefully his heart hadn't exploded from all that cocaine.

The door to the master bedroom was slightly ajar. Harvey approached Rusty's personal quarters, feeling a chill. He nudged it gently with his foot, an uneasy feeling settling in his gut.

The walls were covered in rich wallpaper, deep blues with gold accents. An antique dresser stood to one side. A king-sized four-poster bed dominated the room. The bedding was messed up, the sheets tangled.

Harvey's instincts snapped him back to full alertness.

A rustling. A soft whisper. Then a scream came from the en suite. Rusty's, high-pitched, filled with terror.

Harvey raised his pistol and moved in with swift precision.

Steam veiled the bathroom, coming from the overflowing tub.

Rusty Rivers lay in the middle of the pristine marble floor.

Face contorted in pain, skin marked with fresh burns.

Bound, burned, broken.

His white dressing gown was soaked with red emanating from his groin. Blood streamed down his thighs onto the tiles.

Harvey had seen too many things on the battlefield, but he'd not seen anything quite like this.

Someone had tried to castrate Rivers.

He spun a full three-sixty, his weapon trained, his finger pulsing on the trigger.

But there was no one else here. No attacker, no sign of forced entry anywhere in the property.

It was as if Rusty had tortured himself.

But Harvey knew this wasn't self-inflicted.

'Who did this? Where are they?' Harvey swung around again, his gaze sweeping the bathroom.

'I didn't see...' Rusty's voice was weak. 'I didn't see anyone...' Alive. Just.

Harvey crouched in front of him. 'Sir, who did this?'

Before Rivers could respond, his eyes widened in pure horror.

They weren't alone.

An agonising pain lanced through Harvey.

His legs went numb.

He looked down and the cold steel of a dagger emerged from his chest. Blood soaked his shirt, spreading out from the wound. Shock kept the pain at bay, for a moment.

He was still standing, but knew the only thing holding him up was the knife.

His attacker pulled back the dagger and a spurt of bright red blood shot out as he stumbled to his knees.

Bastard had got the heart or transected the aorta.

Harvey wasn't going to survive this one. He only had a few seconds left. His vision blurred. The room tilted and something thudded into his shoulder. Or his shoulder thumped into something.

He thought of far-off places, of battles fought, of the pride he once held. Now, in this ornate prison, the battle had found him once more.

And as the darkness closed in, one thought consumed Harvey.

He had finally lost.

2

DCI Simon Fenchurch sat back in his chair, cradling his neck in his hands. He couldn't look at the computer screen for longer than about ten seconds before his gaze was drawn to the window. To the wall. To his phone. To anything but work. That whole world out there, where people just got on with things and did stuff. Not being stuck in an office.

A sigh, then he leaned forward again. *Get on with it, you stupid old goat.*

Emails flooded his inbox, like a dam had broken somewhere upriver, drowning him in thousands of the bastard things. A digital deluge of biblical proportions. And he didn't have an ark.

Nobody seemed to have noticed that he'd been off sick for six months. Should've been three, but the best thing for a recovering oxycodone addict was to have to take oxycodone as part of recovery from knee replacement surgery.

Some absolute animal from Scotland Yard had got hold of his email address and return-to-work date, then sent him twenty emails in the last week. Quarterly goals, strategic plans, budget meetings.

The worst part of the flood.

And no bugger had given him any police work. The only email he'd had from anyone more senior than him in the Met hierarchy was the commissioner's update. He was so bored, he was even tempted to try reading it.

His mouse wheel clicked as he sifted his way to the bottom of the lake.

Nothing from the new boss. Nope.

Great.

Not even a cursory "welcome back" email, outlining when the new broom wanted to catch up.

Nope.

What a way to make a guy feel welcome.

Fenchurch sipped his tea from the Rangers mug. Not even his Scottish team – Aberdeen, for his sins – and not even the same mug he'd inherited from his old boss – the last two had ended up smashed against the wall. He had to keep replacing them to maintain that connection with Al Docherty.

He sank the last of his tea. Time for another cup.

He got up and his phone rang.

Dad calling…

Not that Fenchurch would seek him out for a dose of sanity. He answered it, anyway. 'Morning, you old bugger.'

'Simon.' Sounded like he was eating a biscuit. 'How's your bollocks?'

'They're both fine and swinging away, Dad.'

'Good, good.'

Fenchurch made his way along to the kitchen and emptied the kettle, then filled it again. 'What's up?'

'Listen. I was thinking we should celebrate tonight.'

'We are.'

Long pause. 'Are we?'

'It's Al's birthday, Dad. He'll be six.'

'Right, right. So what's the plan?'

Fenchurch wasn't the only one who hadn't read his emails. Or texts. Or remembered the contents of phone calls. 'Six o'clock, the flat.'

Hard not to say 'our flat'.

Easy not to say 'Abi's flat'.

'I'll be there, son.' Another bite of a biscuit. 'Something I read in the paper this morning got me thinking, though. About this girl from Canning Town who got abducted. Not a bad background, full of neglect.'

Fenchurch filled his mug with hot water, burning the teabag. He didn't say anything, because he knew what was coming next. Instead, he mashed his teabag against the side with a spoon.

'It's six years since we rescued Chloe.'

'Dad...' Fenchurch felt that tightening in his throat and his chest. 'What? Wait. That was in June?'

'Yeah, but she didn't want to speak to us, did she? Well, you and Abi. I mean, she was talking to me on the QT. And when Al was born, she—'

'Okay.' Fenchurch tipped the teabag into the bin. 'We'll make it about her too.' He pinched his nose. 'So she doesn't feel left out of her kid brother's birthday.'

'No need to be like that, son.'

'Dad, it's my first day back. I don't want to think about any of that ancient history. I just want to get on with our lives. I think Chloe's in the same boat.'

'Simon, there's no need to sound so judgmental.'

'How am I sound—?'

'Stands to reason, doesn't it?' Another crunch of a biscuit. 'You're basically saying my world doesn't matter. That I don't matter.'

'How the hell am I doing that?'

'Simon, I help families find out what happened to their children. In some cases we even bring them back home. Chloe's a major success for the unit.'

'The *unit*? Tell me you're not—'

'Yeah, son, I'm still working with them.'

Fenchurch splashed some milk into his mug. Stupid old sod couldn't stop. He grabbed his mug and stormed back along the corridor to his office. 'You're *retired*.'

'I know, son. I'm only consulting here. It's part time. Twenty hours a week. And Chloe chips in too.'

Fenchurch felt a different sensation. Not tension or disgust, but pride. Pride that his adult daughter had put her ordeal behind her. Unlike the rest of the family, seemingly.

He eased into his office and slumped behind the desk again. Maybe he was being too harsh – he'd known of so many cops who'd struggled to find purpose after retirement and had just withered and faded. No danger of that happening to Ian Fenchurch, was there? 'Dad, I'm glad it's keeping you out of mischief. But be careful, yeah?'

Dad cackled down the line. 'Always a fair amount of mischief to go around.'

Someone knocked on the door.

'Better go, Dad. See you tonight, okay? Love you.' Fenchurch killed the call. Usually that knock was followed by a push and a barrage of abuse or a request for help. Not today. 'Come in.'

The door flew open and bounced off the wall.

A woman stood there, hands on hips. Short spiky hair, narrowed eyes and a power suit straight from an American drama from the eighties. 'Fenchurch, isn't it?'

'That's right. Can I help you?'

She crossed the floor and held out a hand. 'Detective Superintendent Alison Cargill. Pleasure to finally meet you.'

'And you.' Fenchurch stood up and shook her hand, cold and clammy. 'Sorry, can I get you a tea or a coffee?'

'Up to my eyes in the stuff today already.' Cargill picked up a chair from the meeting table, then flipped it around and sat on it reversed. Tough gal. Okay... 'Just wanted to catch up with you after your lengthy convalescence. How are you doing?'

Fenchurch smiled at her, as politely as he could manage. 'Just going through my emails.'

'Not a more fun task in the world, am I right?' Cargill beamed at her own joke. 'Not sure much has happened in the time you've been away, though. Oh, DI Ashkani is on maternity leave.'

Fenchurch nodded. 'Heard it was a boy. Tariq.' He'd met the little tyke a couple of times. Uzma was going out of her mind. Not that she'd shared that with Cargill, by the sounds of it.

'Indeed.' But Cargill's raised eyebrow indicated she had no idea or interest. 'DI Winter is covering for me.'

'Rod's a good cop.'

'You know him?'

'For years, yeah. Worked with my old man. Shared a few cases over the years. Still leaves us short a DI, though.'

'Which is why I made Kay Reed a full DI.'

'Well done.' Fenchurch sat back and sipped at his tea. 'Been trying to do that for years. She kept turning me down.'

'Well, that's interesting. She accepted my offer. Just takes a firebrand Scot to persuade her, eh?' Cargill's wink was like the slash of a knife. 'Haven't been here that long, though. Thought moving down to the Met from Police Scotland would be a big culture shock, but it's not that different to working in Edinburgh or Glasgow, is it?'

'I suppose not. Most of the brass up there are from down here, right?'

'A few were, aye.'

'Besides, you're not my first Scottish boss.'

'Ah, but I couldn't be any different from the late DCI Alan Docherty.'

'You knew him?'

'We had dealings back in our Lothian and Borders days, as was.'

'As was?'

'It's all Police Scotland now. But Alan was a DI when I was a DC. Good cop, but a bit too generous when it came to people's faults.' She left the words hanging.

Fenchurch raised an eyebrow. 'That supposed to mean something?'

Cargill leaned back on her chair then rocked forward again. 'Thing is, Simon, I'm sure you can understand my predicament. I've come into a new team, where I've got four DCIs covering various areas of East London. Four SIOs. And the clearance rate isn't great, it has to be said. Which is why I'm here. I've got a reputation, shall we say. I get shit done. And statistics being what they are, we need to make some drastic improvements.'

Fenchurch felt the guillotine blade touching the skin on the back of his neck. 'Go on.'

'I'm moving two of the four DCIs on and bolstering them with some deserved promotions. You'll be able to congratulate DCI Rod Winter yourself. The other is about to be advertised. But one of the two DCIs making way will be you, Simon.'

The guillotine blade nibbled at his skin. 'You want to move me on?'

'It's not *want to*. I *am* moving you on.' She looked around the room. 'Between us and these four walls, Simon, you're a dinosaur. And I don't like you.'

The words made him laugh. But he held his expression

steady – he'd faced down old-fashioned hard cases before. 'That's charming, considering I've only just met you.'

'I know your reputation. You're a cowboy who's way past his prime. A relic of the old boys' club and a drug addict who's been over-promoted. I want you gone by the end of the month.'

'Obviously you've got this impression from a bunch of one-to-one interviews with me and from months of direct observation of me in the job. Oh, wait. No, you haven't, because I've been recovering from knee surgery.'

'And from inadvertent drug addiction.'

Fenchurch felt fire claw at his neck. That blade was biting.

'I know all about your addiction, Simon. It's all logged in the case file from a few months ago. Not a problem, really.' But it sounded like it was. 'I'll be keeping a very close eye on you.'

'Ma'am, with all due respect, this is my first day back after —'

'Simon. When my predecessor gave you the opportunity to step up, it's clear from a deep dive into the statistics that he made a gross mistake. You haven't grasped the opportunity and developed your team. The paperwork in this station is *atrocious*. Sure, you might've solved some big cases in that time but you've let a lot of others go. Indicates a high degree of chaos to me.'

'Chaos?'

'Chaos. Let me explain how I see policing. A DCI takes on the role of a senior investigating officer in a major inquiry. That means you're in charge of everything in a case. You set the standards and you need to be across the whole case. All of the detail, but all of the summary. Instead, you've acted like a sergeant. At best. The way I see it, you're clearly a doer but, at your rank, the Met needs leaders. Now, I've got a role ready to go up to advertise your job, so I just need you to decide what fate befalls you.' She left a pause for a few seconds.

He didn't fill it, just slurped at his tea.

'I mean, you could retire.'

'I'm not retiring.'

'O-kay... Well. In that case, I'll present you with three options. I've sounded out the respective supers and they're all keen to work with you.' She tossed a manila envelope onto his desk. 'First, you've got a chief inspector role in Media and Public Affairs.'

'Press office? Are you kidding me?'

'It's an important role, Simon. Leading the liaison with the press and broadcast media.'

'Okay. You've only just met me, but you've clearly pegged me as someone who can't lead. So why is this role a good fit?'

'Because all of the strategic work in that area has been done. This position is all about doing. Engaging with external stakeholders to deliver on—'

'No.'

'No?'

'No way.'

'Come on. It's a good role.'

'Not for me it isn't. And I'm not great at engaging with stakeholders, internally or externally.'

Cargill glanced at a photo on his desk. 'I heard all about your daughter.'

'So did half the western world.'

'It could be argued that you led a successful personal campaign to recover your own daughter.'

'Ma'am, with all due respect...' Which was absolutely fuck all, but Fenchurch didn't voice those words. 'The sole reason my daughter was recovered was because of the *investigation* I led into her abduction. Nothing to do with a fu—'

'Suit yourself.' She tossed another envelope over. 'Well. If that role isn't for you, how about chief inspector in Essex?'

Fenchurch had often thought of moving out to the coast. A quieter life, a train ride away from London. Sure, there were crimes out that way, but they were mostly different from the inner-city stuff he'd spent a lifetime contending with. And it could be a fresh start. Or even a chance to put things right at home. That was a worm dangling on a fishing rod. 'Tell me more.'

'Interested, eh? Well, there's an opening at your level in Essex Police. Station commander, based in Leigh-on-Sea.'

'Nice place.' Fenchurch tore open the envelope and scanned through the paperwork. No change to salary or benefits. He put it back down. 'But I don't think that's for me.'

'Why not?'

'Because I've been a detective so long I can't even spell uniform these days.'

'Simon, those skills are all transferable.'

'It's a no from me. What's the third option?'

'Well, Simon, we've already covered that one. You should retire.'

'And I told you – I'm not retiring. So I choose door four. Staying here, doing the job I'm really good at.'

She gasped a sigh, dripping with frustration. 'There is an option five. I will bury you. You'll be fired. At best. Or you'll be in jail.'

'Jail. Right.'

'This isn't a choice.'

'I thought it was? I'm staying here in the Met, where I've proven to be a bloody good detective. I've lived here all my life and I'm not about to be shipped off to the countryside. Or into press relations. And I certainly won't listen to idle threats about being fired.' Fenchurch gave her as warm a smile as he could muster, which was like winter in Greenland. 'While I appreciate the career advice, ma'am, you don't get rid of Simon Fenchurch that easily.'

'Think about it. Those are good roles.'

'Thought about it.' Fenchurch passed her the envelopes back. 'They're not for me.'

'Okay. Well, I'm sorry it's come to this.' Cargill stood up and pushed the chair back around, like how a normal person would sit on it. 'Turns out I have an assignment for you that nobody else wants. Due to a spate of stabbings in Lewisham, the South MIT are stretched to breaking. As such, you're going to have to pick up a fresh case from them.'

3

Fenchurch had known Greenwich since he was a boy. Many lovely afternoons spent with his family strolling through the park and all the shops. The museums. Even wandering around the posh streets and peering through the windows of all the fancy houses. Felt a world away from Limehouse rather than a mile or so across the river on the DLR through the Japanese cyberpunk future of Canary Wharf.

Even closer was his flat on the Isle of Dogs, which he could just see in the distance, lurking behind the towers over the river.

He passed the University of Greenwich, then the theatre. The park sprawled in front of him, hidden behind trees. People heading towards the many entrances, walking their dogs or going for runs.

Life.

Fenchurch remembered when he had one. Taking his son to see the observatory on the big hill in the middle, but getting stuck by the sand pit, where Al spent hours building and playing with other kids.

He pulled in behind a low row of cars and looked over at

the house. A long block of buildings sandwiched together. Used to be a school, by the looks of it. Or a good part of one. Not a big school, but an old one. Acid-cleaned brick, with black railings that had somehow survived both world wars or had been restored at some point since. A blue plaque by the door he couldn't quite read – maybe a prime minister or two had lived there. Four storeys, but all the action was upstairs, judging by the arc light glow, punctuated with even brighter stabs of camera flash.

Work.

Press and Essex be buggered, detective work like this was his bread and butter.

'Guv?'

He'd recognise DI Kay Reed anywhere. Her red hair glowed in the dull morning, laced with silver. Funereal black suit and an expression that could kill at a hundred paces, but it slowly turned into a grin. 'Guv!' She ran over to him and wrapped him in a hug. 'How are you doing?'

Fenchurch gave the politest pat on the back – as much as he loved her and loved working with her, there was a time and a place for a greeting like that. And outside a crime scene wasn't it. 'Good to see you, Kay. You been here long?'

'Couple of hours.' She tucked her hair behind her ear. 'How much do you know?'

'Cargill gave me a cursory briefing. Told me you're a full DI now.'

'Oh, yeah.' Reed blushed. 'Well, the way she put it, I didn't have much of a choice. Step up or fuck off.'

'Sounds familiar...' Fenchurch could've crept down a rabbit hole, descending into a dissection of Cargill's character, based on one meeting. A meeting where she'd acted like an arrogant arsehole, but still – that wasn't going to solve a murder. 'Is DI Doyle here?'

She waved at the townhouse. 'Upstairs.'

'Acting up?'

'You know Ronnie. He's always acting up.'

'I meant as DCI.'

'I know what you meant, but I still wanted to get my crap joke in.' Reed touched his arm. 'Come on.' She crossed the road and signed them both into the crime scene.

As she scribbled, Fenchurch took in the vicinity. Two cars in front of a double garage next door. A Rolls Royce, looking even older than his father. And a Lexus that could belong to Batman – black armour-plating, darkened glass, just missing that gummy-teeth bat logo.

'Guessing there's security here?'

'We think so.'

'Think so?'

'Hard to say when nobody can talk to you on account of them being the wrong side of a knife.' Reed handed the clipboard back to the uniform, then led Fenchurch into the courtyard in front of the house and skipped up the steps to the open door.

Fenchurch followed her into the entrance hall. He hadn't seen that much pink since helping at a Pride march a few years back. Garish and chintzy as hell, with everything threaded through with gold – a roll of the wallpaper probably cost a cop's salary.

The staircase leading up was blocked off by a fierce-looking female uniformed officer. She nodded at Reed but her glower for Fenchurch was pure hostility. A whisper from Reed. 'Good morning, sir.' She tossed a crime scene suit over.

Fenchurch caught it, then stepped into the trousers like he was a new recruit. He didn't have to compensate for the wobble from his crunchy old knee. Stability, instead. It bred confidence. He tugged on the overshoes without having to sit down, then zipped up his jacket. Not even out of breath.

Reed was already halfway up the stairs, so Fenchurch took

them two at a time.

The first floor contained a library and a bathroom, both getting a good scouring by CSIs.

'Simon bloody Fenchurch.' The nearest CSI looked up, cheeks filling the goggles. Mick Clooney. Been a while since Fenchurch had seen him. 'How the devil are you?'

'I'm good, Mick. Well, that's maybe stretching things. How are you?'

'Fucking awful, but hey ho.' Clooney shrugged. 'We've found coke.'

'As in cocaine?'

'I think so. High-quality stuff. Possibly some ketamine too.'

'So we've already got evidence of hard drug taking. Interesting.'

'Right.'

'Not seen you in a while, Mick.'

'Nope. Teaching at Hendon wasn't for me. I got bored. So I'm stuck back here, doing the Lord's work. And you know what they say about delegation?'

'Learn to do it?'

'Eh? No. It'll catch you and bite you on the arse.'

'You're talking about Tammy?'

'Right. Bad enough when she was sleeping with your dad.'

Fenchurch scowled at him. '*What?*'

'Come on, you must've heard the stories.'

'*My* dad was sleeping with Tammy?'

'He broke it off, then she got engaged to some idiot. And now she's pregnant.' Clooney laughed. 'Unless your dad's the baby daddy.'

Fenchurch knew it was a wind-up, so he just smiled it away. 'Catch you later, Mick.' He followed Reed up the stairs, but he couldn't shake the feeling his old man had been hiding something from him. Not for the first time in his life. Or the last.

The second floor would've passed for heaven to teenage

Fenchurch. A band room – drum kit, bass and guitar amps, keyboards and microphones all hooked up to a giant iMac and a mixing desk. The floor-to-ceiling speakers could fill Wembley Stadium. The walls were decorated with gold discs and guitars.

Fenchurch stopped. 'Cargill said this place belongs to Rusty Rivers.'

Reed turned around. 'Don Avonmore, AKA Rusty Rivers of Rusty Rivers and the Reeds.' She shook her head. 'Had a lot of cheeky banter about that because of my name.'

Fenchurch winced. 'I know his music.' He waved a hand at the gold discs. 'Got three of his LPs at home in the flat...'

Reed frowned. 'Isle of Dogs flat, right?'

'Right. I've... been there since Jon Nelson moved out. Glad I kept it on; hasn't been the easiest at home.'

'Sorry to hear that, guv.'

'Abi hasn't kept you briefed?'

'Haven't heard from her in a while.' She smiled at him. 'What was Mick saying about your dad and Tammy...?'

'No idea, Kay. Some bollocks about them seeing each other.'

'Sure it's bollocks?'

'Oh, I'm sure.'

'Well.' Reed skipped off up the final spiral.

'What's that supposed to mean?' Fenchurch took his time, savouring the mechanical precision of his stride now. He scanned the top floor. Three doors, two hanging open. The first looked like a bedroom, but was blocked by CSIs working away.

Reed pointed at it. 'Found one body in there.' She entered another door. 'This is where the other was found.'

Fenchurch snapped on his mask and goggles, then followed her into a luxury bedroom, decked out like a honeymoon hotel room. Four-poster bed, chintzy antique furniture.

A bloodstained outline lay on the deep carpet, right in the middle of the floor. A trail led into the en suite.

Fenchurch stopped dead. 'What happened to Rivers's

body?'
'Rivers?'
'Yeah. This is his house.'
'He's not dead, guv.'
'Wait. There were two bodies?'
'And he's not one of them. He's at the Royal London.'
'So who died?'
'Om pom tiddly om pom. Billion-dollar question, my old friend.' Dr William Pratt stood in the bathroom doorway, his bulbous beard filling out his mask and pushing his goggles away from his eyes. 'I'd say it's good to see you back, Simon, but you haven't been missed.' He bellowed out a muted laugh. 'Yes, Don Avonmore was still alive. Just. Lost a lot of blood from a wound to his groin.'

Fenchurch felt his stomach clench. 'His groin?'

'A testicle had been removed. A good go had clearly been made at the second one, but the vas deferens remained intact.'

'My God.'

'Indeed. A home-made castration.'

'Will he live?'

'Luckily for me, I only have to answer questions about those who've passed on to the other side, not about the living. But yes, Mr Rivers should survive.' Pratt chuckled. 'His real name is curious, though. Don Avonmore. Both are hydronyms.' He looked between them. 'Names that come from rivers. His first name is a river up in old Aberdeen, while the surname is an Irish word meaning "big river". Curious that he chose Rusty Rivers, no?'

'Always thought it was a dreadful name.' Fenchurch smiled. 'Didn't even think it wasn't his birth one.'

'I mean, it's kind of obvious.' Pratt was nodding along. 'But what a musician.'

'Thought you were just into classical music, William?'

'Oh no, as a young man I very much liked country rock like

Neil Young, America or, my favourites, the Eagles.'

Fenchurch bit his tongue – in his estimation, *Hotel California* was the low point of western civilisation.

Pratt blinked hard a few times. 'But the Reeds were the first musical act I liked as a lad. Thought the tartan angle was novel. Despite Rivers not being Scottish. I think he hailed from Basingstoke, of all places. And, of course, I wasn't aware of Rod Stewart or the Bay City Rollers making it cool at the time. And I was blissfully unaware that Mr Rivers was a bandwagon jumper. Just had to enjoy the music. "Lips as Red as the River" or "Annie from Arizona". Classics.' He looked at Fenchurch. 'You a fan?'

'Of his later stuff, sure. He recorded some good albums later on.'

'What, like that *Blood in the Water* abomination?'

'It's a classic. They called him "the British Neil Young".'

'It's a disgrace. So atonal.'

'I like it. And that album he did with Brian Eno in the late seventies at the same studio as Bowie. Even had some members of Kraftwerk on it. Allegedly. An under-looked classic.'

'Sounded like a broken radio. Hardly toe-tapping stuff.'

'No. Few decent albums after that, William. "Die in My Arms" was a massive hit record, though. Then all the cheesy stadium shit in the nineties.'

'Now, that I liked. A return to form after all that experimental nonsense.'

'Then he retired. I saw him on the reunion tour with the Reeds, but that was it.'

'Quite the fan, I see.'

'I know my music, William.' Fenchurch looked at Reed. 'Who's his next of kin?'

'Nobody that we know of.' Reed shrugged. 'Parents both dead. Married in the early eighties, but divorced a few years later and he's been single ever since.'

Sounded a lot like closeted rock stars like Elton John or Freddy Mercury. 'Was he gay?'

'Not that we know of. Usually they'd have beards.'

Pratt rubbed at his. 'That doesn't make you—'

'No.' Reed rolled her eyes. 'It's a term for the woman hired to pretend a gay man is straight. The female equivalent is a merkin.'

Pratt scowled at her. 'A gherkin?'

'No, a merkin. It's a pubic wig.'

Pratt laughed. 'Well, you live and learn.'

Fenchurch switched his gaze back to the pathologist. 'If Rivers isn't dead, William, who is?'

'I've not yet had a chance to look at victim two.' Pratt waved through to the other room. 'But as pertains to victim one, please come with me.' He stepped into the en suite.

Big enough to fit eight people in, with five CSIs working away.

A younger man lay on the tiles. Maybe mid-forties. Black hair, tanned skin despite the time of year. Fancy suit, his white shirt dyed red with congealed blood.

'Our friend here was killed by a knife through the heart.' Pratt pointed at his chest. 'Now, I need to confirm this later at the post-mortem, but a cursory glance revealed a distinctive cut mark.' He fixed Fenchurch with a hard stare. 'Remember that case a few years back, Simon, where we had one of those anti-zombie knives?'

Fenchurch felt a tightening. He'd witnessed that murder. Him and his wife. A young woman's life snatched away from them before his eyes. 'Absolutely brutal. The name of the knife meant "excessive", right?'

'Indeed. A Blackhawk BESH XSF-1. Illegal in this country, but that doesn't stop them getting in, does it?'

'Sadly not.' Fenchurch sighed. 'I'll let you inspect victim two. Any idea who found them?'

4

Fenchurch stepped back out into the cool morning and took in the scene, his crime scene suit still flapping in the stiff breeze. A brute of a Range Rover slowed on the main road, the rubbernecker hidden behind the darkened security glass. A huddle of uniforms spotted Fenchurch, then scurried off to canvass neighbours.

Reed stood there. 'That's him, guv.'

A wizened old sod was talking to a uniform. The flowing white hair and beard of a medieval wizard. Jeans and an Old Guys Rule T-shirt, with big muscles bulking it out, the veins on his arms like thick ropes. Despite his appearance, he still worked out. And a lot.

Fenchurch made his way over and was met with a crushing handshake.

Bright eyes shrouded by thick eyebrows as he looked Fenchurch up and down. 'Don't recognise me, do you?'

Fenchurch gave him a few seconds, then shook his head. 'Sorry, sir.'

'Neil Fields. Hackney Borough Commander in the London Fire Service.'

Fenchurch frowned. 'Isn't that Declan Walsh who—'

'Sorry. I *was*.' A mischievous grin spread across his face. 'But I have to say I'm a little bit disappointed. Seventeen years ago, I worked with you to assess a vicious bit of arson in Hoxton Square.'

Fenchurch felt a cold hand reach inside his heart and squeeze tight.

The first case he'd worked since his short break after Chloe's disappearance. When he decided he stood a much better chance of finding her while being a cop.

Fenchurch tried to hide his inner turmoil with a grimace. 'Two bodies found upstairs, right?'

'Right. We never caught who did it, either.' Even to a seasoned old fireman like Neil Fields, despite the blame mostly lying on Fenchurch's side of the fence, that failure in detection clearly still rankled.

'The kind of statistic I really hate.' Fenchurch couldn't look too long at those beaming eyes. 'So, what brings a chief of the fire brigade here?'

'I retired a few years back. Bit of a squeeze going on, so they let me go early. Meant one of two things. Well, three. First, I got better terms on my retirement – an extra six years' service to get me out of the door. Second, I'd patented an alert mechanism with a mate of mine. Turns out, it's actually a lucrative earner. And third, my knees gave out. Replaced both of them and I feel like I'm twenty-five again. Actually, better – I can rack squat a hundred and twenty kilos.'

'Tell me about it.' Fenchurch tapped at his new knee. 'Had mine done. Talk about a new lease of life... So, tell me why you're here.'

'Live next door.' Fields pointed at the humble sixties bungalow loitering in the grounds of the old school. Probably bought for a reasonable price way back when but now had the value of a small European country's GDP. 'Came out for my morning walk to get my paper, as you do, and I heard screaming from inside. Not loud, of course. Faint.' His beaming eyes seemed to dim a little. 'Sure a man like yourself knows how to differentiate between certain sounds.' The gaze drilled into Fenchurch but he still didn't look away. 'Know how to identify screams.'

'Of course I do.'

'Hear them in my sleep. Not that I get many hours each night.' Fields bellowed out a laugh. Inappropriate for a crime scene, but it let Fenchurch know he was getting somewhere. 'Anyway, I broke inside to see what the hell was going on. Then I saw the bloodbath and called it in.'

'This was this morning?'

'Right. First thing, like I say. Rain or shine, I grind my way out of bed to do a few circuits of the park to get the old ticker pumping.'

'You see anything?'

'Someone ran off.' Fields pointed at his feet. 'Couldn't chase him, even with my robotic knees, so I focused on preserving the scene and saving Don's life.'

First-name terms.

Fenchurch nodded. 'Can you give us a description of this man?'

'Too far away, to be honest with you. Young, though. Or dressed young.'

'White? Black?'

'Didn't see. It was too dark.'

Trouble with murders in November...

'Okay. You can get back to giving your detailed statement, but I guess you know the drill?'

'Sure thing.'

Reed took over. 'You know Mr Avonmore well?'

'Shared a few whiskies from time to time, yeah.'

'You ever hear any strange noises from in there?'

'Even though the bugger's got a demo studio upstairs, I never heard a peep. Don's a man who likes his privacy, you know what I mean? Spent a lot of time in front of thousands of people, so when he's not doing that he likes to be in control of everything. Who comes and goes into that house.'

'And yet you heard the screams?'

'A window was open a crack.'

'Right, right.' Reed turned to glance at it, as if seeing it for the first time. Flashes came from upstairs, from a different room than before. Hopefully that meant Clooney's team had progressed on to the third victim.

Reed looked back at Fields. 'I imagine that kind of control means he's got a seriously good security system?'

'You'd think, wouldn't you?' Fields tugged at his long beard. 'Became a bone of contention between me and Don, truth be told. The business who makes me my money is in the security game. Told Don he should get a decent setup like I've got. My gaff's nothing like the size of his, but I'm totally secure. I mean, it's all electronic stuff. Cameras at all angles, inside and out. Hardened too, so if the grid goes down, it's still recording. Never know who's out there, especially at night. But Don... He was leaving it to eyes and ears, and not electronic ones.' He shook his head. 'I mean... It's going to be an absolute nightmare for you lot to find who did this, right?'

'Right. Any of your cameras point into his property?'

Fields shook his head. 'Another bone of contention. He wouldn't let me.'

'Okay, sir.' Fenchurch smiled at him, then focused on Reed. 'A moment, Ser—*Inspector*.'

'Sure thing.' She stepped off to the side, turning away from Fields. 'What's up?'

'He's our first suspect, okay? Doubt he's done anything, but clear his alibi as a priority and review his security system anyway.'

'Will do.' She looked Fenchurch up and down. 'Why are you still wearing your crime scene suit, guv?'

'Because I have to put a bloody new one on each time. Besides, I'm not finished inside.' Fenchurch patted her on the arm, then went back into the townhouse. He nodded at the crime scene manager again, then climbed the stairs with speed and confidence, both things he'd lacked in recent years. He reached the top floor without losing any breath, and picked up a fresh pair of gloves from the pile and snapped them on. Another nod from the upstairs crime scene manager, then he lowered his goggles and pulled up the mask, and walked into the second bedroom.

About half the size of the master's en suite, let alone the actual bedroom, but with as many CSIs pottering around.

'Om pom tiddly om pom...' Pratt was standing in the middle of a bedroom, arms folded, thinking hard.

Fenchurch joined him but didn't say anything, just examined the scene.

A male body lay on the bed, soaking the cream sheets to a thick vermillion. Naked save for black trunks. Skinny torso, white flesh. Track marks dotted all over his arms and legs.

Heroin addict.

'Om pom tiddly om pom...'

'How's it looking, William?'

'Mmm.' Pratt looked over like he'd just spotted Fenchurch for the first time. 'Well, we've got the same cause of death as with our friend through in the other room.'

'Stabbed through the heart?'

'Quite. This is a precision kill.'

'Same knife?'

'Indeed. Surgical, but not medieval surgery like the attempted castration.'

'So, you're suggesting a professional assassin did this?'

'That's one possibility. Thing is, you can learn anything from YouTube videos or the like these days.'

'You're saying someone's trained themselves to an assassin-grade murder from *YouTube*?'

'No. I'm saying you can learn how to drum or make a pizza or survive a Japanese winter on YouTube. But when I said "or the like", I mean there are other services which have less wholesome topics…'

'Right. Got it.' Fenchurch swept his gaze around the room. Like a standard spare room anywhere, just like the one he had in his flat – barely any furniture, just somewhere to shove a bag or a case. And its own en suite. They'd be lucky to get any evidence from here. 'Heroin?'

'I'd suggest so, yes.' Pratt cleared his throat. 'But you've got a mystery, Simon. Two dead bodies and no identity likely until Mr Avonmore recovers.'

'Nope.'

Pratt frowned at him. 'Excuse me?'

Fenchurch waved a hand at the corpse. 'I know who this guy is. Adrian Thornhill.'

Pratt turned to face him. 'How the devil do you know that?'

'So much for you being a fan, William. He was the guitarist in the Reeds.'

5

Gold lettering adorned the entrance, announcing Spangler Entertainments to a quiet back lane, with just Fenchurch standing there in the rain. The shiny glass doors reflected Soho's blend of modern greys and sixties neon chaos. The whole area still offered promises to those who dared to dream, promises made by those who exploited those dreams.

DI Ronnie Doyle caught up with Fenchurch. His dirty black hair soaked up the rain, but his tall quiff flopped forward. His jawline was a patchwork of grey stubble. 'You a fan, guv?'

'Of Rusty Rivers? Yeah, a bit. Some decent stuff. You?'

'Old man loved him. Not my cup of tea. Met him once, though.'

'How?'

'Some shit with school. Rivers was from around the corner. Paying it back to the community or some bullshit like that. Did an acoustic gig, spoke to us. Weird how you get some famous locals, isn't it?'

'Nobody famous lived where I'm from until after I moved out.'

Doyle smirked. 'How's your old man?'

'He's... Dad. Heard a rumour he'd been sleeping with someone. A CSI.'

'Yeah. Tammy, right?'

'How the hell am I the last to hear this?'

'Not sure, guv.' Doyle scratched at his stubble. 'Remember when I was working with him, he only had eyes for your mother. Then she... went and he's been a bit of a lost soul ever since.' He grabbed Fenchurch's arm. 'Guv, don't begrudge him a bit of happiness in his dotage.'

'I don't. Just wish he'd told me.'

'Right.'

Thing with Doyle was he lived in the past. All those old war stories, might as well have happened to some other daft sod.

'Remember when we...' Doyle cleared his throat. 'I worked Chloe's abduction, remember? Had to keep you and your old man away from it. It wouldn't have been good for a conviction. At least you respected that. Him... Less so.'

Fenchurch scratched at his neck. 'It's nice working with someone who knows what I've been through and doesn't judge me for it.'

'Everyone needs a mentor figure, guv. Just a bit weird having to call you guv, guv.' Doyle gestured for Fenchurch to go first.

He pushed through the door, his coat already heavy with central London's drizzle.

Inside, the atmosphere was thick with the musky scent of expensive perfume and bitter coffee. The walls were covered in glossy headshots of young talents, their smiles too bright, too hopeful. A few faces Fenchurch recognised, but from a couple of decades into their careers, not these lost pictures of innocence.

Plush red carpets led the way to a black marble reception desk. A middle-aged woman sat there, her raven hair streaked with silver, flowing down her shoulders. Her crimson lips matched perfectly with the long nails that danced across the keyboard. Glasses rested on the bridge of her nose as she looked up, her eyes assessing and cool. 'Can I help you, sir?' A warm voice dripping with honey, her eyes shooting between Fenchurch and Doyle, then back to her screen and whatever she was typing.

'Looking for—'

'I'm afraid Mr Spangler is busy this morning.'

'It's not him we're looking for.' Fenchurch took a moment, letting the weight of his news hang between them. 'Are you Gina Thornhill?'

She raised an eyebrow, her fingers slowing but not stopping. 'I am. And you are?'

'DCI Simon Fenchurch.' He held out his warrant card. 'This is DI Ronnie Doyle. I wondered if we could—'

'Adrian.' Her poised exterior faltered just a touch, eyes widening, but she still typed. 'This is about Adrian, isn't it? What's he done now?'

Fenchurch took a deep breath, feeling the gravity of his words. 'I'm sorry, Gina. We believe we found his body earlier today.'

Her fingers stopped, the typing halting mid-sentence. Those piercing eyes, which had assessed and judged countless hopefuls walking through those glass doors, now bored into Fenchurch, searching for the hint of a joke or a lie.

But his hardened gaze offered her no reprieve, no hope.

A shaky breath escaped her lips. 'What happened?'

'We're still piecing it together.'

'He's really dead?'

'I believe so, but we'll need you to confirm his identity for us.'

'Yes, of course.' She wiped away at her eyes, catching a tear before it smudged her make-up.

'When did you last see your husband?'

'It's...' Gina leaned back, her hands covering her mouth as a single tear made its way down her cheek. 'It's complicated. I spoke to him on Tuesday.'

'You're not together anymore?'

'No, we are. He's... Listen. You know who I am, right?'

Fenchurch shook his head. 'Sorry.'

Gina looked at Doyle. 'You?'

'Your face is familiar, but I can't place you.'

'Gina Allen, as was. I was a Page Three girl in the early nineties.' She hefted up her bosom. 'A whirlwind romance and I ended up hitched to Adrian. I was on the verge of making it big, but he wanted me to stop doing that shit, so I took this job. Damn good at it, I am. But he... Adrian was always away with the band or in a studio. Or doing some session stuff somewhere. Cannes or LA or some part of London that might as well be Cannes or LA. And I barely saw him.'

'But you last saw him on Tuesday?'

'Right, right. I went home because this place was getting fumigated... Mr Spangler's a bit of a neat freak, shall we say, and was worried there would be cockroaches. Wouldn't listen that it was extremely unlikely. He was at his house in Scotland, anyway. It was just me here and he told me to take the week off, so I did. Went home and I find Adrian smoking crack with—' Her eyes shot between them. 'Let's just say a friend.'

'Someone in the music business?'

'Right.'

'Someone he's done music with?'

'No. Just a friend, I think. But in that world, yeah. But... Who smokes *crack* on a Tuesday? And at his age?' She leaned back and stared up at the ceiling. 'Did he die of a heart attack?'

Doyle shook his head. 'We believe he was murdered.'

A loud breath rattled her lungs. 'My God.' She let out a slow breath. 'Where? At his flat?'

'You don't live together?'

'He's got a flat... Despite still being married, we learned to have separate addresses.'

Not that Fenchurch could judge...

'Your husband was with Don Avonmore AKA—'

'*Don* killed him?'

'No. Mr Avonmore was assaulted too. Along with another man.'

'Jesus.' Gina walked over to the window and looked out. 'I always thought Adrian's heart would pack in. All the drugs. Not to mention the drink. Never thought... Never expected someone to *kill* him. Will you catch who did it?'

'I promise we'll do everything we can to find out what happened to your husband.'

Gina was now lost in a world of grief, barely acknowledged Fenchurch's words.

'Can I have a word, Inspector?'

Fenchurch swung around.

A man stood in the opposite doorway. Tall, with an athletic build hinting at hours spent in expensive gyms. Tailored suit hugging his frame in just the right places. Charcoal with pinstripes, crisp white shirt, the top button casually undone. The glint of a vintage Rolex. Black Italian leather shoes. Silver hair, trimmed precisely, his ice-blue eyes sparkling with mischief – a man who had seen it all but still yearned for more.

Rick Spangler.

In the heart of Soho, where talent was ten a penny, Spangler was the man with the golden ticket. And he knew it. He disappeared into the office.

Fenchurch nodded at Doyle – stay with Gina – and got one back in confirmation. He followed Spangler through the door.

Spangler was looking out of the window, tossing a stress ball.

Fenchurch joined him. If you craned your neck, you could

see Brewer Street at the end. 'How much of that did you hear, sir?'

'Enough.' Spangler turned to Fenchurch. His smile could warm any room, but it also served as a reminder – beneath the sharp suits and charm was a sharper mind that was always working, always calculating. 'Bullet points... Adrian's dead and Don's been attacked?'

'That's right, sir.'

'Bloody hell.' Spangler leaned back against the window and ran a hand down his face. 'You know, I've worked with Don and Adrian for the best part of forty-five years. When I met them back in 1976, they were washed-up has-beens in their mid-twenties. Punk was happening and their form of pop music was as unpopular as prog rock. And they loved to party. And when I say party, I mean stick smack in their arms. In this industry, a few join the 27 Club. Kurt Cobain, Amy Winehouse, Jimi Hendrix, Janice Joplin and so many others died at that age. But most of them just fade away. You'll maybe get your hair cut by one or your shoes shined or meet one driving your cab. Don and Adrian were clearly heading either way, but they still had something. And I could see it. I was working in the mailroom at their record label, just a daft teenager.' He held out a hand. 'My real name is Drew Peacock. You can see why I changed it.'

Took Fenchurch a few seconds to get it. Then he did. He shook the hand. 'Not that Rick Spangler was any better a name.'

'Different times, right?' Spangler smirked. 'Anyway, I talked to them and persuaded them to let me manage them. They literally had nothing to lose. Rusty Rivers and the Reeds were a joke act, with absolutely no artistic integrity that anyone could see. Except for me. See, I'd been obsessed with their singles. My mum loved them, all those rootin' tootin' country songs about a lifestyle they'd never seen up close, let alone lived. But I loved the B-sides. Songs they'd just tossed away in a quick studio session so they didn't have to shove an album track on. Songs like "Lost My Hope but I Found You" or "Live by Myself" had a heart and integrity that "Arkansas Seesaw" or "Rock Across the Prairie" just... didn't. They had such alluring depths when they let their instincts flow. That was the real them. Something special. And I fixed it all for them. Brokered the deal for *Blood in the Water*, which became one of the biggest albums of the seventies. Not quite *Hotel California*, *Dark Side of the Moon* or any of those Zep records, but still. It *sold*. More than Bowie or Bolan or Elton, certainly over here. It made careers, like my own. And it set them up for what came after. Literally the highest-grossing tour of the eighties. And that was all down to me harnessing their talent.' He looked into Fenchurch's eyes. Deep into his head. 'Is Don going to pull through?'

'We don't know.'

'Jesus. Don was in here last week. He's been asked to do Glastonbury next summer. The old-timers' slot. Massive deal.' Spangler blew air up his face. 'This is going to break Gina.' A glance at the door – there was genuine affection there for his receptionist. 'Is there anything I can do to help?'

'We know the identities of two of the three victims. While Mr Avonmore has so far survived, Adrian Thornhill and an unidentified male weren't so lucky. Any help you can give to identifying the other victim would be useful.'

'Do you have a photo?'

'I do.' Fenchurch got out his phone and unlocked it. The death mask of the unidentified man made even him shudder. 'But I'm warning you... it's—'

'Please.' Spangler motioned for Fenchurch to show him. Then winced when he saw it. 'My God.'

'You know him?'

'I do. I don't know his name, but I saw him last time I was at Don's... See, Don had private security. Three men around the clock. That guy... I think he lived there. The others were back-ups. If memory serves, Don said he's an ex-SEAL.'

'American?'

'Right. Navy SEALs are some of the hardest people in the world. Only the SAS can compete, really.'

'Why would a rock star require that level of security?'

'Gina helped organise it. She'll know who you can speak to.'

'That's evading my question.'

'Right.' Spangler sighed. 'I believe Mr Avonmore received some death threats.'

6

Fenchurch pulled in and let the engine tick over. Southwark bustled around them, office drones milling around. An oversized man in an oversized checked shirt with an oversized iPad tucked under his arm, talking at a woman in a raincoat and umbrella. She looked bored.

Southwark had changed so much in the last decade – the modern buildings surrounding the Shard had spread out this way, tech start-ups and financial-services-adjacent businesses gentrifying and polishing as they took over.

Fenchurch let out a deep breath and killed the engine. 'Let's do this.'

Doyle looked up from his phone. 'Do what, guv?'

'Speak to this fella. His name... Let's just say, I'm sure our paths have crossed.' Fenchurch got out into the downpour and jogged across the road.

Rain beat against the stained-glass windows of the old building, an ancient relic dwarfed by the steel and glass monoliths surrounding it.

Fenchurch pushed open the heavy metal door, holding it

for Doyle, then stepping into the dimly lit hallway, a stark contrast to the outside.

CCTV feeds filled one wall, showing silent images of offices, factories and streets. Stale cigarettes mixed with the building's old musk – rotting brick and sour damp.

Yevgeny Kordov sat behind a massive desk, the wood as scarred and beaten from decades of use as his face. A bear of a man, his bald head gleaming in the dim light. Tattoos peeked out from under the cuffs and collar of his wrinkled shirt. One eye glinted, while the other was hidden under a vertical scar. 'Fenchurch.' An unpleasant smile twisted his lips. 'It's been a while.'

Yeah, it was him.

Fenchurch took the chair opposite, acting all casual like they were just two old mates catching up over a beer or seventeen. 'How are you doing, my old friend?'

'How do you think?' Kordov pointed at his damaged eye. 'This was because of you.'

'I might've kicked you in the balls, but I didn't do *that*.'

'No.' Kordov leaned back, the old chair creaking under his weight. 'But you arrested me. Charged me with *bullshit*, which they threw out of court. But only after I was attacked by other Russians in prison. I spent six months in hospital.' He thumped the side of his head. 'I can't see out of this side. Makes me useless in my previous position.'

'You were arrested because you didn't have permits for those handguns.'

'And my lawyer pointed out that I now run a legitimate operation. My previous employer, how you say, she painted between the lines?'

'Painted outside the lines, maybe.'

'Right, yes. Outside the lines. Very bad painter. I followed her orders. To the letter. When I spoke to your friends, they took my evidence and let me go. My previous employer is back in Russia. I was just about to get released and this happened.' His lip curled. 'Why are you here? I am running legitimate operation.'

Fenchurch stared him down. 'Sure. And if I have a look around, I won't find anything dodgy.'

Kordov tapped a cigarette out of the pack and lit it. 'Alright, Fenchurch. What do you want?'

'You to not smoke inside, for a start.'

'Are you going to arrest me? See if you can get them to take out my other eye?'

Doyle stopped mooching around and took a seat. 'Need to ask you a question about one of your clients. A Don Avonmore.'

Kordov exhaled, the smoke curling upwards. 'What about him?'

Doyle licked his lips. 'He is a client, yeah?'

'Not saying no or yes, but I do know Mr Don.'

'He's been attacked.'

A frown flickered on Kordov's forehead. The smoke hung in the air.

'Someone broke into his house. Killed a guest. Tried to kill Mr Avonmore. Killed your operative.'

'*My* operative?'

'We believe so, yes. But the thing is, nobody knows his name. We do know you employ him, though.'

'That may be the case.'

A thin smile crept across Doyle's lips. 'Did you arrange for this to happen?'

'What?' Kordov slammed a hand on the desk, making the CCTV monitors flicker. For a moment, it looked like he might erupt, but then he chuckled, the sound deep and gravelly. 'Always straight to the point with you. Fine, Mr Avonmore is client.'

Fenchurch got out his phone and showed the photo of the unknown victim. 'And this guy worked for you?'

Kordov inspected it. He didn't flinch at seeing at dead man – not his first, probably nowhere near the last he'd see. 'That is him, yes.'

'Got a name for him?'

'Harvey.'

'That a first name or a surname?'

'Neither. His name is Joshua Murphy. Everyone called him that because he once said his father went to Harvard. He didn't. He hate the name, but he accept it.' Kordov handed the phone back. 'I am sorry to hear the news. He was good guy. American. They train the best. But they the hardest to recruit. Especially for someone from my country.'

'What shift was he working?'

'Shift? What do you hear?'

'I heard Mr Avonmore had three men around the clock.'

'Whoever told you that is liar.' Kordov sucked in a deep drag from his cigarette. 'That is not true, my friend. Harvey was there full-time.'

'He lived there?'

'*Da.*' Kordov let the smoke go. 'He has room, just for him. He kept asking to leave, but I get lot of money for him.'

'Harvey get much of that?'

Kordov laughed. 'A lot of that. He is good man. I treat him well.'

Doyle reached over for the cigarettes and took one without asking. He took a light from Kordov's brass Zippo. 'Why does a rock star who hasn't been properly famous for over twenty years need round-the-clock security?'

Kordov tipped ash into an espresso cup. 'You know. I am sure.'

'Enlighten me.'

'Because Mr Don Avonmore received death threats.'

Doyle tapped out his ash onto the same cup. 'Any idea who made them?'

'I hear whispers. Names from shadows. But I am experienced man. I believe what I know and can prove, not what I hear from shadow men.'

'Names would be a massive help if we're to find who did that to Harvey.'

'My friend... The threats were lies. I have people who look into these things. Say is gibberish. But Mr Avonmore... He is control freak. I couldn't persuade him otherwise. He ask me, Yevgeny, please give me full-time security. Please give me Harvey. So I did. And nothing happened. Of course nothing happened. Is bullshit.'

'Until it did.'

'I am sad to hear of Joshua's death. He was a good operative. A great man. He have ex-wife and children back home. This will be hard on them. Still. Shows whoever killed them is one tough cookie, eh?'

Doyle let out a slow smoky breath. 'Or that Harvey became complacent working for an aged rock star with delusions and paranoia?'

Kordov shrugged. 'Maybe with other men, but not with Joshua. Even in the most, how you say, banal of places, he would be thorough. He was professional to the end.'

'Okay. But someone killed him. A surgical strike through the heart. A professional, maybe. Certainly someone who knew precisely what they were doing. It could be those threats you discounted were genuine.'

'Fine, my friend. Here's deal.' Kordov took another drag. 'If I tell you, you fuck off, *da*?'

'We'll fuck off, sure. But only if it's true.'

'Oh, is true.' Kordov let the drag go. 'The threats came from someone who was in a band with Mr Avonmore.'

7

'This it?' Fenchurch drove slowly along the street of low-slung houses, which opened out into a square dominated by towering oaks in each corner.

Doyle pointed at a townhouse. 'Last on the right, guv.'

Fenchurch took the last space, just outside the address. 'You absolutely stink, by the way.'

'Feel a bit stupid. Gave up smoking four years back. Still, it got Yevgeny to start talking.'

'Shows how brazen he is, that he can commit a crime in front of two officers like that. Only for one of them to join him.'

'Still, it worked. That old trick of sharing someone's vice got him to open up. And big time.'

'I'd have got him to speak, don't you worry.'

'Keep telling yourself that.'

Fenchurch got out. At least the rain had stopped.

The address was at the end of a row of downtrodden townhouses. The paint surrounding the windows was chipping, the windowpanes smeared with grime. Even the brick itself was crumbling. A once-loved garden was now choked with weeds, the skeletal remains of long-dead flowers lining the path Fenchurch walked up.

The sagging front door hung open a crack.

Fenchurch called inside, 'Mr Reid? It's the police.' He held the door and knocked, hard. 'Douglas? Police!' He waited for an answer, then looked around at Doyle. Saw him thinking the same thing, so he opened the door and stepped inside onto uneven floorboards.

The smell hit Fenchurch first. A potent mix of stale alcohol, unwashed clothes and something rotting. First left was a once-grand living room, the kind that would be kept only for Sunday morning, but was now littered with empty bottles, cigarette butts and discarded vinyl records. Curtains drawn, the overhead light blaring away.

Doug Reid slouched on a torn leather couch, a black acoustic guitar resting beside him. The former rock god's eyes were bloodshot and his unwashed hair hung in greasy strands either side of his pale face. A half-drunk bottle of Irish whiskey dangled from his hand. An empty of the same brand had settled at his feet.

Fenchurch walked over and his shadow darkened Doug's face, drawing his bleary gaze upwards. Squinting, one eye shut. 'The fuck're you?' His voice was slurred. His Edinburgh brogue was all twisted by booze.

'DCI Fenchurch.' He flashed his warrant card, not that Doug could focus long enough to read it. 'This is DI Doyle. We've got a few questions for you.'

Doug took a long swig from the bottle, then wiped his mouth with the back of his sleeve. 'Figured the law would catch up with me someday.' He attempted a smirk, but it came out more of a grimace. 'What's it for?'

Fenchurch chose to remain standing. 'Someone's killed Adrian Thornhill.'

Doug's face paled even further at the name. 'What?'

'They also attacked Don Avonmore.'

'Rusty? Shite.' Doug grabbed his acoustic and, as pissed as he was, strummed a beautifully clear chord.

Fenchurch immediately knew it – the opening to "Lost My Hope but I Found You". 'Mr Avonmore's still alive. And someone else was killed during the altercation. When was the last time you saw them?'

Doug swallowed. 'They were here. We were jamming, just like old times.'

'When?'

'Just like when we were top of the charts. Before the drugs and the booze took over and pushed us all apart.' Doug looked away, a hint of anger in his eyes. 'That's all ancient history, though. We were playing some of the oldest numbers. And some new stuff.'

Fenchurch waved around the grotty room. 'They were in here?'

Doug frowned but didn't say anything. The turntable was spinning but the needle had long since returned. 'What's it got to do with anything?'

Fenchurch walked over and stopped the record player spinning. The giant speakers still crackled. 'When was this?'

'Aye. Sure.'

'*Douglas.* When was this?'

The room fell silent, save for the distant hum of London outside.

Doug took another swig of whiskey, then placed the bottle down on the floor next to its brother. 'I can't remember.'

Time for a fresh tack. 'How did you get on with Adrian and Don?'

'We...' Doug clunked the acoustic onto the floor. 'Look, we had our differences, but...'

'What kind of differences?'

'I'd never hurt them.'

'Okay, sure. Great. We'll go and get out of your hair.' Fenchurch leaned in closer, though, his voice low and dangerous. 'I want to believe you, Doug. But right now, you're my best lead and chief suspect. So you better start talking and not stop until the truth comes out.'

Doug's eyes met Fenchurch's, for a moment clear from the alcohol haze. A broken soul, scarred by his life and his choices. 'Listen, I can't... quite remember when. But they were here. We played some old numbers... I think Don wanted to do a small club tour of those old classics... And I showed Adrian some new chords, got my old bass out, then we played this new song I'd written. Rusty... He started vocalising along. Not like words, but sounds and melodies. It all started to hang together.' He looked down at his acoustic. 'Hang on. Where's my bass gone?'

Fenchurch looked around the room. The only other instrument in there was an upright piano, the kind you'd see left in a train station for people to play while they waited.

'Fuckers stole my bass. They'll probably steal that song too.'

'They've stolen others?'

'Tons of them.' Doug tapped the side of his head. 'But I'm too smart nowadays. Recorded all of my songs and sent the tape to myself by recorded delivery. If they release something with the same chords, I can prove they took it from me. Like all the others.'

'You're saying they stole songs from you?'

'Ungrateful bastards, aye. I gave the band their name. Douglas Reid was the first Reed! But the fuckers sacked me and I was only ever a session musician for them. A hired hand who played live for them. They paid me for each gig, sure, but Don and Adrian screwed the rest of us. Recorded all the parts themselves and cut us out of the royalties... We got to go on tour, be a rock star every night, but I was just a hired gun. I was young and so fucking naive. Those two, though, and that arsehole of a manager. They designed it. *Designed* it. You know? To fuck us over. All I've got for a life in the business is this shithole. And a vintage bass some prick's nicked!'

'You own this house?'

Doug looked around. 'Bought it with money they accidentally gave me. Someone at the label thought the bass parts on "Blood in the Water" were mine, but I wasn't even in France when they recorded that album. Paid me a chunk of cash and, to their credit, they didn't come after it. Enough to let me buy this place. Trouble with a house like this, man, is it costs so much to look after. Wish I'd bought a new-build in Dagenham or Chelmsford. Instead I'm saddled with this. Can't afford all the repairs. Only option would be to sell to some property developer walloper.'

'How did you leave it with Don and Adrian?'

'Told them to fuck off.' Doug scratched at his stubble. 'I think.'

Fenchurch doubted that event actually happened. Just the broken false memories of a broken man. 'Mr Reid, I need you to come with us.'

'Why?'

'Because you made death threats against them.' Doyle stood there, hands on hips. Looking around the room. 'One's dead and the other's in hospital. You're a suspect in—'

'FUCK OFF!' Doug threw the guitar towards Doyle, who was too slow in raising his arms. The wood bounced off his head and clattered to the floor.

Doug got to his feet and ran towards Fenchurch, shoulder low.

But with each step, his trousers slipped until they were around his ankles. He stumbled over and fell at Fenchurch's feet.

Fenchurch sighed as he got out his cuffs. 'Let's bring him in, sober him up and see what the hell he's got to say.'

8

A quiet room in a police station was never silent. Somewhere down below, someone was shouting their mouth off.

Heavy footsteps thumped above.

But the two figures on the screen in the obs suite were as silent as anyone could be.

Doug Reid leaned forward, head resting on his hands. A coffee coiled steam around him, but he hadn't drunk any.

His lawyer sat next to him. Dalton Unwin. Big guy, who Fenchurch knew of old. Even through a screen, Fenchurch could sense the anger simmering away – Unwin's righteous fury against a system he attacked as much as he defended his clients.

The door opened and Doyle walked in. He took a few seconds to stare at the screen, then handed Fenchurch a cup of tea. 'Here you go, guv.'

'Cheers, Ronnie.' Fenchurch sat back in his chair and watched, gripping the teacup tight, letting the warmth spread through his fingers.

'Never took you for a Rangers fan, guv.'

'It's Al Docherty's old mug.'

'Ah. That explains things.' Doyle laughed. 'Never took you for the sentimental type, guv.'

Fenchurch smiled then took that sip. 'I have many hidden depths.'

Unwin turned to the camera and gave a thumbs up.

'Show time.' Fenchurch took another sip then set the cup down and followed Doyle across the corridor into the interview room.

Four stark walls painted in a shade of green that might've been cheery when the station opened, but which had since faded to the pallor of a decaying corpse. Fluorescent lights buzzed overhead, the unforgiving glare highlighting every pockmark and scar on Doug Reid's face. He wasn't exactly young, but all the stresses and strains of a life on the road were marked like tattoos.

The acrid reek of old sweat mingled with the metallic tang of fear.

The table was solid and battered. Bolted to the floor but it still wobbled. The surface bore the scars of countless confrontations: cigarette burns, coffee rings and deeper grooves that hinted at violence. Two chairs on this side, one slightly more worn than the other.

Fenchurch let Doyle take the better one, then sat directly opposite the lawyer. 'Dalton. It's been a while.'

Unwin raised his head. 'Inspector.'

'Chief Inspector.' Fenchurch smiled. The radiator clanked and hissed, providing little warmth but adding a rhythmic soundtrack. 'Are you ready?'

Unwin folded his arms across his bulky chest. 'I'm not particularly comfortable with you frogmarching my client in here, especially given his present condition.'

'Frogmarching.' Fenchurch smiled. 'Never change, Dalton.'

'I'm serious.'

'You're acting like we're fascists intimidating an innocent man.'

'My client is innocent until proven guilty.'

'Which is why we're all here, Dalton. We're going to see which of those he is. And you know he's been passed fit for interview by our duty doctor, so quit it with that, please.'

Unwin was tapping his fingers on the tabletop in time with the radiator. 'My understanding is this matter pertains to the murder of two gentlemen at an address in Greenwich this morning. Correct?'

'Indeed. Start the recording, Ronnie.'

Doyle got everything going.

As he spoke into the microphone, listing everyone present, Fenchurch stared down Unwin. This wasn't a battle between him and the interviewee as much as him versus the lawyer. Still, he shifted his focus to Doug. 'Douglas, we've got some questions to ask you. The more truthful you are, the better. Okay?'

Doug was struggling to focus on anything. Blinking too hard, too slowly. 'Fine.'

'Let's get cracking, then. Back at your home, you denied making death threats against Adrian Thornhill and Don Avonmore, AKA Rusty Rivers. Have you had reason to change your mind on that?'

'Nope. Well. Maybe.'

'How about you just tell us what happened, Doug?'

'Fine. I called them. Aye. When I was—' Doug burped into a fist. '—drunk. A couple of times each, I suppose. Maybe more.'

'So you admit to making the death threats?'

Doug raised a finger. 'I admit to drunkenly calling them.' The finger flopped down. 'But death threats? Come on. It wasn't so much that as telling them I wished they were both dead.'

'Sure about that?'

'Course I am.'

'Thing is, they were serious enough for Mr Avonmore to employ private security.'

'Don was never a man to underreact, shall we say. Everything with him was bloody volcanic.'

'He had a security operative staying in his home twenty-four-seven, all because of those death threats.'

Doug laughed, shaking his head. 'Don tell you that?'

'No. We haven't spoken to him yet, because someone viciously assaulted him this morning. Killed two others, including the security operative.'

Doug narrowed his eyes. Despite his state of intoxication, there was a sharpness there. 'Yevgeny Kordov's guy, right?'

How did the bass player in an old rock band know the name of a Russian security operative?

Fenchurch gave him a nod. 'Why do you ask?'

'Because someone sent this Russian heavy around to try and intimidate me. Asked me if I knew who he worked for. I didn't. Got Dalton here to look him up. And he found him. After I saw a few photos of him in military get-up, I thought maybe I'd better not mess with him.'

'This before or after your jam session with them?'

Doug looked away. 'That... might not have happened.'

'But you're sure a Russian visited you.'

'Oh, I'm bloody sure of that.' Doug rolled up his sleeve. In amongst the prison tattoos and healed-over track marks were a couple of fresher scars – five cigarette burns, tracing a line front wrist to elbow. 'Did that to me.'

'Why?'

'Why do you think?'

Fenchurch shrugged. 'You might've hit him with a missing bass guitar.'

'Told you, I found that in the shower...' Doug pressed his

filthy fingernail into the scars. 'It's because I was suing them. Thing is, I know the law. Or Dalton does, anyway.'

Unwin sat back and held his pen between both thumbs and forefingers. 'My client wrote, co-wrote and played on a total of seventeen songs over twenty-seven years, but wasn't credited for that labour. Messrs Thornhill and Avonmore both benefitted greatly from that work to the tune of several million pounds.'

'You're actually suing them?'

'We haven't served the writs, no, but we've been laying the groundwork for it. I've spent money on private investigators to build an evidence trail. She tracked down people who worked on the records. Not just producers like Bradley Sixsmith, but tape operators and tea boys from the studios at the times in question. Some are producers themselves now, others have left the profession. But we've got more than enough to prove my client was in a series of studios when he says he was, so there's a solid claim for missing royalties there. And we're working on evidencing the fact that his contributions had a material impact on the final recordings, including some contemporary demo recordings that have more than a passing resemblance to finished material. And chatter between takes where my client makes strong suggestions to rework elements of the songs. We can prove that not only was he more than a hired hand, but he was a key member of the songwriting team.'

Fenchurch knew the old adage – where there's a hit, there's a writ. So many musicians sued for swiping melodies from other songs, consciously or unconsciously. And that murky world was full of people who'd been stepped on by ambitious stars on the rise. 'So employing a PI to speak to some old tea boys is all you did?'

Unwin knotted his brow. 'What are you getting at?'

'This whole thing… It sounds like the threats weren't just your client calling them after he's had a few.'

'Indeed. We, uh, also got someone to flood them with

messages on social media. Schoolbook, Twitter, Instagram, Facebook.'

'Abuse?'

Unwin's eyes bulged. 'Of course not! Just messages backing up my client's version of events. The intention was to influence the large fan base online and guilt Thornhill and Avonmore into admitting what they'd done to my client and paying up without having to step into court.'

'Was it working?'

'No.' Unwin tossed the pen down onto the desk with a loud clatter. 'Now, the problem you're going to face, Inspector, is my client has a cast-iron alibi for the time in question.'

The radiator clattered a few times in quick succession.

'What time are we talking about here?'

'When you're alleging this attack happened.' Unwin pointed at Doug. 'Last night, my client was at a concert by the musical act known as the Zeroes. I believe this was part of a residency, where they played their four hit albums back to back. My client went onstage with them to play bass on a song during their encore.'

'The attacks were this morning.'

'And my client was in a hotel in Shepherd's Bush until seven o'clock this morning.'

Shit.

Fenchurch tried to keep his face straight but his teeth were itching. 'Doing what?'

'My client wasn't sleeping, put it that way. That's why he's this, uh, *refreshed.*'

'We'll check this out.' Fenchurch shot a glare in the direction of Doug Reid. 'It would've been helpful for you to mention this at your home.'

Doug stared hard at him. 'Mate, I thought you were the Grim Reaper.'

9

Fenchurch walked into the incident room, carrying the paper bag containing his lunch. He did a scan of the room to check if anyone wanted him, but all eyes avoided him.

The joys of being out of the loop for so long.

He didn't feel at home, didn't recognise many of the faces of his own team. And he was the senior investigating officer. He should've been spending his time here, setting up the murder board and establishing processes and procedures, making sure everything flowed, but instead he'd been out interviewing people.

Doing what he was good at. Where he could make a difference.

Maybe Cargill was right, maybe he wasn't cut out for this job anymore. But had it really changed that much?

'Guv!' Reed was waving at him.

Fenchurch walked over and sat down next to her. 'How's it going with your almost namesake?'

'Namesake?' Reed frowned. 'Oh, you mean Doug Reid? Right. Yeah. What a guy.'

Fenchurch put the bag on the table but didn't open it. 'Unwin's pressing me to let him go. He's calling me every two minutes.' He shook his head. 'How's the alibi looking?'

'Wish I could say it's shaky, but...' Reed pulled up a window on her computer.

Multiple angles of the same shot – five old men on a big stage, throwing rock star shapes like they were thirty years younger. Whatever drugs they were on to loosen themselves up, it had worked.

'We've got *fourteen* videos of Doug Reid onstage with the Zeroes. So far.' Reed switched to another folder with a stack of video files. 'Honestly, people spend a fortune to go to these gigs and all they do is get their phones to do the looking instead of being present in themselves. Read this article about how people's long-term memories are affected because they don't actually see the event themselves. Something like the memory of it doesn't go from short- to long-term memory, so people are relying on their devices to remember things. And if you doctored the image, they'd remember that. They'd pass a polygraph because they *believe* they saw it...'

'Fascinating...' Fenchurch watched the video play out in silence.

Doug Reid dominated the stage, smacking his steel plectrum against the strings of his bass guitar. Then he walked up to a microphone and sang lead vocals, while the four members of the Zeroes played behind him.

'This is all good work, Kay. Trouble is, the murders were first thing this morning.'

'I know, I know. It's why we've got a few people tracking down the people at the hotel last night.' She tapped the screen. 'This gig was at Acton Town Hall, but they went to a hotel in Hammersmith after. Kind of place that doesn't shut the bar if there's a guest staying. Doesn't let any members of the public in, either.'

'Got it. The kind of place a rock star can get up to rock star things?'

'Exactly. And those people we have found are all a bit sore-headed this morning and very reluctant to talk.'

'Think they will?'

'Who knows? Thing is, guv, none of this excludes the idea that Doug Reid paid someone to do it.'

'Have considered it, Kay, but I think it's unlikely. While he owns his own place, Doug Reid lives in poverty. He clearly has a drink problem, which will account for a lot of his income. And the rest will go on suing them. From what I gather, Mr Reid hasn't paid his lawyer either, so that case is going nowhere.'

'Level with me, guv. Do you think the death threats angle is overblown?'

'Might be. Doug Reid insists it was death wishes instead, the kind I'd wish to Jason Bell or any number of other berks...' The joke didn't land, so he cleared his throat. 'Way I see it, if it was actual death threats – and I mean credible ones – then Don Avonmore could've just had him arrested. Couldn't he?'

'Maybe.'

'Seriously, though. Doug Reid was besmirching their reputations. Paying people to call Avonmore out on all the socials, wishing the fleas of a thousand camels crawled up his arse... It's still sort of legal. Ish. And doesn't amount to a clear motive. There's no notion that they've got a smoking gun that proves Doug Reid's allegations were bollocks, which might necessitate Doug taking stronger action.'

'Right.' Reed went into her email and sighed, then looked around at him. 'Cutting this whole case back to first principles, we're looking for someone who attacked a clapped-out singer and killed an ageing guitarist. Sure, I can see Doug Reid drunkenly deciding to slot Rusty Rivers and Adrian Thornhill. But to get wasted at a hotel with all his mates in the Zeroes, who are a bit notorious, and still be able to kill an ex-Navy SEAL? And don't forget he tortured Don Avonmore, going to town on him like a medieval zealot.'

Fenchurch nodded along with it. Made perfect sense. 'How's Avonmore doing?'

'Stable, last I heard.'

'I should pay a visit. See if he's lucid enough to talk.'

Reed's smartwatch flashed up a message and she checked it. 'Come with me.' She got up and charged off across the incident room.

Fenchurch grabbed his lunch bag and followed her out into the long corridor leading through the station.

Reed popped into the obs suite on the left.

Fenchurch went in and sat next to her as she fiddled with the controls.

Onscreen, DS Lisa Bridge sat opposite a middle-aged punk sitting in the interview chair. The display might have been greyscale, but it exposed every open pore and every bead of sweat dripping from the rockabilly quiff he kept sweeping back.

Fenchurch unwrapped his burrito. 'You mind if I eat?'

'No, you go for it. Nobody wants you getting hangry.'

Fenchurch bit into the first lump of stodgy Mexican greatness. He chewed, pointing his burrito at the screen. 'Who he?' Spoken through a mouthful.

'James McNab, singer in the Zeroes.'

Fenchurch squinted, trying to reconcile the muscular teenage punk he used to have plastered on his walls as a lad, with the skinny old man he saw now. Gaunt would be a compliment. 'That's *him*?'

'Afraid so.'

'He doesn't look well, does he?'

'He's sixty-seven, guv. And very, very hungover.' Reid turned up the volume.

'Yeah, Doug was with us. He played "Out of the Black" with us. Guested on it back in the day, didn't he? After Ginge left, we had to rope in a load of guest bass players for that record. Then Ginge came back for the next one and we stopped that. So, when we heard Doug was going to be at the gig, of course we asked him to join us onstage. His bass wasn't even plugged in but he rocked with us and his mic was live so at least his vocals were there.'

Bridge leaned forward. 'And after the gig?'

'We were all staying at the Resonance out in Hammersmith. I mean, I live down by Brighton, but I didn't want to drive home after a gig. And they know us there. Let us party the night away like we were teenagers.'

'Was Mr Reid there with you?'

'All night. Geezer still knows how to put it away.' McNab laughed. 'And he did.'

'When did he leave?'

'Be about half eight? Geezer was looking like he was going to fall asleep. We had to put him in a cab back to his gaff in Bethnal Green. Paid for by the promoter, of course. Least we could do. Cheeky sod took a bottle of Irish whiskey with him too!'

'You're confirming his chain of events. Which makes me a bit suspicious.'

'Darling.' McNab laughed. 'You can mosey on up to the hotel and talk to the manager. Cyril, his name is. He'll hand you the CCTV and that'll back it up even better than me, yeah? And you could get a hold of the cabbie who had to endure listening to Doug's bollocks for the whole drive across London at that time. He'll back it all up.'

'We will do, sir. Thank you very much.' Bridge had the frosty look of an experienced cop who just *loved* being told how to do her job. 'Trouble is, they're not too happy to share it with us.'

'Need me to put in a word?'

'That would be helpful, yes. Save me asking my boss to

chase up a warrant. And she's a bit difficult when it comes to that.'

'Excellent.' McNab got to his feet. 'Now, I've got a raging hangover to get back to, so if you don't mind...?'

'You didn't ask what this was about.'

'Eh?'

'You came in here, willingly, to confirm an alibi for a friend. That's great, but you didn't ask what it's for.'

McNab smirked. 'I'm guessing drugs.'

'Nope.'

McNab raised his hands. 'Listen, I don't partake myself. Just booze with me. Always has been. Wine, gin, beer or whisky, with or without the extra e. Lot of old geezers in my game, they'd chuck the contents of a pharmacy's hoover bag down their gullets without a care what it is or what it's going to do to them.' He frowned. 'What is it, then? What's Dougie done?'

'It's about the murder of Adrian Thornhill and the assault of Don Avonmore.'

McNab collapsed back into his seat. 'Rusty Rivers?'

'Yes.'

'Jesus.' McNab sighed, then ran a hand down his face. Those bloodshot eyes stared around the room, locking on the camera, then looking away. 'Pair of bastards, them two. Good musicians, don't get me wrong, but they treated Doug like shit, to be perfectly frank with you.'

'That come from him?'

'Nah, I'm not a mug. Always triple-source my gossip. Heard it from their third drummer and also the band's manager.'

'Rick Spangler?'

'Heard what his real name is? Droopy Cock.' McNab smirked again. 'Stiffed old Dougie for a lot of money. And I mean a lot. Thing is, the word on the street was that clown Spangler got sacked by Thornhill and Avonmore. Some very bad blood between them.'

10

Fenchurch pushed through the automatic glass doors of the Royal London Hospital. The sting of antiseptic hit him, mixed with a thousand human stories, many of them his. But they all came from the past – a few years ago, his present would've been moored to this infernal place. In every day to see his dying mother or, years later, to see his new-born son, struggling to stay alive.

An overworked nurse manned reception, her fingers dancing over a keyboard. Patients queued in front of her, some with resignation, others with frustration.

Fenchurch darted through the doors and passed the signs for the wards. He had to sidestep to avoid clattering into a janitor mopping up a spilled coffee, then made his way past radiology. The faint hum of the machines combined with the low murmur of a radiologist interpreting X-rays for a patient.

He skirted around the intensive care unit, somewhere he'd spent far too many hours, where nurses and doctors moved silently around beds, tending to patients hooked up to a myriad of machines, the constant pulses of light the only signs their hearts were still beating.

Another right turn and he found himself where he expected to be – the sneaky back entrance to accident and emergency.

Dr Lucy Mulkalwar stood amid the controlled frenzy, snorting and sniffing like she was either coming down with something or recovering from a heavy night on the white powder. Tiny and pale-skinned, her black hair threaded through with silver. Shoulders squared but eyes betraying nights without rest – eyes that had seen every wound and injury the East End could inflict. 'Simon?' She smiled, with a tired nod. 'It's been a wee while, eh?' Her accent was purest Glasgow. It'd been a few years since Fenchurch had last seen her, and the odd syllable of East London had tamed that accent, but only slightly. 'What can I do you for?' Spoken like a true East Ender.

Fenchurch stopped to smile at her. 'Looking to speak to Don Avonmore, if that's possible.'

'Aye, good one. Rusty Rivers, eh? My mum was a massive fan of his.'

Fenchurch winced at the language. 'He's dead?'

'No, but she is.' Mulkalwar thumbed behind her. 'Mr Avonmore's awaiting surgery.'

'I was hoping to speak to him.'

'Nope. But I'll give you an overview of what he's been through. Next best thing.' She pulled out a high-end tablet he hadn't noticed and the screen reflected her face. 'You probably know most of this, but I hate leaving anything out, so here goes. As you're aware, the patient was found bleeding out, with one testicle cut off and a huge cut to his lower abdomen.' She snorted again. Then sniffed. 'The large incision to his bowel transected his colon and his small intestines. Have to resect several feet of his intestines.'

Fenchurch hated it when doctors used technical language. He understood the language of the dead – the living was much more arcane. All that saving people's lives malarkey, not the focus on what'd happened to them. 'Resect?'

She rolled her eyes at him. 'It means "cut out".'

'Ah.' Fenchurch felt a stabbing in his own gut. 'Sounds brutal.'

'Aye, and then some. But it's going to save his life. The real problem is he'll only have a semi-colon now.' She smirked at her own joke. 'Other than some potentially bad grammar, it could kill him.'

Fenchurch could only raise his eyebrows.

'Anyway.' She folded her arms around her tablet, seemingly miffed that he wasn't finding mirth in her humour. 'There's absolutely no danger you're getting to speak to him. Told his manager the same.'

Fenchurch scanned around the area. 'Spangler?'

'Aye, I mean... Rick Spangler... That's not a real name, is it?'

'No.' Fenchurch didn't give her the real one. 'Is he still around?'

'Sure.' She set off at Olympic sprinter pace, swooshing through the doors. 'In here.'

The small waiting area's plastic seats were still cordoned off so people couldn't sit together, a lingering relic of the pandemic. Filled with the restless and the weary – two children with small cuts to their foreheads, an old man with a pained expression, nursing a head wound.

Rick Spangler sat on the edge, staring at his phone, clicking his tongue. He looked up at Mulkalwar with a measure of hope, dashed when he spotted Fenchurch. He tried to cover over his wince with a flurry of movement, rising and thrusting out his hand. 'Chief Inspector.'

Fenchurch shook it. 'Mr Spangler.'

Spangler's eyes shifted to the side of Fenchurch. 'Don... Is he okay?'

But Dr Mulkalwar had already gone, heading through the door back to A&E.

Fenchurch turned back to Spangler. 'He's still alive, from what I gather. Going to surgery soon.'

Spangler huffed out a deep breath. 'How's the investigation looking?'

'We're getting somewhere, I think.' Fenchurch held his intense stare, determined not to let go. 'We're unearthing some leads and motives.'

'Sounds positive.'

'Very positive.' Though Fenchurch didn't have a clue who'd done it, he had a nagging feeling that it involved people in the music business. People like Rick Spangler. He gave a friendly grin. 'Handy that you're here, actually. Saves me tracking you down.'

'Sounds ominous.' Spangler tilted his head back and laughed. 'What can I help with?'

'We found some Class A drugs at the premises.'

'Oh. And you, naturally, think they belong to two old rock stars?'

'It's a fair assumption, especially as one of the two owned the property.'

'Ask yourself this. Why was their security guard fired as a Navy SEAL?'

'We don't know.'

'Well, it involved ketamine and heroin. Bad move if you're a security agent.'

'But he was employed privately afterwards.'

'And Don had asked me to investigate his background. It took a lot longer than we anticipated because of who he worked for. All part of my job as manager.'

'Are you able to share that information with us?'

'It's on background only.'

Meaning it was bullshit.

Fenchurch knew this game – throw a ton of unsubstantiated rubbish at the wall to put people off the scent. 'We think the drugs are Mr Avonmore's but we've got nothing to back that up, as yet. What we do know is Mr Thornhill and Mr Avonmore had terminated their agreement with you.'

'That's correct.' Spangler looked up at the ceiling. Seemed to spot something up there that held his attention. 'I'm still a friend, though. With both of them. You know? There's a business relationship and a personal one. They served notice on the former, but not the latter.'

'Do you mind telling me what happened?'

'What's there to say? They notified me they were terminating our agreement. Gave the standard notice period. All fair in love and war.'

'When was this?'

'Last month. But it's just a formality. Unlike a lot of their peers, Rusty Rivers and the Reeds aren't an active concern. There haven't been any contracts to negotiate for upcoming concert tours or any tentative record deals. All I do is handle payments for their back catalogue. Royalties and so on for the remaining territories.'

'Remaining?'

'Well, Don and Adrian sold off their back catalogue last year to an American firm. Got a ton of cash for it. Upshot is they don't get any money for virtually all of their existing songs in most territories, but they've got all that cash now. A few places like Eastern Europe, the Middle East and South Africa weren't included, so I still process those payments for them.' He gave Fenchurch a crafty wink. 'I won't tell you how much they got!'

'Please.'

Spangler frowned. 'Why?'

'Because one of them's dead and the other's been savagely assaulted. Don Avonmore might not pull through. In my game, money is one of the prime motivations for murder. Especially if it's a few million quid.'

Spangler looked away. 'A hundred.'

'What?'

'We sold the publishing rights to their back catalogue for a hundred and twenty million.'

Even as the music business died on its arse, Fenchurch was still blown away by that amount of cash being in play. 'So sixty million each?'

Spangler tilted his head from side to side. 'After my cut and the taxman's, it's about forty million each, all funnelled into limited companies. Enough to see them through their final days and leave a big inheritance. Just didn't think the days would be so short.'

'That is a lot of money. Especially as they've made a lot for years and years.'

'Money follows money, my friend.'

'Still, if someone felt they'd, say, been stiffed by that deal...'

Spangler rolled his eyes. 'Dougie Reid, right?'

Fenchurch maintained full eye contact. 'Talk to me about what happened with him.'

'What's there to say? The guy's completely deluded. Decent bass player, sure, but he had to be told what to do. Always has been. No creative energy whatsoever.'

'So they came up with his parts?'

'Well, yeah. It's not like he didn't know what to do, but the way he'd play... Bass is a support instrument and he was trying to turn it into lead. At least, that's the philosophy of Rusty Rivers and the Reeds. Anything but vocals and lead guitar were there to do a job. He kept pushing that. That's why he's not a full member of the band. That's why Adrian played the bass parts on the records.'

'Which he disputes.'

'Yeah, but some idiots say the world is flat. Doug came to us last year with this big-shot lawyer, saying he'd co-written about half the songs and was due a cut of that money. It was absolute bollocks. Adrian and Don wrote them. They weren't daft. The demos for those tunes were all part of the deal to prove they wrote them. They'll probably sell the demo recordings to a label and release them. And, of course, Doug Reid was on none of them. It was just Don and Adrian. And I'm guessing you've spoken to Doug and he's given you that line about how the band was named after him? Doug wasn't a founding member. The name was there before him. He's just a delusional drunk trying to claw back some cash in his desperate old age.'

'So you're telling me there's nothing in it?'

'Absolutely sweet Fanny Adams. And I've got no real reason to defend them, not after they kicked me to the sidelines and stiffed me on cash for any future albums or tours. But Don and Adrian are friends, I still enjoy the friendship and I made bucketloads myself off of their efforts. All's fair in business, right?'

'Mr Reid doesn't think so.'

'Inspector. Dougie's a damaged man whose mind has been warped by years and years of abusing alcohol and cocaine. He even thinks he had a jam session with Don and Adrian last month.'

'He told us about that.'

'Well, there's nothing to tell. Because neither were in the country on the dates in question.'

'Where were they?'

'Adrian was in Thailand. Don, I think, was up in the Scottish Highlands. A friend of his has a place there. Certainly weren't at a shithole house in Bethnal Green.'

'Interesting how you know his address.'

'I've had to send his letters to the police. And I've had cause to send the police there after another drunken phone call.'

'They do anything?'

'What do you think?'

'You remember the name of the investigating officer?'

'No, but I'll look into it.' Spangler got out a squat notebook and scribbled something down. 'Oh.' He frowned, then folded it away. 'I've been asking around for you, though.'

'What about?'

'I want to help you find who's done this to them. Don and Adrian are friends, first and foremost. And this business I'm in... This industry... It's a hell of a gossipy one. Everybody knows everybody else's business. Or they think they do. So many rumours around everything. Hard to know what to believe. But I've triple-sourced this one. Don was getting hassled by a Scottish rapper.'

'A Scottish rapper?'

'Kid by the name of Kanyif Iqbal. Was following him in the street. Knocking on his door several times. That kind of deal. Security told him to fuck off, but off he didn't fuck.'

'Did you ask Mr Avonmore about it?'

'No, I just heard this morning. Like I said, I was chasing down some old contacts to see if they had anything for me.'

'To your knowledge, has Mr Avonmore ever had anything to do with Kanyif?'

'If my memory serves, they had some cross words at the BRITs a couple of years back. Don was there for a lifetime achievement award. Kanyif was up for best newcomer. I'd had a few, but I remember it well. They had to be pulled apart. I thought it was new versus old, rock versus rap, black versus white. But it seemed to be something deeper than that. They *hated* each other. And most of the venom came from Kanyif.'

'You able to share who told you about this rumour?'

11

Soho's narrow streets pulsed with a blend of modernity and its own unique tradition. A film special effects company sat above two sex shops. Over the road, the entrance to Sixsmith Studios nestled between a trendy coffee shop and a vintage bookshop, the gold-embossed sign the only hint of the magic happening within. That, and the blue plaque:

> Rusty Rivers and the Reeds recorded "Blood in the Water" at this location in March 1974.

Made it seem like the studio wasn't a going concern.

Fenchurch held the studio's heavy glass door for Doyle. 'Wouldn't know it was here, would you?'

'Unless you were looking for it.' Doyle went first and climbed the staircase slowly, his breath coming in heavy bursts, inspecting each of the black-and-white photos of stars from the sixties and seventies. 'You believe this story?'

'Ronnie, I don't believe anything unless it's backed up by about ten different witness statements and we've got it on video.'

Doyle paused to inspect someone who looked a lot like David Bowie. 'Still, money's a solid motive.'

'Yeah, but who benefited from it?'

'Dougie Reid?'

'He hasn't made a penny from them.'

'True.' Doyle set off up the stairs again. 'Got my lot looking into all of their bank accounts. Not a simple matter, I'm sure you can imagine.'

Fenchurch stopped on the landing for him to catch up. 'Anything on this Kanyif Iqbal?'

Doyle sighed. 'Nope. Not a sausage.'

'What, you can't find anything on someone who's had six top ten singles?'

'It's a fake name, guv. There's nothing on the birth register. And we can't get his real one. Not even on Wikipedia, and the hard-core fans would put it up on there if they knew it.' Doyle slogged on up the second flight of stairs.

Fenchurch followed him into the reception, sleek and minimalist, the shiny wooden floors reflecting the spotlights. They were greeted by a muted blend of ambient sounds.

A young woman glanced up from behind her apple-shaped desk. Her electric blue hair shimmered. Piercings in places Fenchurch hadn't considered possible. 'Yeah?' New York accent.

'DCI Fenchurch.' His warrant card didn't seem to excite her any. 'Looking for Mr Sixsmith.'

'Studio C.' She thumbed behind her.

Doyle leaned in close. 'How many are there?'

'Two.'

'So why is it C?'

She shrugged. 'Sounds better?'

'Thank you.' Fenchurch led on past reception and entered a long, dimly lit corridor, the walls adorned with framed gold and platinum records. Timeless albums he still loved and played shared wall space with cutting-edge hits his daughter played at him.

The thud of a snare drum teased from behind soundproofed doors.

But that was Studio A.

They passed into a lounge area. Two plush velvet sofas in rich purples with a coffee table between them strewn with music magazines and vinyl records. In one corner, a vintage jukebox sat next to the obligatory pool table.

A hallway led on to Studio C.

Doyle opened the door to reveal a cathedral of music production. A vintage mixing console dominated the space, covered with an array of dials, switches and sliders all in different positions. Above it, a wide windowpane looked out onto the recording room, currently empty of people but filled with equipment.

Filthy hip-hop blasted out of meaty speakers, loud enough to get Fenchurch's smartwatch warning him of the volume.

Bradley Sixsmith had his back to them, rocking his chair forward to adjust levels on the console.

Fenchurch walked forward and waved his hands in front of the producer.

Sixsmith turned, his hawkish eyes taking in the two detectives. Thinning hair slicked back, dressed in a tailored black suit with the sleeves rolled up to the elbows. Brown loafers, no socks. He looked over to the side. 'Harley, why don't you go do a warm-up? We'll go again on "Brick Bat" in a couple of minutes once I've got this loop fixed.'

'Sho' t'ing.' A skinny black kid got up from a sagging brown sofa in the corner, then sloped off through another door, his baggy clothes hanging off his coat-hanger frame.

Sixsmith looked them up and down. 'Guessing you two are detectives?' His voice was smooth, almost melodic.

'DCI Fenchurch.' He nodded to the side. 'This is DI Doyle. That's a fancy old desk.'

'This? Oh, it's mostly for show. It's all done inside the MacBook these days, but you need to fling everything through vintage gear to get the right sound. Drums, for example, you need the tape saturation to make them crisp. Even though this record is mostly loops of other people's music, I still look for that crunch. It's what *we* bring to the samples.'

'You seem pretty calm to have two cops showing up. Like that's normal.'

'I've worked in this game long enough to recognise cops and to even tolerate your presence.' Sixsmith grinned. 'Drugs, right?'

'Murder squad.'

'Oh.' Sixsmith's thick eyebrows rose to form a half circle. 'To what do I owe this unexpected pleasure?'

Doyle stepped forward. 'We've got some questions, Bradley. And you know full well what this is about. Thornhill and Avonmore.'

Sixsmith leaned back, fingers drumming on the console, a sly smile playing on his lips. 'Now, you I know. What was that case?'

'Tyler Glass of The Octaves.'

'Raped and murdered a fan, right?'

'Allegedly. He got off with it. Said fan had been stalking him. And there was no evidence he'd raped her.'

'Well, I'm not sure what to say.' Sixsmith's focus shifted between them. 'Anyway, let's make some music.'

Doyle picked up a guitar from a stand and started noodling away. 'Used to play bass in a Madness covers band when I was a nipper. Called ourselves House of Fun. Turned out there were another two with that exact name. We were pretty busy for a while, playing most weekends when we could. Then I had to focus on catching murderers.'

'What do you want to know?'

Doyle pointed at the window into the vocal booth. 'Was that HT UniQorn?'

'The one and the same.'

'My nieces are massive fans of him.' Doyle looked at Fenchurch. 'Young rap star from Bristol, right?'

'Wouldn't know. My knowledge of hip-hop ended with Public Enemy.'

'Love them. Saw them at the Hammersmith Odeon, way back when.' Sixsmith grinned away. 'Part of the reason I've been asked to produce his album.' He looked around at the desk. 'Just need to check the talkback mic is off...' He looked back at them with a mischievous leer. 'I'll be honest with you, gents, this kid's music is the kind of murder you should be investigating. He has no talent. No rhythm, no rhyme. All his ideas are from old Wu Tang Clan or Dr Dre productions. He thinks I don't know, but I engineered records by both of them back in the nineties.' He cracked his knuckles in a series of sickening pops. 'Anyway. I heard about Don and Adrian. Are they okay?'

'Mr Avonmore is in surgery this morning. Mr Thornhill and another man were killed.'

'Shit. Adrian's dead? Seriously?'

'I'm afraid so, Mr Sixsmith.' Doyle held his gaze. 'I take it you knew them both?'

'Sure. Closer to Adrian than Don, but that's what everyone says. Adrian was a great friend of mine. We go way back. Of course, I didn't discover them or rejuvenate their career, but I worked on "Blood in the Water". I'd just started in this business. Left school without an O-level to my name, and started making tea for them in this place. Then the tape op called in sick one day, so I worked a session for that record. My big break – I was soon working anywhere I could. Most producers like to stick to the gear they know, but I was always keen to experiment on new stuff. I produced the album, not the famous name attached to it, who just played pool and... Well, you don't want to know the rest. But once I'd made my name, Don asked me to produce their comeback record.'

Fenchurch felt like he'd stepped into one of those documentaries on BBC4 on a Friday night. 'This would be in the eighties, right?'

'Correct. Bumped into him at an after-party and Don was struggling. Drink and drugs. Hadn't put anything out in a couple of years. But we got chatting, went for a meal. Had a long chat. Turns out I knew a few people at their label. Now, I'm a very ambitious man and I saw a way of turning his career around.'

'I wasn't aware he needed it?'

'Oh, he was a critical darling. But he wasn't selling anything like he did in the early seventies. Lost count of the number of interviews where Don said his latter success was all down to me. And it was. One hundred percent.'

'Plaque downstairs says "Blood in the Water" was recorded here?'

'Correct. That studio shut down not long after that. Became a voiceover place. But with a big chunk of their advance, I used their recording budget to buy this place myself. Turned it into Sixsmith Studios. Massive gamble, but I haven't looked back. And I'm eternally grateful to them for allowing that.'

'I gather you're also managed by Rick Spangler.'

'Droopy Cock.' Sixsmith laughed. 'Indeed. I hate that arsehole, but the labels and publishing companies hate him more. So I get good deals. Don't know why I keep letting him persuade me to do this job for talentless shits like Harley through there—' He checked the microphone light again. '— but Rick's got the gift of the gab. I want to retire, but he keeps getting me deals too good to turn down. Of course, the money comes in handy. Got properties to maintain. My monthly bills are high!'

Fenchurch smiled and nodded along. 'Gather you've been working with Kanyif Iqbal?'

'Good guy.' Another glance at the desk. 'See what I was saying earlier about Harley? Kanyif's the polar opposite. Kid's the real deal. Talent just drips off the guy. You go into a room with him and you're performing ten percent better. Rick managed to get Kanyif to guest on this UniQorn album. Two tracks. Both will be singles if I get my way. One's going to be top five, I can feel it.'

'So he's here? Can we speak to him?'

'That's the trouble. He *was* here, but he left just after his first take.'

'When was this?'

'Last night.'

'Know where he went?'

'No, but... Ach, it's probably nothing.'

'Go on?'

'It's just... Kid took a phone call from someone, seemed to get into a heated discussion, which ended with a threat.'

'What kind of threat?'

Sixsmith grinned. 'I recorded the call onto the multitrack. I was going to chop it up and use it on another song. Getting three for the price of two. A bit cheeky, maybe, but spreading the Kanyif magic dust a bit further would help this dreadful record.' A dark look passed over his face. 'But I listened back and the words... It's... He had a gun with him. And a knife big enough to kill a bull with.'

That made him prime suspect. A knife like that had been used to tear apart Avonmore's groin and abdomen.

'Thought the gun was fake. One of those American ones.

He kept posing with it, you know, pointing it side on. But he had bullets in it.'

'He say where he was going?'

'No... But... He made the call just after we talked about Rusty Rivers.'

'Hang on. *He* made the call?'

'Right. Right.'

'You remember the context?'

'Harley's track had sampled a riff from "Blood in the Water". Kanyif recognised it. Said we shouldn't use it.'

'Why not?'

'Didn't say. Then he made the call.'

'You said you recorded this call?'

'Right. It's in another file.'

'Can you bring it up?'

'Sure.' Sixsmith swung around and started working away at a giant screen, as big as a television. 'I'll just pull up the file...'

'Is that his real name?'

'Kanyif? God no. Iqbal's an Indian surname but the kid's half-black. It just means "Can you fuck, pal".'

'What's his real name?'

Sixsmith scratched at something on the recording console. 'You know, I don't actually know.'

'Come on. I find that hard to believe.'

'Seriously... The way that kid's wired. He only answered to Kanyif. So I assumed it was his name, until someone pointed out it's a joke.' He made a slurping noise. 'Here you go.' He clicked the mouse and room noise burst out of the giant speakers.

'Yo, man, it's Kanyif.' Pause, letting the Glasgow-Bronx hybrid accent rattle around the control room. 'Don't say you don't know me, man. Don't fucking say that. You do, man. You do know me.' Another pause. 'And I know.' A longer pause, filled with menace. 'I fucking know, man.' He laughed now, even more sinister than the pauses. 'Saying you don't know? Rusty fucking Rivers. You was my hero, man! I'm going to fucking kill you. Because you fucked a kid, man. You fucked a *child!*'

Then the sound of footsteps stomping away.

12

Rain splattered the tarmac and bounced off the unassuming van, the water sliding off like sweat from a boxer in the ring. The Transit's sides bore the emblem of a generic plumbing company, one you could even call and speak to an operator, who'd politely refuse your urgent need for work.

Fenchurch thumped the back of the van and looked around the cluttered urban backdrop of Hammersmith.

The hotel's façade was an impeccable fusion of Georgian and Victorian design – cream bricks framed by ornate stone balustrades and elegant wrought ironwork, brought up to date with a large chrome and glass atrium. Mature ivy crept up the side, restrained and trimmed, allowed to flourish just enough to give an organic touch.

Crystal-clear lanterns hung on either side of the grand entrance, their soft glow lighting up the doorman. To his side, a discreet brass plaque simply read:

The Resonance

Beyond him, a cobblestone driveway curled towards an underground car park where luxury vehicles were secreted away, depriving the paparazzi of candid shots. Lush green topiaries and a few strategically placed trees lined the perimeter, providing tranquillity and further shielding guests from prying eyes.

For those in the know, the Resonance was more than just a hotel – it was a sanctum where rock stars could fade into the shadows after electrifying gigs.

And Fenchurch was in the know.

James McNab would probably be back upstairs now, sleeping off the worst of his hangover until he had to do it again tonight. Or maybe he was struggling with thoughts of what he'd said or done the night before.

Fenchurch looked to the side. 'We getting anywhere with them?'

'The hotel?' Reed scratched at her neck. 'Not sure. I gave Lisa the warrant.'

'Is she in there now?'

'She's not, no, but two of her lot are.'

Doyle cleared his throat. 'I've been out this way before. Happy to help if you need it.'

Reed shot him a withering glance. 'I've got this, Ronnie.'

'Didn't say you hadn't, Kay.'

Yeah, Fenchurch could slice the air with a knife.

The door opened and Inspector Michelle Grove looked out, her long face pointed like a bullet. 'Kay.' She frowned. 'Simon?'

'That's me. Can we come in for a chat?'

'Sure, sure.' She disappeared into the gloom.

Fenchurch followed Reed and Doyle in.

The van's interior was dim, despite there being hundreds of high-tech lights everywhere.

Up front, the cockpit was all business – buttons and switches littered the console, each one a potential lifesaver or game-changer. The moulded seats stank of the sweat that came from long nights and high-speed chases through the labyrinth of London's streets.

Behind the driver were two chairs, thrones for urban warriors. Each was equipped with a harness, better suited to a fighter jet than a city vehicle. A giant touchscreen display between them, London's pulse right at their fingertips, showing real-time information – maps, suspect details and live video feeds from police drones.

Directly behind the seats were quick-release gun racks. Heckler & Koch carbines, straight out of Hollywood. Below were clear-fronted drawers. Ballistic shields and medical kits sat next to Glock handguns and magazines studded with bullets.

The atmosphere was thick, heavy with anticipation.

Grove perched between her two burly officers in their thrones, all sharing the same icy stare. Typical of firearms officers. None were Rambo, just steady Eddies who could handle their emotions. 'Heard you'd retired, Simon.'

'Rumours of my demise are greatly exaggerated.' Fenchurch crouched between Reed and Doyle, mirroring Grove's team. 'I'll pretend you know nothing. We're after Kanyif Iqbal.' He unfolded a surveillance photo. 'Scottish rapper.'

Grove snatched the page from him. 'The world of rhymes and beats wasn't enough for him, eh? Had to move into the world of murder.' She passed the photo to her colleague, then leaned. 'Is the target armed?'

'And very dangerous. Lead suspect for a double homicide in Greenwich this morning. Believed to be armed with a pistol of some kind and one of those knives you can kill zombies with.'

'Never got that.' Grove's number one passed the photo to number two. 'Why focus on zombies? They're slow-moving and effectively falling apart. Easy kills.'

'But only if you get a headshot, Ian.' Number two inspected

it closely. 'And what if you've not got any guns or you've run out of ammo?'

'Fair enough, but why zombies? Why not werewolves?'

'Still don't want to get into close quarters with a zombie, do you?' Fenchurch stared Ian down, then snapped his teeth together and made him jump.

Number two winked at Ian. 'No danger you'd turn into one, mate. You've got no brains.'

Fenchurch waited for the laughter to die down. 'Okay, so we have the target as staying in the penthouse suite over there.'

Grove looked out of the window at the hotel. 'He there just now?'

'Unknown.'

'Assume he is. Any expected collateral?'

'Minimal. Hotel's mostly vacant midweek. We know of a few guests. Rock stars from a concert in Acton last night. Suspect they're all sleeping it off.'

'Ah, it's one of *those* places.'

'They're playing the same venue tonight, so they might be sound-checking.'

'Won't it all be set up?'

'It's the Zeroes. They smash the hell out of their equipment at the end of the show.'

'Right, right. Still, we need to keep it clean.'

Reed handed Grove a hotel blueprint. 'We've already got people inside. Been pestering the staff for CCTV footage, but not playing ball. We need this done right, Michelle. Quick, and with minimal damage.'

She met her gaze. 'Always.' Then she sucked in a deep breath and let it slide out. 'So are we active or passive?'

'You're here to support us. Could be the report of the gun is incorrect. Could be he just decides to play ball and come with us. But in case he doesn't, I need you guys locked and loaded. Ronnie here will stay with you to help with identification and other operational matters. Don't fire unless he expressly okays it.'

'Understood.' Grove reached over for a Glock handgun. 'Let's do this.' She clapped her hands together, then walked over to the door and tore it open while her colleagues armed themselves. 'Simon, Kay. You two do your thing. Pair of dickhead coppers asking questions. Gather the intel and we'll mop up your spillages, like always.'

'Appreciate it, Michelle.' Fenchurch followed Reed out of the van, then crossed the road, heading to the hotel's ornate entrance in silence. His blood was thudding in his ear, the stress building and mounting.

Approaching an armed man who'd already killed twice today.

Yeah...

What a first day back.

Fenchurch checked his phone and still didn't have a missed call from Cargill. He was SIO, so this was his operation. He'd tried to pass it up the chain but nothing clanked down from her.

The doorman stood alert, his tailored uniform the same deep navy that featured everywhere on the hotel. His primary job was to recognise faces from glossy magazine covers and grant them swift entry. He gave them a look that suggested he knew they were Old Bill, then let them past. Sure as eggs was eggs, he'd have some way of signalling that fact to the desk.

The hotel lobby was the definition of opulence, filled with plush seating and crystal chandeliers.

The receptionist was a young man with a meticulous beard, eyeing them with visible annoyance. 'Your team have already disrupted my staff over this CCTV business.'

'This is important police work, sir.' Fenchurch raised an eyebrow. 'We need access to the penthouse.'

The receptionist hesitated, his focus darting to a phone on his desk.

Reed smiled at him. 'This is to be done quietly. Okay? The guest in that suite is wanted for two murders and a—'

'*Murders?*'

Reed nodded. 'And a serious assault that may escalate to murder. He's armed and dangerous. We've got an armed response unit surrounding this hotel to provide operational support.'

Fenchurch rested his hands on the desk. 'Is Mr Iqbal here?'

'I don't believe so.'

Fenchurch felt a bit of hope deflate. He'd keyed himself up for a showdown. 'Can you check?'

'Our CCTV system is designed for maximum privacy, so no. It's all part of the discretion we give our customers.'

Fenchurch swung around looking for cameras, but all he saw was the hotel bar. Empty, save for an elderly couple sharing a bottle of wine, both staring at their phones like teenagers. 'Okay. We just need access to the suite to see if he'll come quietly.'

The receptionist gave a grunt, then handed over a key card. 'This is for the penthouse lift. Opens up into the suite.'

'Thank you.' Reed nodded at two of her officers in the foyer, then walked across to the lift. 'You okay, guv?'

'I'm good.' Fenchurch thumbed the lift button and the doors slid open.

Reed tapped the key and the doors shut, then it climbed up through the building. She put her radio to her mouth. 'Serial Alpha to Serial Bravo. Suspect is not believed to be in situ. Repeat, suspect is not believed to be in situ. Over.'

As they rose, the weight of what was about to happen pressed down on Fenchurch. He tried to soothe himself with the knowledge that Kanyif wasn't in the suite just now. But it wasn't quite knowledge, just a supposition. A guess.

The elevator doors slid open with a whisper, revealing a

penthouse that was less a room and more a monument to excess. The dim spotlights cast a muted glow across the vast living space. Windows dominated one wall, offering a panoramic view of as much of London's skyline as you could see from this far west. Directly ahead, the polished mahogany bar was lined with expensive spirits. A bottle of Krug rested in an ice bucket. A grand piano sat in the corner, obsidian black and polished to a mirror shine. The walls were adorned with art – not the sort that hung in museums, but the sort that screamed money. In the far corner, a spiral staircase led up, the wrought iron balustrade like a serpent, disappearing into the shadows of the level above.

Fenchurch felt like he was stepping into the den of a predator that dined on gold and silk.

No sign of anyone, let alone Kanyif.

He felt the remnants of the tension slacken off.

'Not here, guv.'

A deep thud came from upstairs.

Fenchurch felt a fresh pulse of tension. He approached the staircase and the bedroom, gripping his baton tight.

A balcony door swung open, a gust of cold air hitting him.

Fenchurch dashed back down, then out onto the balcony. He looked down at the grid of streets. No sign of anyone jumping.

The lift doors pinged.

By the time he'd looked round, they'd slid shut. Someone had gone in.

Fenchurch ran over. 'Shit, he's played us.' He spotted a stair door. 'Call this in, Kay.' He opened the door and tore down the steps. This was the seventh floor; his knees were racing the speed and power of a private lift. He reached the bottom and stormed back into the atrium.

The lift doors were closing again, but nobody was inside.

Reed's two officers lay on the floor, groaning.

The receptionist stood there, mouth hanging open. 'He... I'm so sorry.'

'Was it Iqbal?'

He pointed to the door. 'That way!'

Fenchurch spotted a shadow through the glass, then shot off through the hotel and out onto the street.

Kanyif was swift on his feet, weaving through pedestrians.

Fenchurch was close behind, the pounding of his heart keeping time with his quarry's footsteps. But his own were faster. He was catching up with him.

Kanyif turned a corner.

Fenchurch followed him, mere metres away now.

Kanyif stopped and spun around, drawing his gun. Aimed straight at Fenchurch. 'Get away from me, man.'

'Don't do this!'

'Fuck you, man!'

A shot rang out, piercing the afternoon.

Fenchurch went down. Ringing in his ears and the taste of gunpowder in his mouth.

But there was no blast of pain.

The bullet had missed.

Deliberately?

Kanyif stood over him, the knife in one hand, the gun in the other, pointing side on like a gangster.

Forget Cargill's offers of retirement or redeployment to useless positions.

This was how it was going to end.

On a street way out west, shot by a punk rapper.

Kanyif crouched in front of him. 'I'm not who you want.'

Keep him talking.

Fenchurch slowly raised his hands. 'So who is, Kanyif? Eh? Who is it I want?'

His finger itched on the trigger. 'You know! You know, man!'

'I don't know. Please. Put the gun down. Talk to me.'

'Can't trust you, man!'

'None of this is your fault, Kanyif. I will help you.'

Tears filled Kanyif's eyes. 'Man, you don't get it, do you?' He pressed the gun against Fenchurch's lips. 'You don't get it!'

The sharp crack of a gunshot ripped through the silence.

13

Fenchurch sat in the hotel's bar area. Plush leather seats. Marble table. Silver service, his small cup filled with tea. He plonked another cube of sugar in and sipped at it. Disgusting, but... Something to do with shock. The sugar and the caffeine.

His ears still rang. He could still taste the gunpowder in his mouth, no matter how much sugary tea he drank.

He shivered as if he was naked on top of an Icelandic glacier. It felt like it'd never stop. He had another sip of tea and the shiver subsided.

His phone sat on the table, face up. Never trust someone whose phone was face down. Either hiding something or struggling to control themselves.

Still nothing from Cargill. He'd been fucking shot at and she *still* hadn't called.

And he'd even reached out to her. Christ.

'Om pom tiddly om pom.'

Fenchurch looked up.

Dr Pratt glowed under the spotlights, haloing his bushy hair like he was some kind of angel. 'How are you faring, Simon?'

Fenchurch let his breath go and it stuck in his throat. He took another sip of tea. 'Okay, I guess. I mean, someone was just about to kill me, but I... I guess I got away with it.'

Pratt put his hand on top of Fenchurch's and leaned in close. 'I'm glad you did, old friend.' He sat opposite and poured out a cup for himself without asking. 'I won't pester you anymore, just to say that I have completed my investigation into the death of Mr Iqbal. Certain protocols prevent me divulging too much. Killed by a police officer, blah blah blah. Suffice it to say that it appears Mr Iqbal was killed by one of the two bullets fired. All of the officer's pistols have been seized for ballistic analysis.'

'Separate shots? Or two from the same gun?'

'Not for me to say. It's not like I did the post-mortem on the pavement. Word is, it was Inspector Grove and one of her team, a Constable George Shaw, who were the two potential killers. If it was Shaw, it'll be his first kill. But he's in good hands with Michelle. Then again, you don't become a firearms officer without expecting to crack some eggs. And, of course, this is just conjecture. As a medical professional, I have no time for speculation or rumours. Harumph.' Pratt reached into his briefcase. 'Speaking of rumour, though, Mick Clooney asked me to give you this.'

Fenchurch took the evidence pack, but he didn't have to open it. Handwritten documentation, visible through the clear plastic, written on hotel notepaper. 'What's this?'

'I found it inside Mr Iqbal's coat. To my untrained eye, it looks like some lyrics to a song he was working on.'

Fenchurch read them:

> In the shadows of fame, an old star crept,
> Snatched her away, her momma wept,
> Rock 'n' roll legend, lived a dark creed,
> That river runs red, so cling to the reeds

Fenchurch set it down on the table. Clearly about Rivers abducting someone. The girl Kanyif had accused him of abusing.

But all hearsay. No evidence. No identity.

If it was true, it'd be a strong motive, for sure. Someone took the law into their own hands somewhere in the UK most days, but hardly any of those acts resulted in corpses. This had reached three and counting.

'Thanks, William. Was there any more?'

'Nothing I'm party to.' Pratt slurped at the tea, twice, three times, then gasped. 'But that clearly means something to you, right?'

'Sort of. It's clearly calling out Rusty Rivers for some misdeeds with a young girl. But there's no detail there, William. No evidence. Who's the girl? Where is she? What did he do with her? Does she even exist?'

'Indeed.'

Fenchurch drank some of his tea. Made his fillings throb. 'Got any good news for me?'

'This might raise your pecker, old friend. We've done a cursory examination of the dagger Mr Iqbal had with him and... We've found traces of blood and flesh between the serrations of the blade. Mick Clooney and I shall determine whose blood we're looking at, but I'd hazard a guess at one of three sources. Josh "Harvey" Murphy, Adrian Thornhill and Don Avonmore.'

'Oh?'

'The dagger has the unique pattern used to kill Harvey and Mr Thornhill... Whether it was used to do that to Mr Avonmore, we shall see.'

Fenchurch topped up his tea from the pot. 'So Kanyif is likely to be our killer.'

'It would at least appear he was acquainted with them.'

'Cheers, William. You be able to get a PM done on them all today?'

Pratt looked out of the window. 'This place is pretty far from my jurisdiction, so I'm trying to arrange for me to take over this matter, given the obvious connections with our case in Woolwich.'

'Greenwich.'

'Oh, yes.' Pratt ran a hand through his beard. 'Of course.' He slurped more tea, then gasped again. 'How could I forget?'

Fenchurch smiled, though he was a bit worried by that slip. 'Listen, if you need me to make a nuisance of myself with senior officers to help with that jurisdictional ball ache, give me a shout.'

'I will do.' Pratt finished his tea and seemed to dribble most of it into his thick beard. 'Anyway, I'd best be off. I turn into a pumpkin if I'm this far west for longer than two hours.' He got up and staggered off through the atrium. 'Om pom tiddly om pom.' No halo this time, just the devil tail of intrigue from his evidence.

Fenchurch sipped his tea, staring into space.

Kanyif crumpled, lifeless, onto the wet pavement.

Fenchurch's heart was thumping in his chest. He looked up.

Michelle Grove stood over them, her gun trained on where Kanyif had stood. 'We had to take the shot.'

'Guv?' Doyle stood over him. 'You okay there?'

'Ronnie.' Fenchurch rubbed at his eyes. 'Just mulling over a few things.'

'Right. Right.' Doyle sat down where Pratt had been and stared into the cup. Maybe wondering what the leaves at the bottom meant. 'When you and Kay went into the penthouse... How did he escape?'

'Must've been hiding behind the piano.' Fenchurch sighed. 'We should've gone in with a much bigger team.'

'We assessed the risks, guv. It's all documented. We didn't

want any casualties and we only got one, our target. Everything pointed to him being out of the room.'

'True, it's just... It's shit when that happens. I want people to face justice. I met Thornhill's wife this morning. She deserves to know the truth about what happened to her husband. Doesn't she?'

'She does, though. He was murdered by Kanyif Iqbal.'

Fenchurch raised his eyebrows. 'Hopefully.' He tried to attract the waiter's attention to get more milk. Nope. 'How's Michelle?'

'She's as tough as an old man's scrotum, guv. Her new lad, though... The bullet went clean through Iqbal's heart.'

'Was it him?'

'Grove said so.'

'Poor kid.'

'Yeah, but you don't get into that line of work without expecting to end at least one life. His statement's already down. Kanyif was standing over an unarmed police officer, pointing a gun at him and he appeared distraught. He drew his issued pistol and didn't even issue a challenge. Said it was clear the man was going to shoot the officer, so he fired one round at his centre mass, striking him in the upper chest.' Doyle pushed the empty teacup away. 'I've got some news, though.'

'Good or bad?'

'Bit of both.' Doyle cleared his throat. 'The, ah, Independent Office for Police Conduct have already been in touch with Cargill.'

'News travels fast.'

'There'll be an inquest into the killing.'

'Don't doubt it. What's the good news?'

'That's the bad. The good... My team got hold of the CCTV. We'll review it and prove that Doug Reid was here at the time in question.'

'Hardly good. We kind of know it wasn't him, though.'

'Still, it's good to *know* know, right?'

'Right.' Fenchurch sipped at his tea but it'd gone cold and tasted even more disgusting now. 'What about Kanyif's movements? Can we pin him—'

'Left two hours before the shooting. Thinking he must've gone over there.' Doyle leaned forward. 'Thing is, guv, there was a girl with him.'

'With Kanyif?'

Doyle nodded. 'Thirteen, maybe. We spoke to the staff. Turns out, a girl was staying here with him.'

Fenchurch picked up the lyrics. 'The threat on the phone call he made to Don Avonmore… I thought it was because he thought Avonmore was abusing someone. But if…' He tasted bile at the back of his throat. 'Jesus, what the hell was this all about?'

14

Fenchurch leaned against the cold hospital corridor wall. A door opened and he caught a glimpse of himself in the mirror – the fluorescent lights cast a pallor on his already tired face. Made him look like he should be a patient here, not a visitor.

And he was both.

In the time he'd been away, it'd become standard to send officers either home or to a hospital when they suffered a critical stress injury.

Just like he'd apparently done.

Not the first time someone had pointed a gun at him. Probably wouldn't be the last.

And of course there was nothing wrong with him. Not trauma.

Sure... Keep telling yourself that...

The distant hum of machines and the muted steps of busy nurses were the only company he had. Every tick of the nearby clock made him tense up, like someone had a gun trained on him.

That gun...

He'd been a cavalier sod in the past, sure, but that was close. Too close.

What the hell was he thinking? Even with his new knees, he should've let Grove's team handle that.

He had kids, for Christ's sake. Sure, Chloe was an adult – following the family trade of being a cop – but Al was still young, still thought his old man was his hero.

Fenchurch wanted to savour as many years with him as he could.

He stood up tall and tried to shut down the busy thoughts inside his head. Through the recovery room's window, Don Avonmore shifted on the bed, swathed in sterile white sheets, with wires and tubes snaking around him like a spiderweb.

The room's gatekeeper was Dr Mulkalwar, her eyes trained on her tablet. Until she gave the nod, that door might as well be a hundred miles away.

Fenchurch's fingers drummed an impatient rhythm on his thigh. He didn't like waiting, especially not when answers lay just beyond reach. Or maybe he'd just find more questions – seemed to be one of those cases.

Mulkalwar walked over to him, her face stern. 'Inspector. Have you been there long?'

'Twenty minutes or so. Got the all-clear on... what happened to me.'

'Aye, I heard about that. You okay?'

'I'm fine.'

'Sure, keep telling yourself that.'

Fenchurch gestured into the room. 'How's the patient?'

'Mr Avonmore's in a very fragile state. He's been heavily sedated and will need a while to come round from that.'

Fenchurch tried to keep everything calm and level. 'Thing is, I really do need to speak to him. It's crucial to the investigation.'

She gave a polite smile, with a hard edge. 'And I'm sure you realise that I have a duty of care to my patient.'

'Of course I do. Thing is… We have reason to believe Mr Avonmore was abusing a minor.' Fenchurch paused, letting the words sink in. It was stretching things, sure, but he wanted to get to the bottom of what happened. If there was a missing victim of abuse, he needed to find her. But he also needed to know if that was true. 'Thing is, the victim's currently unaccounted for. The only other person who might know her location is dead.'

Mulkalwar turned away and looked into the room, her lips twitching. 'I see…' She hugged the tablet tight. 'You can have a couple of minutes, but I'll be monitoring his vitals. Please don't push this or take the piss, right?'

'Of course. And I appreciate it.' Fenchurch held her gaze until he got the impression she knew the sentiment was genuine, then he passed her and entered the room, keeping a distance from the bed. 'Hi, Don.'

'Who's that?' Avonmore looked up at him, his eyes glassy through the mist of sedation. 'Adrian? Is that you?'

'It's DCI Simon Fenchurch.' He rested against the chair back. 'I'm investigating what happened to you. How are you doing there?'

'I feel like someone's cut me off at the chest. Everything below my ribs is numb. Doctor says I'll be okay.' Avonmore cackled. 'Should I believe her?'

'You've got a long road to recovery, but you're in the best place for it.'

'Wouldn't go that far.' Avonmore winced. 'I've asked my doctor to get me out of here.'

'Private?'

'Of course.' Avonmore looked Fenchurch up and down, like he was something he'd spotted on the bottom of his shoes. 'Have you caught the man who did this to me?'

'We believe we have.' Fenchurch let a breath go. 'But sadly, he was killed during the operation to bring him in.'

Avonmore frowned. 'Well, that's... not the worst outcome. Probably save the court system a bunch of time and money. And it's certainly a better consequence than they could impose.'

'Trouble is, with him being dead, it doesn't help us answer why.' Fenchurch stood up tall and folded his arms. 'Why did he kill your friend and your security guard? Why did he remove a testicle and stab your abdomen?'

Avonmore flinched. 'He was going to do a lot more to me, I think. Harvey disturbed the animal doing this to me. He saved my life. Cost him his own, but... All I could do was watch him die in front of me.'

'You told my colleagues you didn't get a good look at him. You remember anything now?'

'Feels like you're trying to trick me here.'

'Nope.'

'But you know who did this, don't you?'

'And you're playing silly buggers with me. So I'll ask you once again. Did you see who did this?'

'It was dark. I was... I'll be honest, I wasn't entirely sober last night. Me and Adrian had been drinking and... whatever. I went to bed late and I woke up in a bit of a state. Which is why I drew a bath. It can get things pumping, you know? So the bedroom was dark and I didn't see him approach me until I felt the knife in my stomach.'

'He didn't say anything?'

'Not a word. Just cut me and caused me immense pain.'

'When someone does something like that to someone, they're usually sending a message.'

'Not that I heard. The bath was running, like I say. It's a bespoke model, very high flow.'

Fenchurch reached into his pocket and handed over a still

of the girl with Kanyif as they left the hotel. 'You recognise either of these people?'

Avonmore looked at the page then his mouth dropped open. 'My word. That's... That's Kanyif Iqbal. Is that who did this?'

Fenchurch nodded slowly.

The frown deepened. '*Him*? Seriously?'

'Seriously. We understand you had a beef with him?'

'A beef?' Avomore barked out a laugh. 'We had a few cross words because he'd sampled one of my records without even having the courtesy to ask me. He got all aggro with me, so I just said pay up or steal someone else's music. That was all it was.'

'But he didn't react well to it, did he?'

'Neither of us acted very well, I'll be honest. But in fairness to him, he did actually pay up. The sample is on one of his tracks. I can't remember which one. So it all ended well for both of us.'

Fenchurch reached forward and tapped the edge of the page. 'And her?'

Avonmore inspected it. 'It's a bit blurry and— Natasha?' He put it close to his face. 'Is that Natasha?'

'I don't know. Who's Natasha?'

'She's my niece's daughter.'

'Why would she be with Kanyif?'

'I haven't the foggiest.'

'You don't know.'

'No. But... But *him*? Why is she with him?'

Fenchurch shrugged. 'I'm asking you. She's your niece, after all.'

'Listen, I probably shouldn't say this, but... The music business operates on secrets and rumours. Everyone knows what everyone else is up to. And there were unkind words said about him.'

'What sort of words?'
'How he liked young girls.'
'Kanyif Iqbal?'
Avonmore nodded, a fierce Morse code. 'I heard the same from multiple sources.'
'You do anything with that information?'
'I had no proof and it wasn't my business. Like anyone else who... dabbled in that murky world, I just shunned them.'
'This is after he sampled you?'
'Believe me, if it was before, I would've told him where to go.'
'Thing is, Mr Iqbal's said the same about you.'
'My God. That's outrageous!' Avonmore waved the sheet of paper around. 'She'd been staying with me. Her mother died in a car crash a few months ago. Terrible business over by Stonehenge on that awful road, you know. I saw her at the funeral... Asked her if she needed any help. She had nobody. Literally nobody. Her own father was off the radar. My sister... She's not in the best of health. So of course I took her in. Gave her a room in my home.'
'But she's been staying with Mr Iqbal.'
'She... she went missing a few weeks ago.'
'Did you report Natasha missing to the police?'
'Of course I bloody did. She's thirteen. They sent people around. Not that it did any good.'
'You remember the name of the officer?'

15

Back in Greenwich, PC Adam Burridge was waiting for Fenchurch. Leaning against his squad car's bonnet, thumbs tucked into his stab-proof vest, staring into space. He looked up at Fenchurch's approach. 'Oh, hey.' He stood up tall, like he was on parade. 'Didn't see you there.' His Newcastle accent was clipped and musical. 'How are you doing, sir?'

The wonders of rank.

'Constable.' Fenchurch stopped next to him and watched the queue of traffic snake up and around the park. 'Thanks for meeting me here. Thought you were East End, though?'

'Was.' Burridge wouldn't make eye contact. 'Got shifted down here a few months back.'

'That a good thing?'

'For them, aye. A batch of new recruits hadn't bedded in and they asked me to supervise them. Took a few months, but it's in a good place. One bad apple was ruining it for some potentially good cops who weren't getting the support they needed.' Burridge scratched at his chin. 'Bit boring around here, to be honest. Greenwich and Blackheath are too posh. East Greenwich, Bermondsey and Peckham can get a bit lively, mind, but it's nothing like what I'm used to up in your neck of the woods. Hope to God I'm doing a good job, but the difference I make feels a lot less tangible here.'

He made eye contact now. 'How's your daughter doing?'

Fenchurch held his gaze. 'Chloe's good, yeah. Splits her time fifty-fifty between uniform work and with that Trafficking and Prostitution Unit.'

'She's a good cop. Or has potential to be.' Burridge smiled, the crow's feet around his eyes splitting. 'And going after something that personal to her, it's got to pay off, right?'

'It can. But that kind of thing can break some too.'

'Aye, but not Chloe.' Burridge grinned. 'She's tough as old boots. One of the best I brought through.'

'Glad to hear it.' Fenchurch fixed him with a hard stare, one designed to make him realise he meant every single syllable of those words, before he got on with things. 'Listen, Adam, the reason I've asked you here is because you responded to a missing person's report. Girl, aged thirteen. Name of Natasha Iskander.'

Burridge frowned. 'Odd surname that.'

'It's Egyptian, would you believe? On her father's side.'

'Doesn't ring any bells.'

'Happens to the best of us, eh?'

Burridge pursed his lips. 'Not to me. Can remember everything I've attended. Got one of those brains, you know?'

'Got one myself, so yeah, I do know.' Fenchurch gave him a warm smile and it was reflected at him. 'Anyway, this case was three weeks ago. Twenty-eighth of October.'

Burridge got out his notebook and flicked back through. 'Twenty-eighth... Okay, here we go. Well, I was in Bermondsey all day. Twenty-ninth, we did security at the O2 for a concert there. Quite a controversial headliner.'

Fenchurch pointed at the brick townhouse. 'Her great-uncle reported her missing and you responded.'

'Nope.' Burridge shook his head, then looked around the area. 'Never been here in my life.'

Fenchurch had a weird sensation in his guts, like snakes were coiling up in there. And biting at his flesh. 'Adam, it's on the system.'

Burridge shrugged. 'Hate to say it, mate, but someone's telling you porkies, mate. I never responded to anything here.'

'You're sure about that?'

'Course I am. I'd remember a place like this. And a name like that.'

'I get it.' Fenchurch sighed. 'I'll take it up with your sergeant and see what's what.'

'Sure. You still need me here?'

'No, you can get back on duty. Thanks for attending. Appreciate you coming over this way.'

'No problem, sir.'

Burridge put his cap on.

Fenchurch fixed him with his hardest stare. 'This is your last chance to correct your statement, though.'

Burridge ran a hand down his face. 'Actually... I haven't been here before, but this is where that Rusty Rivers guy lives, right?'

'What about it?'

'Weirdest thing... About six months ago. I was asked to look into some death threats he had received. He came into the station, had a few letters. Told us about phone calls he'd had. Pressed him on it and he said it was just the usual nonsense you got with fame. You know, fans who get too close, who think they own the star.'

'Didn't stop him coming into a police station.'

'Right. And wasting our time.'

'Maybe not such a waste of time. He was attacked and seriously injured.'

'No, that's...' Burridge sucked in a deep breath. 'That's true. Listen, I'll dig out what he gave us and send it all on to you, sir.' He slid into his car, then drove off with a wave.

Fenchurch didn't know what to make of it. What the hell was that about? Someone was lying, but Fenchurch knew Burridge and his reputation. Almost too honest, they said. If he'd been here, he would've said.

'Guv?' Reed stormed along the road, flanked by the steady procession of cars. 'You okay?'

'Not really.' Fenchurch rasped at the stubble on his chin. 'According to the PNC, PC Adam Burridge responded to the missing person's report, but he just denied all knowledge of it. Said he's never been here.'

'You believe him?'

'Him? Yeah, I do. So either someone's lying to us, someone's made a mistake, or Burridge has lost his mind. And he seems pretty sane. And doesn't make mistakes.'

She nodded along with that logic. 'What's your gut tell you, guv?'

'That I can't handle the spiciest hot sauce in my burrito these days.' Fenchurch puffed out his cheeks. 'I honestly don't know, Kay. I don't like any of this or the way it's making me feel.' He tried to shake off the squirming sensation, not all of it from the chilli burning away. 'Can you get someone to dig into this story? Have a word with the sergeant and get the attending officers in a room. Someone was here, so I want to speak to them.'

'On it.'

Fenchurch let out a deep breath. 'You getting anything here?'

'Just been speaking to the neighbour. Mr Fields, gather you chatted this morning?'

'Yeah. Fire chief. What's he saying?'

She beckoned him to follow her. 'Better you hear it from the horse's mouth.'

Neil Fields was standing outside his bungalow, sucking deep on a cigarette. 'Hiya.' He ran a hand through his bushy beard. His wrestler's arms seemed like someone had pumped them full of air – or steroids. 'Probably think it's a bit stupid of me, a former fire chief, to smoke, but... The danger is all part and parcel of the job.' He laughed, a harsh sound.

Fenchurch smiled. 'Know plenty of cops and doctors who smoke too.'

Fields fixed him with a bright stare. 'Your colleague here was asking about a girl staying there? Saw her.'

'You speak to Mr Avonmore about her?'

Fields shrugged. 'Told me it was his niece.'

'His niece?'

'Right.'

'He mention her name?'

'Natasha. I mean, as I understand it, Natasha's his niece's kid but people can be vague with family titles and relationships, right? I mean, she's his grandniece, but when it's not grandparents, people tend to slip all those *grand*s, right?'

'Right, yeah. When did you last see her?'

'At least a week. Maybe longer. They never really went out.'

'You ever speak to her?'

'Not directly. I just saw her in the garden a few times.'

Fenchurch waved at the towering walls surrounding the properties. 'Behind those?'

Fields looked away. 'Mine is a wee bit elevated because of the hill. Even though it's a bungalow, I can still see in.'

'Did you see anything this morning?'

'I didn't, no. But like I told you, I heard it.'

'Right, right.' Fenchurch looked at Reed – that seemed to be it – then back at Fields. 'Thanks for your time, sir.'

'No worries.' Fields walked back into his home in a fug of smoke.

Fenchurch walked back towards his car and Avonmore's front door. 'Interesting how he can see into the back. We still don't have a confirmed method of entry for Kanyif. I'm assuming he didn't get in via the front door.'

'I think forensics were looking into that. Mick called me and said the back garden's immaculate. Hard to spot any footprints, so hard to prove a method of entry.'

Fenchurch didn't like that. They had two corpses and one that was touch and go. They had a dead killer, but no confirmed method of entry. Made things feel a bit shaky – like Docherty used to say, it was on a shoogly peg. Whatever *shoogly* meant. 'Can you speak to the gardener?'

'Lisa's got two people around there now.'

'Good.' Fenchurch was shaking his head. 'Kay, I know this is London and you're never more than two metres from one, but I really am smelling a rat here.' He couldn't stop shaking his head. 'Someone's messing us about. And someone's lying.'

She was nodding along with it. 'You think Natasha is the girl Kanyif thought Avonmore was abusing?'

'Right. Thing is, it doesn't matter whether Avonmore was or not, just so long as Kanyif *believed* he was.'

'So why's she been staying in Kanyif's hotel?'

'A very good question, Kay. And one we don't have an answer to yet. Three dead, one seriously injured and now we've got a missing teenager. We know that girl exists and she seems to be the only one who knows what the hell is going on here. We need to find her. But I can't see how.'

'Okay, but we do have *something* – the CCTV of her and Kanyif leaving the hotel this morning.'

Fenchurch tried to take some comfort from that. 'Get someone going through missing kids and identify her.'

'You don't think she is Avonmore's niece?'

'I want to know who she is. If she's his great-niece, then fine. But if she isn't? I want to speak to her parents. I want to know who she really is.'

'You honestly think Avonmore was abusing her?'

'I've no idea, Kay. But something on this case doesn't sit right with me and I want to get to the bottom of it. I want to know who's lying to us and why.'

'Guv, I get it. A missing teenager. It's hitting close to home.'

'It's not because of what happened to us, Kay. It's because it's potentially happened to someone. This Natasha is someone's kid. Maybe she is Avonmore's niece, but maybe not. But we're going to find her. And she's going to tell us what the hell is going on.'

16

Despite its proximity to Canary Wharf and its ever-expanding number of towers that not even Brexit's decimation of the economy could harm, Canning Town was still the embodiment of urban decay. The estate stretched out before Fenchurch like a grey jungle, the monotonous blocks casting bleak shadows.

Despite the cold evening, the park across the road was busy. Some young kids were playing on rusty swing sets, their laughter tinged with the thump of hip-hop from a boom box. A group of older kids played in the basketball court behind them, the rhythmic thud of the ball hitting the surface out of time with the beats.

Whatever they were up to, it was none of Fenchurch's concern. He climbed the cracked steps then followed the faint wails of a radio tuned to a mournful dirge along a walkway looking out across the street.

Number 307 had its curtains shut – could be to stop prying eyes, could be because the resident was still asleep at this hour.

Fenchurch knocked and waited, arms folded.

Reed joined him, focusing on her mobile. She gave a sigh, then put it away. 'Just got word from Greenwich, guv. Other neighbours have confirmed the sighting and the niece story.'

'But did anyone challenge him about it?'

'Nope.'

Fenchurch felt his teeth clench.

The door swung open. A man stood there, dressed in trousers and a work shirt, the sleeves rolled up to the elbows. 'Can I help?'

'DCI Fenchurch.' He held out his warrant card. 'This is DI Reed. Looking for a Chris Mason.'

'You've found him.' Mason's smile soon faded to a frown. 'Come in, come in.' He led them inside.

The flat was a shambles. Boxes and boxes stacked up, pressed into place by old furniture. Hard to find anywhere to sit, so Fenchurch stayed standing. 'Here to ask about your daughter, sir. Jasmine, is it?'

A series of twitches passed across his face. 'Jasmine? What's happened?'

'We understand you reported her missing.'

'Have you found her?' His glare at Fenchurch was a challenge. 'Is she dead?'

'We might've picked up her trail.'

'What?'

Fenchurch pulled out the paperwork – the print from the CCTV, the print from the MisPer system – but he didn't unfold them. Not yet anyway. 'We have a lead on her whereabouts, but it's part of an investigation into a double murder.' He unfolded the sheets and showed him the MisPer report. 'I gather you reported her missing six weeks ago.'

'That's right.' Mason let out a long sigh. 'Listen, I've been trying to find her. But... Have you any idea what it's like to lose your kid?'

Fenchurch held his gaze. 'Seventeenth of July, 2005. My daughter was abducted from outside my flat in Islington.'

'Shit.' Mason ran a hand down his face. 'You ever find what happened to her?'

'My wife and I are among the lucky ones. We recovered her, but it was over a decade later. We lost those formative years with our daughter.'

'I... My God. And you're a cop? How could it happen to a cop?'

'Can happen to anyone, sir. Doesn't matter how careful you are.'

'I wish I'd been more careful, I tell you. It's... She...' He slumped into a rotting armchair and swallowed hard. 'It's all my fault. I didn't look out for her enough. Let things happen that... I let things slip. And it's all my fault. All. My. Fault.'

Fenchurch knew those thoughts. In him they had spurred him into action, into obsessively hunting down leads every night. For over ten years. But it'd made Fenchurch's wife turn to stone – she came to terms with the loss, then she thawed out and was able to move on with her life. Without Fenchurch. While he still hunted when all hope was dead.

But in others Fenchurch had met, the feelings of guilt and shame and embarrassment and anger and rage had made them crumble.

Mason's jaw clenched. His eyes twitched. But then his shoulders slumped and he leaned back into the chair, looking every bit the broken man he was. 'She's gone. But it's not my fault.'

Fault...

People obsessed about whether they were the ones to blame, not about what they could do to fix things.

Fenchurch stared hard at him. 'Whose fault is it, then?'

'Someone snatched her off the streets and you're blaming me.'

'Nobody's blaming you.'

'The cops who investigated her disappearance seemed to.'

'Seemed to doesn't equate to blame, though.'

'Young girl from Canning Town. Rough background. Neglected parenting. That's all you guys see, isn't it? But she had everything she wanted. Everything I could give. And we only live here because... My wife and I split up. She's still in Camden, but Jasmine and I moved in here. Mum's place. Had to put her in a home. Costing a fortune, but...'

'I'm sorry to hear that, sir. Do you mind telling me what happened to your daughter?'

'It's not like she was abducted from the street. She just... I... I'm a teacher, but I also have to work at night. I take on a few shifts for Travis each week, driving people around in my car. Didn't know what Jasmine was up to. Turns out my wife didn't know either. She'd been... She'd been trafficked. From the age of twelve. Some sick fuck had been... having sex with my girl... Had been letting others do the same. My wife... I... told her that kid was... trouble. She wouldn't listen. Said I was just as bad when we were that age.'

'Which kid are you talking about?'

'This place is a state. I'm sorry. I was halfway through getting rid of Mum's stuff when this happened. I've been going through Jasmine's things. Speaking to her friends. And... The only thing I've found is the names of some men who had sex with my daughter. How can I live with that? These guys in their thirties, forties, fifties. Having sex with her. Paying her. How can I go on, knowing that's what was happening to her?'

'Did you report it to the police?'

'They don't care, do they?'

'Did you, though?'

'I did. The problem is there's no evidence.'

'So how do you know they'd been abusing your daughter?'

'I...' Mason tugged a hand down his face. 'Sorry. I just know that... She... My God.'

'Mr Mason, I'm determined to find your daughter. It'd be extremely helpful if you share the name of the man who trafficked her.'

17

Tears filled Kanyif's eyes. 'Man, you don't get it, do you?' He pressed the gun against Fenchurch's lips. 'You don't get it!'

The sharp crack of a gunshot ripped through the silence.

Fenchurch opened his eyes again and cradled the mug tight. He looked across to the other flats' balconies, then took a final drink of tea. Every time he shut his eyes, he saw that event happening. Again and again and again.

It was going to torment him.

He'd come so close to dying.

And the doctor had given him the all-clear. Well, the all-clear and a tub of pills to take. He didn't want to go back there – his base chemistry would have to do.

But it made him think – what was it he didn't get? Was Kanyif trying to send him a message? Or was he part of some conspiracy himself?

Fenchurch had seen the abused turn into abusers enough times to know it was a thing. But whether that was the case with Kanyif, he had no idea.

He took in his immediate surroundings, trying to centre

himself. At the steam hissing out of the bathroom extractor opposite. At the dots of light signifying planes coming into land at the nearby City airport.

Made him think of another time sitting here, at another of his lowest ebbs. He'd had no hope of finding Chloe for years, but it didn't stop him looking. Didn't stop his old man looking, either. Then a case reared its ugly head and gave him some hope.

That craven devil, hope.

Fenchurch fished his phone out of his pocket, but it wasn't there. It was sitting on the table, face down. Yeah... He couldn't control himself.

He checked the display – a missed call from Abi. His heart stirred and he hit dial.

'Hey.' Her voice was warm and soft.

He leaned forward. 'Hey, sorry, I didn't hear your call.'

'It's okay. Suspect you're busy?'

'Been a hell of a day.'

'Want to talk about it?'

Like she wanted to talk about anything. And hadn't just shut down on him completely. 'What was it about?'

'Eh?'

'Your call. What was it about?'

'Oh, right. I returned *your* call.'

'Okay, sorry.' That little burst of hope faded to a flicker. 'Just wondered if you wanted to see me tonight, that's all.'

'I'm busy, Simon, sorry.'

'Look. We're not living together anymore. Haven't for a while. I just need to know where I stand.'

'We're going through a rough patch, Simon. That's all.'

'Feels like our whole life has been a rough patch for a few years.' Fenchurch took a sip of cold tea and resisted the urge to spit it out. 'Abi, did we make a mistake in getting remarried?'

'Simon... Not now, please. This isn't the time.'

'If not now, then when?'

'Simon...'

'Feels like we aren't even married, Ab. Do you want to get divorced again?'

'Look. I've got some friends coming over and I need to put Al to bed.'

'I hope I can see you soon.'

'I hope so too.'

His hand gripped tight around the mug. 'You're the one putting these barriers up between us.'

'It's just... It's weird between us. We've had a lot to deal with. Both of us. I'm no saint, Simon. And I don't know what we are anymore. But space will help us focus on that and figure out what we are. Okay?'

'Okay. Well, kiss our boy goodnight from me.'

'Will do. Night.'

Fenchurch put the phone away, but he knew he wouldn't get much sleep.

That call, on top of Kanyif Iqbal trying to kill him. On top of a missing teenager.

He didn't know where it started to go wrong again with Abi, but it had gone very, very wrong. The first time they got divorced, he could blame it all on what they went through. The loss of a child – the *unanswered* loss – would destroy most marriages. And his stubborn refusal to accept the situation and his obstinate insistence to keep on fighting for the truth was met by Abi's acceptance of their fate. And her desire to rebuild her life in the ashes of the tragedy.

In one sense, he was right to keep pushing.

In another, he should've stayed close to Abi.

The fact they'd chosen different paths had—

His phone rang again and the hope swelled back up in his belly.

Reed calling...

The hope fizzed away as Fenchurch answered it. 'Evening, Kay.'

'Guv. How's it going?'

'Still not heard from the new boss, despite being shot at.'

'Wow. She hasn't been here. Must still be out west, managing the shooting.'

'Can't help but feel like she'll toast my nuts when she catches up with me. The longer I don't see her, though, the better.'

'Well. Just about to head home, but I've got some good news for you. Thought you'd want to know. That name for the trafficker we got from Jasmine's dad?'

'The Blacksmith... Like he's some kind of Marvel Comics supervillain.'

'Right, yeah. Well, Lisa's team have spoken to a few people in the know and they've tied the identity to one Joshua Kincaid Green.'

The name meant nothing to Fenchurch. 'Who is he?'

'Nasty bastard, guv. Thirty-two. On remand for sex trafficking. Mainly local girls, but some desperate ones from Afghanistan, Yemen and Syria. He put them on the game in London. Killed two of them. Hence him being on remand. Due in court whenever they get around to processing it because of the backlog. He pleaded not guilty, but from what I can gather, he's like a puppy in a puddle.'

'This is good news, Kay. I'll head to Belmarsh first thing.'

'He ain't there, guv. He's in HMP Frankland. County Durham.'

'On remand *there*?'

'Don't know why, but he's there. Called myself and checked. Prisons are in a bit of a state just now.'

'Tell me about it.' Fenchurch exhaled slowly. 'Okay. I'll head up after the briefing. Leave at eight. With a good wind behind me, I'll be there about two.'

'You sure about that, guv? That's a long drive.'

'Sure. I want to see the evil bastard who trafficked a twelve-year-old girl with my own bloody eyes.'

DAY 2

Tuesday

18

The sun was setting, casting the fields in shades of fiery orange and deep purple. Fenchurch roared into the car park, his tyres squealing against the worn tarmac. The dimming light created pools of shadow between the parked vehicles, turning the place into a maze of light and dark. He killed the engine and the sudden silence was jarring.

Fenchurch just sat there taking in the sky, a masterpiece of fading colours, its beauty a stark contrast to the prison, and let the stillness replace the constant movement since he'd left London.

Worst part was, he was bloody late. All that bravado about getting there in six hours... He'd tempted fate and forced the gods of high buggery to stick three stretches of roadworks on the M1 alone, plus another on the A1(M) just north of Northallerton.

The sign was already lit up:

HMP Frankland

Tucked away in rural County Durham, it was one of

Britain's most formidable detention centres. They called it the Monster Mansion, a reputation earned by housing some of the nation's most notorious inmates. Some Fenchurch had even put away himself. Some he didn't want to think too hard about.

Even from the car park, the place had an aura of dread. The imposing walls were crowned with razor wire with guard towers placed at intervals, housing watchful eyes scrutinising every corner of the expansive compound. Punctuated with CCTV cameras and barred windows, most of them mere slits. The entrance was fortified and heavily guarded.

With a deep sigh, he stepped out and the soft crunch of gravel beneath his shoes mixed with the distant sounds of the road back to the motorway.

And he'd been too stubborn to stop for a break.

Every joint in his body was crying out for relief and standing up felt like a visit to the chiropractor. Eight hours of solid driving had turned his spine into a series of protests, every vertebra aching. He stretched the kinks out of his back and it sounded like he was popping corn.

A car door opened and a figure approached, with a hint of wariness in his stride. Barrel chest and arms that showed signs of many hours spent in the gym. Weathered face and deep-set blue eyes. A tight crop of salt-and-pepper hair crowned his head. He looked Fenchurch up and down, a hint of disdain evident. 'You must be the cockney wanker.'

'That's DCI Cockney Wanker.' Fenchurch met his disdain with a warm smile. 'Williamson?'

'Right. DI Chris Williamson.' He offered a hand that seemed as much a challenge as a greeting. 'Fenchurch, aye?'

'That's me.' He took it, his grip just about as firm. 'Heard this place housed monsters. Didn't realise that extended to the local detectives too.'

Williamson smirked. 'We handle things differently up here.'

He set off towards the prison entrance. 'Danger we'll miss my kid's play, so if we could do this quickly.'

'Didn't drive for eight hours to do anything quickly, mate. Came here for answers.' Fenchurch shot him a sidelong glance. 'What's the play?'

Williamson paused, studying Fenchurch for a long moment before nodding. 'She's in *Nine to Five*.'

'The old Dolly Parton film?'

'And Jane Fonda. Been stressing herself silly about it for ages.'

'Thanks for helping me with this.'

'Not like I've got a choice. My gaffer's told us to keep a close eye on this. Don't want anything fucking this up, especially not a sparrow-eating cockney.'

Fenchurch let it slide. 'What involvement did you have with him?'

'We arrested him after he fled London. He'd been repeating his trick in Newcastle and Durham. On remand here because, let's be honest, he's going to spend the rest of his life here once the courts get around to him.' Williamson stopped to open the door. 'What's your interest in him?'

'Your boss knows.'

'Sure, she does.' And Cargill still hadn't bothered to contact Fenchurch. 'But what's the actual truth? Why are you interested in Josh Green?'

'That bit about him trafficking girls in the East End. One of them is wanted in connection with a double murder. And she's missing.'

'Rather you than me, mate.' Williamson clapped his hands together and gestured inside the prison. 'Alright, then, let's show you what Freakland has in store for you.'

19

Inside the prison, stark corridors echoed with their footsteps, peppered with the murmur of hushed conversations and the occasional shout. Fenchurch stepped into the common area, under the stern watch of guards and the ever-present cameras. The door clanged shut behind them and Fenchurch had that familiar tingling deep in his guts. Heavily outmanned, with some people who'd very much enjoy spending a little bit of time on their own with him in a room. He tried to cast the thoughts from his mind and just focus on following Williamson as they navigated another corridor, passing the doors to ranges of cells. Designed to give the inmates a modicum of privacy from casual observation, but it tended to keep the noise and the stink confined.

A door opened and an orderly stepped out. 'Fenchy. Younis says hi.'

Fenchurch ignored the voice, pretended it wasn't real, and continued on.

Williamson's shoulders seemed to ease off as he stepped through another door. He looked back at the closing door and shook his head. 'Having to walk past that lot on the way here...'

Fenchurch locked eyes with him. 'Know the feeling.'

'Did you hear someone say—'

'Gents.' The guard who'd guided them through was thumbing at a sturdy door, reinforced with metal with a tiny window of wired glass. 'Your guy's been in there ten minutes now. Don't like to keep them out of their cells for longer than about half an hour at a time, so if you could...'

'Sure.' Williamson smiled, then steeled himself at the door, standing next to Fenchurch. 'Place gets to you, you know?' He let out a deep breath. 'Anyway. Green's here, at least physically, so how about we get this over.'

'Sounds good to me. We'll see if we can get to the final song.' Fenchurch followed him into the interview room.

A box-like space, bathed in unflattering light from a single fluorescent tube overhead. The faded blue-grey walls bore faint scars and scratches from countless previous occupants. Disinfectant attempted to cover the musty dampness that seemed embedded in the very bones of the prison. Small CCTV cameras peered at them from all four corners, their red lights glaring, all trained on the heavy-duty table in the middle, bolted firmly to the ground, its surface marred by years of use.

Josh Green sat with a bravado out of place with the surroundings. Leaning back in the metal chair, revealing a ring of prison tattoos around his neck. Hard to tell what it was supposed to be, if anything. His red eyes scanned them both. A sex offender like him wouldn't have many friends inside. One who'd been trafficking kids would have even fewer. 'Which one of you's Fenchurch?'

Fenchurch raised his hand. 'Thanks for agreeing to meet us. Need to ask you—'

'Younis said hi.'

Fenchurch sat back and snorted. 'Did he? Well, I won't say anything back.'

'We ain't cellmates, but I see him from time to time.'

'You worked for him back home, didn't you?'

'In London? Nah. I'm my own man. Got my own plans. March to my own beat.'

'Sure. They all say that. Some even believe it.' Fenchurch sat back and let Green take him in. 'Read your file, though. Not a lot of people have a file on them. Means you've been a naughty boy for a very long time. You might deny working for Younis, but I gather you used to work for Flick Knife.'

'Flick Knife...' Green's laugh was like a bullet. 'Haven't heard that name in a while. Frank Blunden, God rest his soul.' He leaned forward, stroking his fingers across his tattoos. 'I did some stuff for him, yeah, but that was back in the day, wasn't it? Before this life finally caught up with him and he popped his clogs. Heard it was your old man who slotted him.'

'Nope.' Fenchurch gave him a smile. 'Someone tried to stitch him up. My old man's a bit of a naughty bugger, but he ain't that bad.'

Green sat back and folded his arms. 'Well, this has been a lovely catch-up on old times. Now, if you don't mind, I might head back to my cell.'

'Not so fast.' Williamson drummed his thumb and fingers on the tabletop. 'Why do people call you the Blacksmith?'

'It's...' Green bared his teeth. 'I... I was told this isn't part of the prosecution, so I'm not going to tell you.'

Williamson nodded slowly. 'See, I heard it's because you branded people.'

'*Branded*?'

'You know. Hot iron, pressed against skin.' Williamson made a hissing sound. 'That true?'

'No comment.' Green frowned. 'So, if this ain't about Younis, what is it about?'

Fenchurch saw something in those desperate eyes. The kind of greed that made someone sexually exploit children for their own financial gain was usually underpinned by other things.

Like a desire to throw anyone loosely connected to him under the bus. Someone like Dimitri Younis. Well, he was keen to see where it would lead. 'You got anything you can share about him?'

'Not if it gets back to him.' Green laughed. 'Heard the poor sod lost all of his money in some stupid investments. Bitcoin and all that shit. Don't understand it myself, but then I think not many do. Way I hear it, Younis still has a ton of power in London, don't he?'

Fenchurch shrugged. 'Does he?'

'Sure. People owe him favours. Might not have either bollock left, but he's still got influence and power. You ask me, I think he's got some cash squirrelled away somewhere.'

'He say anything about that?'

Green sniffed, then shifted on his seat and cast his gaze between them. 'Nah.'

'Jasmine Mason.'

Green jerked back like he'd take a cattle prod to the gut, then stood up sharply. 'You can fuck *right* off.'

'Charming.'

'I'm serious.' Green was shaking his head. 'I'm getting out of here. Guard!'

The door clattered open and the lump of muscle strolled back in. 'What's up, Josh?'

'Want out of here.'

'But you're being interviewed by these lovely men.'

'I know what their game is and I ain't playing it.'

Fenchurch stared at him. 'You recognise her name, though. Made you—'

'Fuck off.'

'The way you reacted... That's not the reaction of an innocent man, is it?'

'Fuck off! I'm leaving.'

'Jasmine was twelve when you started doing that to her.'

The guard scowled. '*Twelve?*'

Green raised his hands. 'I did fuck all to her.'

'But you know her.' Fenchurch stood up but kept his distance. 'Now as soon as I mentioned her name, you clear off. So that makes me think you did what they say you did to her.'

'Ain't talking to you about her.' Green focused on the guard. 'Get me out of here. Now!'

Fenchurch moved over to the door. 'Look, Josh, if you've got something on Younis, we can work something out here. You talk to us, we can see what we can do. But Jasmine's missing and we want to—'

'Fuck. Off.' Green walked over to the door and left the room.

The guard gave Fenchurch a what-can-I-do shrug, then followed him out.

The door slammed.

Williamson snorted. 'Guessing you have that impact on a lot of people you meet.'

'Happens more often than not, yeah.' Fenchurch sat back in his chair. 'I drove eight hours for that.' He sighed. 'Okay, so I'm trying to process this, but I'm coming to two conclusions here. First, as soon as we mentioned Jasmine's name, he cleared off. That implies guilt.'

'Second?'

'Second thing is he's clearly been speaking to Dimitri Younis. This is the Monster Mansion and Younis is nothing if not a monster. I know it's late and you want to get to Dolly Parton, but is there any chance we could have a word with him?'

20

Same room, different monster.

A much, much worse one.

Even as he sat in the safe atmosphere of the prison interview room, Dimitri Younis exuded an air of menace. Deep-set eyes taking in every detail from beneath a pronounced brow. Each scar on his sinewy hands told a story, his fingers stroking the table. 'Fenchy.' His voice was a sinister whisper, his vocal cords shredded by all the screaming he'd done a few months ago. 'What brings you into my domain?'

'Last I checked, this was His Majesty's Prison. Not the domain of a sex offender who's lost both testicles.'

Younis winced, then covered it over with a snarl. 'You know what? Fuck this. I'll see you in court, Fenchy, where you'll have to watch me get found not guilty because one of your coppers decided to go medieval on me.'

'That won't count for anything, Dimitri. You've done a lot of things over and above that. Sure, he'll get reprimanded for it. But that prosecution is copper-bottomed.'

'Sure it is, Fenchy. Sure it is.'

Fenchurch waved around the room. 'This place is your new

home, so I hope you're making yourself comfortable here.' He paused, then smiled. 'Actually, this'll be your last home. You might've managed to get yourself released a couple of years back, but you won't be getting out again. Not this time. We've got a watertight case and you haven't got the cash to afford anything above a low-end Legal Aid lawyer. And the charges will stack up. You'll die in here. Or you'll die in a secure hospital unit down the road. But you'll never experience freedom again.'

Younis sat there with a snide smirk on his face. 'As much as it arouses me to see you, big guy, this little chat is making me miss *The Repair Shop*.'

'What the hell is that?'

'Daytime TV shit. Some posh sods repair family heirlooms. Fair brings a tear to your eyes.' Younis tucked his hands in his pockets. 'So this better be important.'

Fenchurch held the gaze and reflected the snark. 'Oh, it's very important. Thing is, we've just been speaking to Josh Green.'

Younis frowned then tried to cover it with a smile. But he clearly knew him. Whether he knew what he'd done was something Fenchurch would get to. 'What do you want with him?'

'You know him, yeah?'

'I do. Both of us are on remand here. I'm here for shit I didn't do. Him, I don't know. I mean, this place… It's practically in Scotland, isn't it? Why have they put me here? I keep asking but nobody tells me the reason.'

'Dimitri, this is the highest-security prison in England. Scotland and Wales too. Maybe not Northern Ireland. So, of course, it's the only real choice for someone like yourself, especially after you've been released before and *especially* with all the crimes you've been charged with. Unless you get shifted somewhere else, which is very unlikely, you're going to spend the rest of your natural life in this place.'

'I don't have an unnatural one. I ain't a vampire or a werewolf.'

'Dad jokes now?' Fenchurch laughed. 'Thing is, Dimitri, I'll be one of the people presenting evidence in court. Now, my plan is to take the stand and go through all of the evidence both my lot and the City of London police have collated on you. See, it's not just sexual and physical crimes, it's financial too. Sure you can imagine how extensive our treasure trove is, especially now we've got access to all those encrypted drives of yours.'

A brief flash of fear shot across Younis's face.

Fenchurch leaned forward and lowered his voice. 'Of course, as part of that I could raise the fact you've helped us with this case. Don't get your hopes up, though. You're not getting off with anything, Dimitri, but it might make your sentence a little bit lighter.'

Younis laughed. 'What difference does a year or two make when it's twenty-odd?'

'Love your optimism there.' Fenchurch smiled, enjoying watching him squirm. Someone like Younis spent their lives in a dream world where nobody could touch them. Seeing him humbled like this, crushed by reality, it made Fenchurch appreciate the work he and his team had put in over the years. 'It's not just how long you're away for, Dimitri. *Where* counts. This place can't be much fun, even for a man like yourself. Maybe we could get you a cushier cell. Maybe that cell could be in a cushier prison.'

'Lots of ifs, buts and maybes here, Fenchy.'

'It's all I can offer. But I'm a man of my word. You know that. If I say I'll do something, I will do it.'

Younis scratched at his neck. 'Guess I do know that, yeah.'

Fenchurch felt like he'd won him around, but he knew with Younis never to count those chickens until they were running around and clucking. 'Reason we're here is to find Jasmine Mason. Canning Town girl. Got herself into a spot of bother.

Someone trafficked her, made her work the streets for him. You know the drill.'

Younis nodded slowly. 'And that someone is Josh Green?'

'You got it in one.'

'And how do I help? What do you want from me?'

'Dimitri, Josh started trafficking her when she'd just turned twelve. She's not even fourteen now.'

'Fucking hell.' Younis swallowed hard. 'He didn't tell me *that*.'

'Not many in your line of work like to admit to being a nonce, do they?'

'I mean, I like fresh meat as much as the next guy.' Younis gave a disgusting leer. 'But I want them to be *legal* and to consent, of course. *Thirteen*? Thir-fucking-teen? Jesus…'

Fenchurch nodded along with it. 'She's gone missing, Dimitri. Last seen in a hotel with a man who went on to kill two men and injure another.'

'She helped kill them?'

'We don't know. But she's thirteen, Dimitri. Please help us. I know there's a part of you that wants to do good. Please.'

'How…?' Younis blew air up his face. The question seemed aimed at himself rather than Fenchurch. 'Josh worked for me, yeah? Pretended he didn't, but he did. They all did. And, of course, when he saw me in here, he came up and tried to act the big man. Tried to get my protection. So I made him open right up. Until he was *gaping*.' A smirk. 'And he talked to me about a few of the girls he'd run in London. Said one of them was called Jasmine. Told me how he'd picked her up, wooed her, got her on the game. Oldest trick in the book, yeah? But he… I didn't know she was *that* young. And that kind of shit doesn't wash with me. You're a prick, Fenchy, and I fucking hate you. I wish *you'd* had your bollocks removed, not me. Wish you'd lost your voice because you'd screamed so much. I wish that on you. I wish all the pain on you. But this…' His snarl showed that Josh Green was going to pay somehow. 'I've caused a lot of people a lot of heartache and hardship in my time, but they're all adults. They all knew the game and what they were getting into before they put their toes into the water. And they get a lot out of it too. I'm all about the quid pro quo. Especially the quid. But this is a kid, Fenchy. *Thirteen*... I want to help you find her.' He narrowed his eyes. 'Just like you found Jennifer.'

Fucker.

Motherfucker.

Fenchurch gripped his thighs under the table. He knew the name Chloe had been raised under by those animals who took her.

Fenchurch could easily smash that face into the desk, break the rest of him, not just his lost testicles.

But they were on video and Fenchurch couldn't rise to the temptation. Motherfucker had lured him in and now he was trying to get his goat. Make him lose the rag.

Fenchurch took a deep breath and tried to stay as still and calm as possible. Show no reaction.

'What do you want from me, Fenchy?'

'Let's start with everything Josh Green told you about Jasmine.' His voice sounded higher pitched than he would've liked.

'Okay, so the disappointment for you is I have no idea what's happened to her. Just so we're clear on that.' Younis sat back. 'And the rest of it, if you want it. It's just going to be you and me, Fenchy.' He waved at Williamson. 'Cheerio, buddy.'

Fenchurch tapped Williamson on the arm. 'Give us a minute.'

'Sure?'

'Sure.'

Williamson sighed then got to his feet and sidled over to the door, then left the room. Seconds later, the red eyes of the CCTV went black.

Younis let out a deep breath. 'Must be what a bird feels like when they take their bra off at the end of a long shitty day. You've no idea, Fenchy. I'm watched all the time in here. Constantly. Can't go for a shit without it being on some log somewhere. Imagine that being your job. Logging all of my logs.'

Fenchurch left him a pause, long enough to make him think he found it funny. 'I've held up my side, Dimitri. Time for your quid pro quo.'

'You know I run a lot of pimps in my organisation. Right? Well, we have a thing where we discuss the boys and girls they run. Josh Green was keen to talk about a girl called Jasmine. Said she made him a lot of cash. And I got my cut of that. All was good. But I swear I didn't know her age.'

'You didn't ask. Didn't wonder why she was so lucrative for him.'

'No. I did ask. Josh told me she was legal. And believe me, Fenchy, I fucking hate being lied to.'

'Assuming I believe you, what else did he tell you about her?'

'Guys like that are very keen to update you on stuff. It's bizarre, but hey. I'm an important guy, ain't I? Josh said he sold her to another guy to settle some drug debts.'

'*Sold* her?'

'Right. Happens in that game. To the boys and girls, it looks like they've got someone else to look after them, but there's always money involved. As far as I know, the new guy seemed pretty happy with her.'

'Another of your people is trafficking in thirteen-year-olds?'

'Nope. Not mine.'

'Who was it, then?'

'Called himself Colin Scott.'

Fenchurch thought it through. 'Right, well. Don't know if it's his real name or not. Most of them use a pseudonym, to protect themselves. But he was a john, right? Some of these daft buggers fall in love with the girls. Fuck knows what they do with them once they've bought them. Keep them in a gilded cage, probably. Maybe a horrible one. I don't know. I'm a few steps removed, so it's not my problem.'

Normally, Fenchurch would attack him. These venal crimes were happening with his knowledge, perpetrated by his people. And he was talking about people being bought and sold like cattle. But he needed to focus on the prize here. 'Was it Rusty Rivers?'

Younis laughed. '*Who?*'

'Real name is Don Avonmore.'

'Right. Nope. Who's he when he's at home?'

'Singer. Big hits in the seventies and eighties.'

'He your killer or your victim?'

'Maybe both.'

'Oh, intriguing. Sorry, Fenchy, but that's me all dried up. That's all that nonce told me. Happy for you to lube me up, though.'

'Never change, Dimitri.' Fenchurch left a pause. 'Actually. Please do change.'

'I'm trying. Believe me. And I hope you find this girl. I mean that. And Josh is about to get what's coming to him.'

'Please, just let us handle that.'

'Oh, I won't kill him. But I've learnt that losing your bollocks causes a lot of pain. If he suffers a manscaping accident, you won't be able to tie it back to me, even if you think I did it.' Younis got up and walked over to the door. 'I'll look forward to seeing you in court, Fenchy.' He stopped there, head bowed. 'I'm taking you at your word that you'll be kind to me. I've given you a lot.'

'Just leave Green alone. That's all I ask.'

21

Fenchurch stepped back into the car park and the cold air slapped his face. It was dark and freezing now, but he was outside the Monster Mansion again and away from the demons lurking in there.

Of course, he knew Younis was stuck there, but he hadn't expected to see him again in his life, except in court. So to have to speak to him there...

Williamson snorted, his breath misting in the air between them. 'That get you anything?'

'Something. Whether it's bullshit or not, we shall see.'

'If you want my opinion, mate, he seemed genuine.'

'Thought so too, but he's done this before. And thanks for clearing out when he asked to.'

'Sometimes you need to get the intel, right? Sod the evidence trail.' Williamson craned his neck around to look at Fenchurch. 'He had you rattled at one point, though. Mind me asking who Jennifer is?'

'My daughter. I mean, her name's Chloe, but she was called that by the people who raised her. It's a long story, but it's been all over the papers.'

'That was *you*?' Williamson looked at Fenchurch like he'd only just noticed him. Up and down. Eyes narrowing. 'Thought I recognised you from somewhere.'

Fenchurch looked away. 'Thing is, her name was never public domain.' Saying it out loud, hearing it... Yeah, it was absolute bullshit to think it was a guess. Younis *knew*. 'And I don't think Younis was involved in what happened back then, but you just never know. It happened seventeen years ago. He'd have only been eighteen, I think.'

'But?'

'But I wouldn't put anything past him. *Anything*.'

'You catch who did it?'

'We did. But... It was a group. An organisation. One of those things where you just can't be sure you've got them all.' Fenchurch covered over the pain with a smile. 'Anyway. I think that's a lot to be getting on with.'

'Really?'

'You'll know yourself, Chris... These guys don't give anything away. We got a lot today. I appreciate your help.' Fenchurch held out a hand for shaking. 'You get yourself back to Dolly Parton.'

Williamson shook it. 'Mate, it's all part of it, eh? You take care of yourself, Fenchurch. You're a cockney wanker, but you're okay. You got a bed for the night?'

Fenchurch checked his watch. Six, on the dot. 'I'll find somewhere, yeah. Probably need to get something to eat, but I can't stomach much just now.'

'You know where I am if you need me.'

'Thanks, Chris.'

'Anytime.' Williamson trudged over to his car, checking his phone. He got in and shot across the park – maybe he'd make some of the school show after all.

Fenchurch got in his own car and let the cold linger on his skin. He should turn the engine on and get all warmed up. Instead, he sat there, trying to decide what to do.

If he left now, he could be back in London by midnight probably, assuming traffic would be light. He could make some calls on the motorway, try to make some progress on this case. See if any of the stories he'd just gathered stacked up, then get Kay and Ronnie to input into it all.

Seeing Younis again, like that was tough, but he didn't know whether to believe him or not.

Still, Younis had actually helped him a few times in the past. When he didn't have to. He'd given him some leads that actually led somewhere.

He had to take him at his word.

He tried to focus on the fact things were in a better place than he imagined, even with two murder victims and what happened to Don Avonmore.

But the bottom line was a sucker punch in the guts. No real leads on Jasmine's whereabouts, but... He'd find her. He'd give everything to find her.

Fenchurch turned on the ignition and put the heating up full. He drove off, navigating the stupid menus to call Reed, drumming his fingers off the steering wheel as it connected. He should find a Premier Inn or Travelodge around here, to get some shuteye, then maybe come back and have another go at Josh Green. Pin him down with Younis's words.

'Guv?' Sounded like Reed was in the station.

'Evening, Kay. You alright?'

'Getting there, guv. Very, very slowly.'

'Anything to update from your end?'

Her long sigh must've covered over his words. 'How did it go, guv?'

'Got nowhere with Green. Ended up speaking to Younis.'

She gasped. 'Younis?'

'He's on remand here. Turns out he made a few enemies in

Belmarsh, so they're tolerating him a bit better here. Or keeping a closer eye on him. Thing is, all I've got for a stupid amount of driving is a name. Colin Scott.'

'Means nothing to me.'

'Isn't there a police federation cop by that name?'

'Oh, yeah. Him. Not his full name, guv. He's David Colin Scott Davies. His old man was David Davies, so he uses his middle names. Everyone calls him Dave, though.'

'Could be real, or it could an assumed one. Given what he's alleged to have done, I think it's an assumed one.'

'What's he done?'

'He bought Jasmine off Green.'

Another gasp. '*Bought* her?'

'According to Younis. Some pimp stuff. Probably sold her to a client.'

'Okay, so I can see why you've got the doubt.'

'Indeed. Can you dig into that name?'

'On it. But there must be a million Colin Scotts in London.'

'Just looking for connections to the case.' Fenchurch turned on the ignition and switched the heating up full. Cars swished on the road past the prison. It might be cold, but at least it was dry. 'How's it going back in sunny London, Kay?'

'Pissing down. Otherwise, we've been following a lead on Jasmine's whereabouts. Spotted her by the O2 in Greenwich about three weeks ago.'

'In Greenwich?'

'Yeah. No concerts on that night.'

'It's near Avonmore's home.'

'Few miles away, but yeah. It's not far. Turns out she went to a shelter in Lewisham.'

Fenchurch played it through, adding to what he had. 'That would be around the time she stopped being seen with Avonmore.'

'It would, yeah. She stayed a night there, then her brother turned up to collect her. Black Scottish guy.'

'Kanyif.'

'Indeed.' Reed sighed down the line. 'Some cases we really struggle to narrow things down, but this one...'

'Any aggro between them?'

'Not really. She didn't seem happy to go, but they didn't fight or anything.'

'Okay, so I'm wondering if either Kanyif or Avonmore is Colin Scott.'

'Like I said, I'll dig into him. See if we can get anything to tie them together.'

'I don't like this, Kay. Someone buying and selling people. Younis told me it happened. Bold as brass.'

'Have you got any evidence to support it?'

'Of course. It was just me and him. But the local cop recorded it all.' As he drove, Fenchurch put his hands over the air vents and tried to get some warmth back into them. 'Kay, the big thing is... it's reminding me of what happened a few years ago. That case where I thought it might've been Chloe. I know my girl's alive and well now, working as a cop, but back then... I didn't. And I wake up some nights and I'm back in the middle of that nightmare.'

'It's okay, guv.'

'I know. It's all part of it. But this case... Her dad... You saw him, Kay. Right?'

'I did.'

'This is what these bastards do to people, Kay. They take and they take and... They don't care who gets eaten up in the process.'

'I'm sorry it's reminding you of all that, guv.'

'I'll be fine, Kay, but... We just need to find her. That's all.'

'Well, I've *maybe* got some good news. I've got an address for Kanyif Iqbal near Glasgow. Under his real name.'

Fenchurch entered the details into the car's satnav. 'Glasgow's not *too* far away...'

22

This was one drive too far.

The house sat all hunched on a grimy street in the depths of North Lanarkshire. From the disused coalfields of County Durham to here. Not even Glasgow, just the overspill into old coal-mining territory.

A row of post-war relics left to rot. Half the windows were boarded up, while others held on to greasy panes, gazing out like tired eyes. The pavement was scarred with potholes. The faint sounds of distant arguments and the nearby motorway melded with the chilly Scottish air. The pebbledash covering the walls was cracked in the corners, with dark stains from rainwater. Graffiti tagged the house as belonging to Hamilton Young Team. Still baffled Fenchurch that kids would be so daft as to get into that crap, especially these days, but then again people with nothing always gravitated towards those who had a little bit more. Power, money, whatever it was. It's how people like Younis thrived.

Fenchurch got out into the cool air, threaded through the cigarette smoke, though he couldn't determine the source of it. He felt a long way from home. And back in time – he'd spent a winter up here and never felt warm the whole time, not even in the bath. That water never got hot enough.

He checked his watch and yawned. He really should get to his bed. Get an early start tomorrow. But the night wasn't so much young as ready to give him the opportunity for a bit more.

A Toyota sports car pulled up and whizzed into a parallel park behind him. The driver narrowed her eyes at him, then got out. 'You the DCI?'

'Do I look like a cop to you?'

'Everything about you screams cop.' She thrust out a hand. 'DS Olivia Blackman.' She defied the stereotypes of the hard-edged Glasgow detective. With an infectious energy, her youthful face lit up the cold evening. Bright, intelligent eyes sparkled with devilry and challenge. 'My boss told me to meet you here and make sure you don't cause any mischief.' Her auburn hair danced playfully as she laughed.

'Mischief's my middle name, sadly.'

'My ex-husband almost literally had that name.' She smiled. 'Less said about that clown the better.'

He hoped she wasn't fishing... 'Does the name Colin Scott mean anything to you?'

'Nope.'

'What about Don Avonmore?'

'Isn't that...' She clicked her fingers. 'That old singer?'

'Rusty Rivers.'

'Right. Mark's a massive fan.'

'Mark?'

She winced. 'Mark's my ex. Well. Kind of ex-husband but current boyfriend. It's complicated.'

'Sounds it. Is he a cop?'

'He's the least-cop person you'll ever meet.' She tugged at his sleeve. 'Word of advice, never get into bed with an author. They're all mad.'

'So I gather.' Fenchurch folded his arms. It was freezing. And was that rain? Bloody hell. 'So. I believe this address belongs to one Edward Keith Deeley AKA Kanyif Iqbal.'

'Yeah. Not sure how he got from one to the other, but he did. Reason my boss asked me to help you is I investigated Kanyif AKA Keith for a few crimes over the years. He was wanted for a stabbing. Got off with it. Pushed someone over in a fight, broke their ribs. Couldn't prosecute, either. The thing with Glasgow nightclubs is they can be edgy as fuck. And Kanyif played that game, trying to be the hardest in there. Always the big man. Drugs, knives, gangs. All of it.'

'Guessing there's a reason for that?'

'Right. Poor guy had a tough life. Dad never on the scene, really. And mixed-race kids are a lot rarer up here than down south. Upshot is they get a lot more abuse from both sides of the divide.' She sighed. 'Before you start, my surname really is Blackman. It's a Danish Viking name, or so my old man says. It's not a racist joke.'

'I wasn't going to ask.'

'Good. Last I heard, Keith started rapping and became Kanyif. Did a few shows here. One thing Glasgow's got is a great music scene. A local manager loved his voice. Got a London producer interested. The rest is history.'

'Never heard a note of his music.' Fenchurch looked over at the grim house. 'And this is where he grew up?'

'Indeed.' Olivia walked over to the house and rattled the door. 'You been waiting here long?'

'Just five minutes. Drove up from Durham.'

'*Durham?* Not London.'

'Had to speak to someone there.'

'They don't have phones in London?'

'It was an inmate at HMP Frankland. Wanted to see the whites of his eyes.'

'Ah. You drove there from London?'

'Indeed.'

'Long way from your patch.'

'Yeah. I used to work up here, mind. A few months, about ten years ago. Just after a stint in Florida.'

'Wow. That's quite a difference.'

'Less than you'd think.' Fenchurch checked his watch. Nine o'clock. 'So, the reason you're meeting me here at this time is he's dead.'

'So I gather. We need to break the news to his mother, right?'

'Among a few other things. Thing is.' Fenchurch spotted a neighbour smoking a cigarette outside her front door and leaned in a bit closer to Olivia. 'Before that, we have reason to believe he's been harbouring a trafficked girl.'

'Harbouring?'

'He might've rescued her. Might've abused her.'

'Fuck.'

'You ever hear any whispers of that?'

She shook her head. 'He always had a few girls on the scene, all white. But they were usually older than him.'

The door opened and a woman stood there. Her face was etched with lines. The weight of the world dragged down on her stooped shoulders. Her sunken eyes, shadowed and tired, darted about. Long hair hanging in limp strands, the grey more prominent than the original dark brown. 'Are you two wanting something because I can fucking hear you over my telly!'

'Police, ma'am.' Fenchurch showed his warrant card. 'Need to speak to you—'

'Olivia?' She was squinting at her. 'Is that you?'

She nodded. 'Hiya, Mary.' She walked over to her, head tilted to the side. 'How are you doing?'

'I'm *fine*.' The word was a snapped rebuke. Mary kept scowling at Fenchurch. 'Who's he? What's this about? Why are you here?'

'This is DCI Simon Fenchurch, Mary. He's a cop from London. We need to talk to you about Keith.'

'My useless bastard of a son.' Mary pulled the door to behind her and cut the din of some Netflix show. Obviously her remote's pause button didn't work. Not letting them in, then. 'What's Keith done?'

'Mary, DCI Fenchurch here needs to talk to you about him.'

'Well, I don't care. Haven't seen my laddie in fucking months. He moved out of his flat a few years ago. Thought he was maybe with his brother in Thailand.'

'He has a brother?'

'Aye. John. Half-brother, anyway. Useless prick. Worked on the rigs until they spotted how useless he was.'

'Does his brother have any children?'

'*John?*' Mary laughed. 'God no. He's gay. Loves a bit of sausage.'

'Right. That doesn't preclude—'

'Nope. I know what you're going to say. Some gay men have kids. Not John. He's not the kind to give anything back, is he? Probably a psychopath, you know?'

Fenchurch made a note to follow up on it. 'Does the name Colin Scott mean anything to you?'

She screwed up her face. 'Should it?'

'Take that as a no. Do you have any idea where Keith could be?'

'Moved out of his flat, like I said. Are you deaf or just fucking stupid?'

Fenchurch missed the brutality of a Scot. 'So he's not been here?'

'Not in fucking ages. Said to his brother that he was staying with his manager.'

'Know his name?'

'He's mentioned him, but I'll be fucked if I'm listening.'

'He live in Glasgow?'

'Fuck no. St Andrews.'

Fenchurch frowned. 'The golf course?'

'The posh town in Fife, you daft bastard.'

'Got an address for him?'

'Somewhere.' She disappeared inside, leaving the door open a crack.

Olivia leaned in close. 'You have to tell her sooner or later.'

'Let's get this address first, then you can handle it.'

'Oh, thank you, *sir*.'

Mary came back and handed an old envelope to Olivia. 'Here you are, hen.' She scanned between them. 'Listen, you two really need to tell me what this is about.'

Fenchurch gestured for Olivia to break the news of her son's death.

23

The inky night wrapped Vicky Dodds in a shroud of unease. The house behind her was filled with a sleeping family.

Her sleeping family.

Husband on an early start, both kids asleep in their rooms, so she stood at the end of the driveway, checking her watch and letting out a slow breath. Waiting outside was the only way to contain things and avoid too many questions. Especially at this time.

The ambient glow of the lone streetlight cast long shadows on the tarmac. The world seemed to hold its breath, the only sounds distant cars on the new road and her own heartbeat throbbing in her ears.

The first cold droplets of rain hit her face, light and sporadic, but increasing in tempo until they tapped an impatient rhythm on the pavement. Her coat, already inadequate against the chill, offered little protection and the water began to seep through. Just when she was about to give in to despair, the hum of an engine broke the stillness.

Headlights pierced the night, cutting through the veil of rain as it made its way toward her, the driver squinting at her as it came to a gentle stop. Even before the engine died, she recognised the ugly mug behind the wheel.

The car door opened and Simon Fenchurch stepped out, a dance of droplets colliding with his coat. He waved at her as he approached her. 'Evening, Vicky.'

'Simon.' She leaned in and kissed his cheek. Just once. 'How are you?'

He gave a shrug. 'What are you doing outside?'

'Waiting for you. Everyone goes to bed early in our house.' She tapped her smartwatch, showing it as just before eleven. 'And it's pretty late.'

'Yeah, sorry about that.' He stopped a few feet from her, the rain now a curtain between them. 'Look, I could've got a hotel.'

'It's fine. I didn't have to answer your call or offer you a bed for the night. And this is a good way of pre-empting me getting allocated to helping you tomorrow.' She set off towards the house. 'Come on, let's get you a cup of tea.'

'I'm gasping, thanks.'

'Gather you caused a bit of trouble in Glasgow?'

'Word spreads fast.'

'That's Police Scotland for you.' Vicky opened the door and stopped the dogs before they started jumping. 'Calm down!' She let him in, then nudged the door shut. 'Bloody dogs...' She led him into the kitchen. 'Full fat or decaf?'

'Decaf, ta.'

'Coming right up.' She filled the kettle and stuck it on to boil, then eased some mugs from the tree onto the counter. The dishwasher rumbled and hissed through its evening cycle. She leaned back against the counter and folded her arms, inspecting him more closely under the spotlights. He looked tired, but the heaviness in his existence seemed to have lifted slightly. 'So. Glasgow, eh? You and Olivia Blackman got stuff thrown at you?'

Fenchurch winced. 'Weirdest death message I've ever seen. Soon as DS Blackman told her, Mary Deeley started throwing things at us. Kettle. Frying pan. Knives.' He shook his head then spread his hands. 'I mean, I get it. Deaths of children are the *worst*. Can't imagine what it must feel like, but…'

'Me neither.'

'Didn't know that you Scots can be *that* anti-English, though. I heard a lot of words I don't know paired with words I do know.'

'Oh, you Sassenach wankers aren't well loved up here.'

He smiled. 'That was one of them, but it was paired with something a bit stronger and that rhymed with "hunt".'

'Justified, though.' Vicky laughed. 'And don't take it personally. Most places up here, that word is used like punctuation.'

'Kind of the same in parts of London, to be honest with you.'

The kettle clicked and Vicky poured the water into two waiting cups, then mashed the tea bags and dumped them into a compost caddy. 'Milk? Sugar?'

'Just milk. Sweet enough as I am.'

'Yawn.' She poured some in then passed him the cup. 'Here.'

Fenchurch blew on the surface. 'Thanks.'

'Olivia's a good cop. Whatever happened, she'll sort it out for you.'

'Her and half of Glasgow's uniformed contingent were trying to do exactly that.' He took a sip of tea and gasped. 'You worked with her much?'

'A bit. She got into a bit of mischief last summer. Her exhusband's kid went missing up in the Highlands. Investigation was pretty difficult. He kind of went off-piste, though I'm sure you can understand that…'

He didn't say anything, just raised an eyebrow.

'Dundee's the lowest point in the North region of Police Scotland, so me and my team spent a fortnight up way past Inverness, sorting stuff out afterwards. An absolute quagmire of shite, to be honest.'

'They don't have cops up there?'

'They do, it's just...' Vicky shrugged. 'Cases that fucked up, they like to get another team from another city in, to make sure there's no cross-contamination. Had the same from Aberdeen in one of mine.'

'Seen similar things in the Met, but your cities are our boroughs.' Another sip of tea. 'How fucked up are we talking?'

'That's a whole other story.' Vicky sipped her tea and set it aside. She knew she wasn't going to drink any more of it. 'Think Olivia's ex is an author. My husband's read some of his stuff. Not my cup of tea, but he's one of those types who does a bit too much research. Whatever the writerly equivalent of method acting is, he does it. And Olivia said he was in huge amounts of debt to a loan shark too. One of my... friends, I guess, had to lead another investigation down in Edinburgh to tear that whole operation apart.'

'Sounds complicated.'

'And then some.'

'And here's me thinking the Met was tricky.'

'Oh, you've got it easy down there.' Vicky smiled at him. 'But after I got off the phone to you, I checked with the boss. I'll be accompanying you to St Andrews in the morning.' She waved at the window. 'You can practically see it from here. It's over the mouth of the Tay, but it takes the best part of an hour to get there.' She rested her hands on her hips. 'And I'd appreciate it if someone doesn't throw stuff at us.'

'Hopefully not.' Fenchurch smiled, then took a big glug of tea. 'How've you been since I last saw you?'

'Been pretty quiet, to be honest. And quiet's good. But I

prefer things happening.' She reached into the cupboard for a packet of biscuits, but there was only one left. And it looked a bit fusty. She handed it to him. 'Been a lot going on with you, right?'

'New knee, yeah.' Fenchurch took the biscuit, then stretched out his leg. 'I'm like Robocop now.'

'You're moving a lot better.'

'Thanks. And thank you for the flowers and the card, meant a lot.'

'Least I could do. I haven't known you that long, Simon, but you've been a mentor to me. And I appreciate it. Not easy being a DI with my kids, that's for sure. You've been such a great sounding board.' She fixed him with that hard stare. 'Never judgemental, always understanding. It means a lot.'

He returned the hard stare with interest. 'I know what people have to do at times in this job. The decisions you have to make. You've made some tough ones. The same ones I'd do, given half a chance.'

'I don't think many would.'

'You and I are cut from the same cloth.'

'It's quite flammable.' She laughed. 'So, let me get this straight. You've driven from London to Durham, then to Glasgow and now to Carnoustie?'

'Yeah.' Fenchurch slurped at his tea. 'Only seen this place on the TV because of the golf.'

'I'd show you around but there's not much to see. And you'll probably want to get back to London soon, right?'

'Let's just see what tomorrow brings, yeah?'

'Okay. You must be hungry?'

'Had fish and chips on the way up the road.' He was scowling. 'What the hell is sauce?'

'It's an Edinburgh thing. They've got it in bits of Fife too.'

'It ruined my dinner. Is it brown sauce?'

'Watered down brown sauce is the best way to describe it.'

'Yeah, well, it won't catch on.'

'Chips in Edinburgh are rubbish.' She picked up his empty teacup. 'Now, you go and get yourself to bed. We've got an early start. You need a toothbrush?'

'About that...'

DAY 3

Wednesday

24

Tears filled Kanyif's eyes. 'Man, you don't get it, do you?' He pressed the gun against Fenchurch's lips. 'You don't get it!'

The sharp crack of a gunshot ripped through the silence.

Fenchurch jerked awake.

A dark room. Sweat pouring off him. The place was stinking of the broken biscuits stink of his sweat.

Where the hell was he?

He lay back and tried to think it through. Didn't help that he was bursting for a pee.

Vicky Dodds.

Her home. That's where he was. All that driving yesterday. Up from home to Durham, to here.

Hard to face the truth, though – he was running away from his problems.

Cargill was right – he was a manager. He should be managing, not driving up to bloody Scotland to *do*.

And that dream... Like a PTSD flashback. Hard to avoid that conclusion after a rapper tried to kill him.

It made him think though – he still didn't know what he

didn't get, whatever message Kanyif was trying to impart. But it wasn't looking good for Kanyif. Having a thirteen-year-old with him...

His stomach growled and rumbled. Whatever the hell sauce was, it didn't agree with him.

He felt around for his phone and woke the display. 5:56. Not too shabby, but he could do with another couple of hours. Always could, though.

His phone vibrated with a message from Vicky:

> Hey, you up?

Fenchurch turned on his light and took his time sitting up. He was sore from all the driving.

> Up yeah. Where's the toilet?

> One opposite you is free until Bella dominates it for an hour before school.

> Thanks.

Fenchurch got up and hauled on yesterday's clothes. He probably stank, but he couldn't smell himself. Maybe the odour of broken biscuits was him. He crossed the corridor and pushed into the bathroom, then sat on the pan.

A text from Cargill sat there, sent ten minutes earlier. He hadn't noticed it:

> Simon, I'm handling the W London situation, per protocol. I don't need to hear from you. Sure you can handle the case. Will be in Lem St tomorrow afternoon to touch base. Best, Alison

All the warmth of an asteroid in deep space.

He flushed, then washed his hands.

He was the best part of five hundred miles from home, chasing down the thinnest of leads, just so he could avoid Cargill.

Yeah, that was healthy behaviour.

He went back into the hallway.

'Hi.' Vicky was in her dressing gown, yawning into her fists. 'Got some porridge on the hob. You fancy some?'

'Not really a fan of porridge.'

'Oh, you'll love the way I make it. Dad's recipe, passed down through decades of Doddses from Ancient Roman times.'

'You know what, that'd be lovely. Thanks.' Fenchurch followed her into the kitchen, filled with the aroma of fresh coffee brewing in a filter machine. 'Any idea where I can get clean pants and a shirt from?'

'We'll be going past a Markies in Dundee on the way there. Sure you can get changed in the toilets.' She stirred the pot on the hob. 'Did a bit more digging into this bloke we're looking for. A friend of mine investigated a rock band this guy used to manage. Expect Delays, I think they were called.'

'I remember them. Had a couple of decent singles. Didn't the singer get done for murder?'

'Two, I think. A whole mess.'

'She coming to help?'

'She?'

'Your friend?'

'Oh. He's a he. And no. He's the last person you want to help.' She plonked two bowls on the counter, then dolloped thick porridge into them. 'Here you go. Maple syrup? Sugar? Peanut butter?'

Fenchurch sat at the breakfast bar. 'I'll take whatever you want.'

She drizzled maple syrup in and handed it over.

Didn't look the most appetising, but Fenchurch was in her

home, so he started stirring the syrup into the gloop. 'Thank you. Smells good.'

'It's just porridge.'

'And for helping.'

She sat opposite him. 'You helped me out. It's the least I could do.'

'Sure I'm not getting in the way of your work?'

'No way. I'm in court tomorrow, so all I'd be doing today is prep for it. I kind of need a break from that case, to be honest.'

Fenchurch took a bite of the porridge and, surprise surprise, he actually liked it. 'This is delicious.'

'See? What did I tell you?'

25

The vast golf course stretched out to the left, its manicured greens and bunkers desolate in the morning light, with the muted roar of the North Sea in the distance and the twinkling lights of Carnoustie over the water, just like Vicky had said.

Fenchurch piloted his car through the historic streets of St Andrews. Gothic spires reached for the sky. Old stone buildings lined Links Crescent, leafy like some North London suburb, but both felt a million miles from his stomping ground in the East End – this was much nearer that distance.

He followed Vicky's car onto North Street, which looked like the town's main artery, but his satnav showed another one a block north. If *block* was the right term for a town this old.

Vicky pulled in on a double yellow, opposite a pub and a hotel. Up ahead, university buildings bustled with student life. The streets were alive with youth and energy as they trudged towards their first lectures of the day.

Fenchurch grabbed the space behind her car and put the usual sign out – hopefully Scottish traffic wardens obeyed that.

He got out of his car into the chill of the morning and stretched out. 'That was some drive over.'

'November isn't exactly seeing it in its best light.'

'Looked fine to me.'

She smiled. 'You get your clean underwear in Markies?'

'And this shirt, yeah. You'd have thought I'd learn to pack a go bag but...' Fenchurch scratched at his neck. 'I've been known to have a bit of tunnel vision.'

Her eyes narrowed. 'Something I should worry about?'

'God, no. Just not thinking about certain things.' Fenchurch looked up at the townhouse. 'So the manager of a rock band lives *here*?'

The townhouse was four storeys of historic charm. An impeccably restored stone façade with a touch of modern opulence. The lime-green door was flanked by stone pillars and adorned with a gleaming brass knocker. Windows either side were framed with deep-blue velvet drapes, offering glimpses of art that likely cost more than most officers made in a year.

'I'll lead, if you don't mind.' Vicky crossed the wide avenue, then walked up the steps and rapped the door knocker with a loud clatter. 'Don't want anything thrown at me.'

Fenchurch winced. 'I told you, that wasn't my fault.'

'Sure. I believe you.'

'I'm guessing you've got previous with this Lennethy guy?'

A tight nod. 'He's been involved in a drugs investigation.'

'Suspect?'

'Witness.'

'Do tell.'

Before she could even start, the door opened. A man stood there, his silver fringe hanging over piercing blue eyes. Decked out in lime-and-purple plaid three-quarter-length trousers, clashing with a crisp orange polo. He looked ready to conquer the greens. Or at least get lost in the surrounding bunkers. He focused on Vicky. 'Inspector!'

She smiled back at him. 'Lennethy.'

'How the devil are you?'

'Need a word, sir. Inside, if that's okay?'

'Listen, I'm teeing off in twenty minutes and I'm already running late.'

'You're *golfing*?'

'Why else would I live here?' Lennethy laughed, but it soon darkened. 'After what happened in Glasgow, I decided to clean up my act. Get fit. Walk every day, for a few hours. And I accidentally got into golf. Massively. This dude, Brad Sixsmith, big name producer. I bumped into him at a party in London and he said how golf had saved his life. Curbed his worst excesses. So I played a round with him. Man, he's a really good player. And I want to get that good. Hence living here. Home of golf and all that. Try to get three rounds in a day.'

Vicky laughed. 'Of the Old Course?'

'Sure. And there are other great courses nearby, such as Kingsbarns and Carnoustie. Actually a few up and down the Angus coast are really good, but I really like this town.'

Vicky was frowning at him. 'How do you accidentally get massively into golf?'

'Same way I got into dru—' He swallowed. 'My previous hobby. I've got OCD and I can't help it. Things suck me in deep. And golf is better than cocaine, right?'

'So I've heard.' Fenchurch motioned inside the house. 'Mr Lennox, we—'

'It's Lennethy. I only answer to that name.'

'Okay.' Fenchurch gritted his teeth then smiled. 'Lennethy, can we do this inside?'

'Nope.' Lennethy reached over for a golf bag, filled to the brim with various clubs, and wheeled it over to the door. 'I'll try to help, but it's got to be super quick.'

Fenchurch waited for eye contact. 'Kanyif Iqbal died yesterday.'

Lennethy cast his gaze between them, his mouth hanging open to reveal rotten teeth. 'He *what*?'

'He was shot and killed during a police operation in West London.'

Lennethy swallowed hard, looked up and down the street, then let out a deep breath. 'You better come in, then.' He stowed his clubs away, then strolled through the wide hallway to a room at the back. 'Why hasn't anybody told me?'

'We're telling you now, sir. And we've been tracking you down.' Fenchurch followed him into a plush kitchen. Spartan, with white units and no appliances, save for a professional-grade coffee machine. A large table dominated the space with six place settings, overlooking a lush garden at the back. Similarly fancy houses lined the sides.

'It's... Jesus. Why's this not all over the news?' Lennethy started fiddling with the giant espresso maker. 'Can I get you anything?'

'We're both fine.' Fenchurch held his gaze. 'It's not over the news because we're keeping a lid on it. Certain details have been released, of course. There's been a police incident in Hammersmith. And we gave some details of the victim such as age and gender. But we want to make sure the investigation is kept tight.'

Lennethy covered his mouth like a naughty schoolboy. 'Sounds ominous.'

'Because it is. He died trying to shoot a police officer.' Fenchurch felt that internal flinch. 'The details surrounding the incident pertain to a double homicide and a serious attempt on someone's life.'

The coffee machine hissed as Lennethy fiddled with something. 'Kanyif did that?'

'Why do you ask?'

'Well.' Lennethy puffed out his cheeks then let out a deep breath. 'He was a violent man when he wanted to be. Thing with rappers is they really need to walk the walk. And he did. Knew his guns and his knives. Did he kill the people?'

'That's a matter I can't discuss with you.'

Pound signs and dollar signs flashed in Lennethy's eyes. A dead star on his hands, just like in that old Smiths song. Countless cast-off demos would now become hit singles. And the way he died would boost the notoriety. Maybe. Conspiracy theories would spring up – he'd be on that island with Kurt Cobain, Jim Morrison and Elvis.

'I gather Mr Iqbal had been staying in Edinburgh with his manager. Which we gather is you. And you're not in Edinburgh.'

'Not anymore. Not after... Well, Victoria here will inform you that I had to leave Glasgow rather swiftly a few months ago. Some chaps who were under suspicion of supplying cocaine lived opposite my house and I grassed on them.'

Fenchurch didn't want to get derailed by this. 'Are you still Kanyif's manager?'

'That's right. Unless you've heard otherwise?'

'No, it just pays to not assume. I like to check all the facts a few times over.' Fenchurch watched him sipping his espresso from the tiny cup. 'So Kanyif was staying with you?'

'Yes.'

'Here?'

'Yes.'

'Was he on his own?'

'Not quite.'

'Who was—'

'A... A young girl was with him. His brother's girl.'

'He said that?'

'Right.' Lennethy finished his coffee and put it down. 'I mean, John is his half-brother. Bit of a tearaway. Five kids, if you believe it.'

Based on what Kanyif's mother had said, Fenchurch didn't

believe a word of it. And the lie made his guts squirm. 'Is that what Kanyif said?'

'Several times. It's why... her... complexion didn't match Kanyif's. At least, that's how he explained it to me.'

'They stayed in separate rooms?'

'She's his niece, you sick weirdo. Of course she did.'

'Like I said, I just wanted to check everything.'

'Of course they stayed in separate rooms. Got six bedrooms here.'

'What was her name?'

'Jasmine. I think.'

'How long were they here for?'

'Three weeks. Kanyif wasn't into golf, so he didn't really fit in. Said it was for boring twats who've given up on life. I mean, there's such an elegance to the game. The power of the drive. The sheer mathematics of the approach shot. And handling the pressure of the green. I wish he could've tasted all of that. Probably would've stopped him getting into trouble.'

Fenchurch narrowed his eyes at him. 'What kind of trouble are we talking?'

'Nothing specific. It just followed him around. People he knew from back home. People he'd met living in London and LA. All that jazz.'

'Anyone we should be speaking to?'

'Man, I don't know how to do your job for you, do I?'

'Anyone he had a beef with?'

'Rap is...' Lennethy poured himself another coffee. 'It's all about the beefs. It's like American wrestling. Either of you watch that?'

Fenchurch nodded. 'I know it.'

'Right. It's pantomime. These dudes are calling each other out, calling each other names, when the reality is they're best buddies. So no real beef.'

'What about with Rusty Rivers?'

'Rivers?' Lennethy barked out a laugh. 'That old dickhead?' He downed his shot of coffee. 'Claimed Kanyif had illegally sampled a guitar lick. They're on the same label. Same publishing company too. Thing is, that dude was just racist.'

'Rusty Rivers was?'

'Not his real name, you know?'

'I know. But was he a racist?'

'I think so, yeah. Didn't like a black kid from Greater Glasgow sampling his record, despite it making him a nice chunk of change. Some dance act in the nineties did the same thing. Carl Arms or something. Massive Ibiza hit.'

Fenchurch started to see something tangible in the beef, aside from the allegations of child abuse. That felt so murky still, so intangible. Gossip, hearsay. 'What happened when they left?'

'Kanyif? Nothing. No drama or anything. Dude was recording a track with HT UniQorn down in London. Bound to be a single. Especially now.' The greedy look was back in Lennethy's eyes. 'I tell you, though, that kid's going to be massive. So much talent.'

Complete opposite of what Fenchurch had heard from Sixsmith. 'The reason we're asking all these questions is the girl is missing.'

'So?'

'She's thirteen.'

'And? Kids go missing all the time.'

'She was trafficked.'

'Shit. By Kanyif?'

'We don't know.' Fenchurch saw the colour of those pound signs turn from black to red. All those unreleased recordings were now worthless if his client was a child trafficker. 'Does the name Colin Scott mean anything to you?'

'Nope. Should it?'

'Doesn't mean anything at all?'

'Nope.' Lennethy scowled. 'Who is he?'

'Okay, so the first thing we know about Jasmine is that she wasn't related to Kanyif.'

'Eh?'

'Whatever he told you about her being his brother's daughter was incorrect. She grew up in Canning Town. Well, she hasn't exactly finished growing up, has she?'

Lennethy dropped his coffee cup on the floor. 'Shitting biscuits.' He picked it up – still intact.

'She was trafficked at the age of twelve by a man who is presently in police custody. We believe he sold her to another man.'

'This Colin Scott?'

'Indeed.'

'Well, I don't know one. And I'm sorry.' Lennethy placed an arm on Fenchurch's shoulder. 'It must be really hard for good people like yourselves to investigate despicable crimes like these.'

Fenchurch let him hold his hand there. 'It's only made difficult when we don't find the victims in time.'

Lennethy walked over to the window and looked outside for a few seconds. Then swivelled back round. 'Listen, this is tough to process. I don't think he was abusing her, but you can't be sure, right? But... Something weird happened. Not sure what to make of it. It's possible Kanyif had been speaking to someone about what happened to her, but I don't know...'

'What does that mean?'

'Well. I was chopping some liver for my tea one evening and he walked into the kitchen. This very room. He was on the phone to someone, I don't know who. Must've thought he was alone in the house, or that I was out golfing – pulled a muscle on the back nine for my lunchtime round so I couldn't do the afternoon one. Stopped talking as soon as he saw me, but I remember what he was talking about. "Abused by a man she trusted." I thought it was his brother.'

'And you didn't ask him?'

'I did.' Lennethy shook his head. 'But I got the look. You know, the one from his second album? *Now Strikes the Hobgoblin*. I got that exact look. Made my bones chill. I knew to shut up.'

'Listen, if there's else anything you can do to help us find her, please.'

Lennethy nodded. 'I've got a lot of calls to make. Who should I deal with in the police about this?'

'Call DI Kay Reed the second you get anything.' Fenchurch passed him one of her cards. 'And I'd appreciate this being kept under wraps for now. I know you'll want to alert his army of fans, but we don't want anything to jeopardise Jasmine's safety.'

'Understood.' Lennethy stared hard at the card. 'Listen, the weirdest thing happened...' He looked up at them and Fenchurch could almost see the dollar signs in his eyes. 'Kanyif left a laptop behind. Do you think if it has any demos on it, that I'd be able to get them?'

26

Fenchurch couldn't believe they had a Pret a Manger in St Andrews. Felt like such a London thing. Then again, St Andrews felt like a London thing. West London, particularly, near where his sister lived. Not that he'd seen her for a while.

He sipped at his filter coffee and watched Vicky through the glass, talking on the phone to someone.

The laptop sat on the table in front of him, a high-end MacBook that looked like it came from a few decades into the future. All wrapped in an evidence bag, ready for a boffin to mansplain his work to them.

Bastard thing was locked with a password, wasn't it?

'Sorry about that.' Vicky sat opposite and wrapped her fingers around her tea. 'Local cops are going to come around to speak to Lennethy.'

'Have to say, he didn't seem too shaken by it.'

'I suppose it was just a professional relationship, but sometimes the lines can blur a bit.' She pulled the laptop towards her. 'I'll get this sent down to Gartcosh this afternoon.'

'Gartcosh?'

'Scottish Crime Campus. Police Scotland HQ. Well, most of it, anyway. Down near Glasgow. Not far from where you were last night, actually. A lot of our forensics have moved down there. Our best guys down there will go through this. My brother's working there too. Says they're almost as good as the Met.'

'Almost?'

'They'll be *as* good, Simon. At least.' She pawed at the device. 'Thing is, that's a modern MacBook, so it'll be encrypted. Doesn't matter who looks at it, it'll be impossible to get stuff off.'

'Let's see what they can do. Are you going to drive it there?'

'It'll go tonight in the internal mail.'

'Cheers, Vicky. It's possibly a dead end, but you never know. We found some lyrics in his jacket, which had some clue as to what old Rusty Rivers was up. Maybe there's a whole album's worth on that thing which could give us an explanation of what was really going on and with who.'

'Here's hoping.' She sipped at her tea. 'There are better cafés in St Andrews, you know?'

'Yeah, but I know what I'm getting with a Pret filter.'

'You didn't fancy one of Lennethy's coffees?'

'The stuff looked like tar. Besides, espresso doesn't really agree with me.'

'How?'

'Just gives me headaches and flu-like symptoms. Think it triggers my hay fever or something.'

'Wise to avoid it, then.' She put the lid back on hers. 'How's it been being back?'

'In Scotland?'

'No, on the job.'

'Right.' Fenchurch took a drink of his coffee. 'Well, it's too early to say. Monday was my first day back.'

'And you drove to Dundee yesterday?'

'Didn't choose to. But when you show up and you get shifted onto a double murder, you'll do anything, right?'

'How's your team coping without their boss?'

'You mean me?' Fenchurch waited for her nod. 'Well, I've got a good team, Vicky. Ronnie and Kay are more than capable of being SIO themselves. Had a catch-up with them in the car on the way over. Things are ticking over down south.'

'Good. But ticking over isn't making you happy, is it?'

'No. I prefer things to be going at a hundred miles an hour.'

'Like you on a motorway.'

'Not got much chance. The whole way up was like an IKEA car park.'

She wrapped her fingers around her teacup. 'Simon, I don't know how to say this so I'm just going to come out with it... Do you think you're just running away from your problems?'

'Who said I've run away?'

'You're not denying having problems.'

'True.' Fenchurch gulped down more coffee. Almost too much. 'Thing is, while I've been off getting my knee done, there's a new broom in place, managing a few of the MITs. I spoke to my new boss first thing yesterday and... Bottom line is I'm being aged out. Need to make way for the next generation. Not mine. And you know the worst part? Hasn't even bothered to call me today to find out what's going on. Or to find out where I am. I was at a public shooting in West London two days ago, for crying out loud.'

'Guess you lot have processes in place for that kind of thing?'

'We do. Happens way more than I'd like too. I can only assume Detective Superintendent Alison bloody Cargill is looking after that side of things.'

Vicky's mouth hung open. '*Her*?'

'You know her?'

'Aye. My, eh, friend in Edinburgh had a similar experience

with her. He was a DS, her a DCI. Constantly felt like she was trying to edge him out. Trouble was, he kept on solving cases. People who keep solving cases have to get promoted. He's kind of a golden child now.'

'Sounds like a wanker.'

'He is that, too, but one you don't mind having on your side.' She shook her head. 'You have my deepest sympathies, Simon. She's a careerist who doesn't care who she steps on. She'd push her grannie in front of a bus just to get five minutes' face time with the chief constable. Ruthless, direct and arrogant. And that's the kindest thing I've heard said about her.'

'Have *you* had many dealings with her?'

Vicky nodded. 'Two years ago, I brought down a child sex ring in Dundee. Before that case last year, where I came down to London. We caught a load of people, put them away. Someone... Someone got killed when I tried to arrest him. Cargill was away from the MITs at the time and was working on the Professional Standards team who investigated me.'

'What happened?'

'I killed someone.'

Fenchurch frowned. 'Excuse me?'

'It's not like that, Simon. He was trying to kill me. It was self-defence.'

'We've all been there.'

'Have we?' She tucked her hair behind her ears. 'Thing is, this wasn't. Just made it—'

'Vicky. Stop. I'm guessing this is one of those things you shouldn't tell me.'

'I can trust you.'

'Vicky...'

'I know I can. We've both done things we're not proud of.'

'We have. But I know enough. I get it. I don't judge you. The trouble is, once you know something, you can't un-know it. Trust or not.' Fenchurch felt a wrench twist his spine, tightening it. Some animal had operated on Chloe when she was young – the result was it had wiped her memories, meaning she'd forgotten most of her time with them. Most of it. She clung to the fragments still left. 'Don't compromise me, Vicky. And I mean that in the nicest possible way. It's a burden knowing the truth about something and the more people who know, the more likely it all comes undone. If I had to take the stand, I won't lie.'

'I get it.'

'Who else knows?'

'My dad. Sharon.'

'Keep it that way.'

'He was going to come after my kids. He knew people who would do it. I had to act.'

Fenchurch sat back and it felt like his head was inside a ringing bell. 'I'd do absolutely everything for my kids.'

'Exactly. But I'm telling you this because these things are all connected. People in that vicious game talk to each other.

'You sound like my old man.'

'Doesn't mean either of us is wrong.'

'True. Look, I'll try and bear that in mind. Just make sure you don't tell anyone what you did. Okay?' Fenchurch finished his coffee and let his breath out. 'Anyway. Are we any further forward with this?'

She shrugged. 'Not my case. I'm just here to make sure you don't get stuff thrown at you.'

Fenchurch laughed. 'That laptop feels like it's the only clue I've got.' He ran a finger along the machine's sleek lines. 'But there's something about Kanyif and Jasmine that makes me feel a bit sick. Trouble is, I don't think I'll get any answers up here.' He stood up and offered his hand. 'This has been fun, Vicky. Thank you for the bed and board.'

She charged around the table and hugged him. 'I'll send you the bill.'

'I appreciate it. You live in a lovely part of the world, Vicky.'

'Not many people say that about Dundee.'

'It's not the city I'm talking about. It's the countryside. Hills, glens, sea, beaches. Don't knock it.' Fenchurch crumpled his cup. 'I better head back home. But we should do this again, yeah?'

'Definitely. Stay for a bit longer next time.'

27

Fenchurch put his cup of tea down on his desk and slid in behind on his chair. Absolute heaven to get back into that position. Stupid amount of time driving back from Scotland, but he was here, back in London. A cup of tea and a sandwich, then he'd chase up Reed and Doyle to find out what the hell was going on with the case and why neither were answering his calls as he drove down.

He unlocked his computer and did a brief scan of his emails. Nothing stuck out. Wait a sec...

The door opened and Cargill wandered in, hands on her hips. 'Little birdie told me you were here. And here you are. I feel blessed.'

Fenchurch swore he could see ice forming on the inside of his window. 'Evening, ma'am. Sorry, I got your message this morning, but I've been otherwise occupied.'

She leaned against his desk. Pretty aggressive pose. 'Where have you been?'

'Chasing down some leads.'

'Chasing down leads, eh? In Scotland, I gather?'

'Indeed. There, and the north-east too.'

'And you flew up? Got the train?'

'Drove. Just got back ten minutes ago.'

She stood up tall and let out a deep breath. 'That's a lot of mileage to claim back.'

'If things are that tight, ma'am, I won't claim it.'

She pouted at him. 'I expect to see a revised resource plan by close of play tomorrow.'

'Eh? Why?'

'Because my SIO having to "chase down leads" shows the team isn't sufficiently staffed at junior levels, hence needing a revised resource plan that I can redeploy against. Or it shows that said SIO is not capable of doing the work at that level.'

'I'm both sufficiently staffed and capable. Remember, my team and I solved a double homicide in one day. This particular matter needed sensitivity.'

'The sort of sensitivity that necessitates a grieving mother hurling kitchen appliances at police officers?'

'That wasn't my doing, ma'am. I'm sure you've been in situations like that yourself.'

'Me? Of course not. I'm a professional.'

'Right.' Fenchurch couldn't hide the laugh. 'Sure you are.'

'What's that supposed to mean?'

'Exactly what it says on the tin.'

'And I gather you hooked in DS Olivia Blackman for that work?'

'That makes it sound like I was up to something dodgy, ma'am. The truth was, I put in a call to a chief inspector I know in Police Scotland. Luke passed me to her boss and she was allocated to help out, given prior knowledge of the suspect who was shot in Hammersmith right in front of me. She helped deliver the death message to his mother, but not before we obtained a last known address for him. It's all above board.'

'Well, DS Blackman's got a black mark against her name.'

'Sounds a bit racist.'

She blushed. 'Of course it's not racist!'

'Sure.' Fenchurch folded his arms across his chest. 'But my work up there means we've got a potential lead on Jasmine's whereabouts.'

She perched on the edge of the desk. 'Do tell.'

'Kanyif's laptop will be analysed by your former colleagues in Gartcosh.'

'Oh, those numpties... Great.' She shook her head. 'And what do you expect to get from that? His Wordle history? His login to *Fortnite*?'

'I don't expect anything, ma'am. I just want to see what's on it. Go through it. See if we obtain any leads from what's on there. We got one from some scribbled lyrics found in his coat pocket. Could be some other material on the computer that—'

'That all sounds like a tall order.' She drummed her fingers on the desk. 'Any actual leads?'

'Well, the man I spoke to in Durham allegedly sold Jasmine to a third party.'

'Sold her?'

'We're digging into his background, ma'am.' Despite the room being freezing, Fenchurch felt a bead of sweat run down his neck. 'But there's something about the whole story that doesn't stack up for me.'

'Go on?'

'Both Avonmore and Iqbal claimed that Jasmine was their niece. The truth is she was neither. So both were lying.'

'You think both men were abusing her?'

'I don't know. But there was a personal history between the two of them. An antagonistic one, for sure.'

'Okay.' Cargill stared into space for a few seconds, wetting her lips a few times, then drilled her gaze into him. 'Speaking of personal histories, I understand if this whole thing is a bit too close to the bone for you.'

'What's that supposed to mean?'

'The matter with your daughter.'

The *matter...*

'Ma'am, Chloe's a serving officer. And she's not allocated to this case, as you'll know from the resource plan.'

She held his gaze, running her tongue over her lips. 'But she was abducted, correct? In similar circumstances to Jasmine.'

'My daughter wasn't trafficked. Not in that way. She was much younger. And this whole thing has nothing to do with her. Surely you can see the nuances are vastly different, which allows me to retain my objectivity?'

'Okay.' She snorted and gave him yet another stern look. 'Well, I'm heading to the Yard to update the comms strategy. We will be going public on the identity of the victim this evening. Ideally, we'd hold on to it for longer but there's no chance we can carry on keeping it a secret when someone on the A-list's been killed. Plus, us trying to would make something we can easily justify look potentially corrupt. But please keep it under wraps until then.' She stood up tall and dusted off her trousers. 'If I need anything, I'll be in touch. But please, no more "chasing down leads". You're a DCI, not a DS.'

'Of course, ma'am.'

She gave him a final appraisal, then walked off and slammed the door.

Fenchurch sat back and felt the room warm up.

What Vicky was saying about her was turning out to be true. Ruthless, direct and arrogant.

Some people might've described Fenchurch as that, but they'd have been wrong. Mostly.

Yesterday morning, his instinct had been to stay in this role, but if this was how it was going to be working for her...?

Retirement had felt like he'd be giving up and edging a step closer to death, but now it seemed tempting. He was young enough to have a long one in good health. A solid way of putting an end to all this bullshit. And if it wasn't Cargill, he'd be working for some other berk. His allies were growing fewer and fewer the higher he rose in the organisation. And his enemies were all still at higher ranks.

Fenchurch set about doing the absolute minimum of admin, just to shut her up. He pulled up four old reports and copied and pasted text from them. Adjusted all the personal details. Nothing inspiring, but it would keep the Cargill-shaped wolf from the Fenchurch-shaped door.

He knew as well as anyone that if he didn't at least phone in the boss stuff, she'd have no trouble dropping him down a rank rather than moving him out to a posting in Middle England, somewhere with a constituency name like Frogspawn and Arsehole.

His door clattered open.

Fenchurch clenched himself for another onslaught from the new broom.

'Guv.' Reed powered into the room, carrying her laptop under her arm. 'Heard you were back.'

Fenchurch held his arms out at either side. 'Help me down off this crucifix, would you?'

Reed frowned. 'Eh?'

'These stigmata bloody hurt.' Fenchurch rubbed at his palms. 'Cargill's just been in, giving me no end of hassle over absolutely nothing.'

'Right. She was sniffing around earlier, asking questions about you. Tried to fob her off, but she's kind of got a point. It should've been me or Ronnie heading up to Durham.'

'Well, it wasn't.'

Another knock on the door and Doyle came in. 'Guv?' He stopped. 'Oh, Kay. Didn't see you there. You first.'

'No, I can wait.'

'Right.' Doyle sighed. 'Well, we've followed up on the security system at Avonmore's place. Looks like Kanyif got in by jumping a wall on Gloucester Circus, next door.'

'So Kanyif definitely killed Avonmore?'

'Looks that way, yeah.' Doyle scratched at his neck. 'Weirdest thing, though. We've been unpicking their movements after they left the hotel in Hammersmith. They took a series of tubes over, then the DLR. We've got a gap where she was during killings. She was spotted in the hotel beforehand, then... We've got Ring cameras from neighbouring properties and we spotted a teenage girl walking past. At half past five this morning.'

'Jasmine?'

'Hard to tell, but it could be.' Doyle stated at Reed. 'After that, we don't know where she's gone.'

'Assuming it's her, she was with Kanyif in the street, outside the victim's house, around the time of the death.'

'Already thought that thought, guv. She's gone in a puff of smoke.'

'Where did they go after?'

'We're trying to find that, guv. Obviously, Kanyif went back to the hotel, which is where...' Doyle coughed into his fist. 'Where the incident happened on Monday. But we don't know what happened to her.'

'Interesting.'

'Anyway, I better get back to it. Bradley Sixsmith is giving a statement just now.'

Fenchurch frowned. 'The producer? Why's he here?'

'He did live sound at the Zeroes gig.'

'Wait. That was to do with Doug Reid, right? I thought we'd cleared him of that.'

'So did I, but Cargill wanted me to be thorough. She just wanted to make sure everything was kosher.'

'So she's been speaking to you?'

'You weren't here, guv. I covered.'

'Appreciate it, mate.'

Doyle smiled. 'Catch you later, guv.' He left the room with a smile.

Reed watched the door close. 'He wasn't sucking up to her, guv. She's on the warpath for you.'

'Great.'

'Listen, I spoke to the sergeant about the MisPer report for the niece. He doesn't remember anything either.'

'But there's a document there?'

'Indeed. Either they're both lying or someone's faked a report from two cops.'

'Can you get IT to do a forensic sweep of the system to find out what the hell's going on?'

'I'll do it, yeah.'

'Thanks.' Fenchurch narrowed his eyes at her. 'Kay, you look like someone who's still got something.'

'You know me too well. We've been digging into Kanyif's bank details. Mostly normal stuff. He spent a *lot* of money in Pret. Must've had his lunch there every day. I mean, I like the place, but *every day*?'

'The coffee's decent there. And there's one in St Andrews, would you believe?'

'St Andrews? What the hell were you doing there?'

'Long story, Kay. But him spending money in Pret doesn't feel like a lot to go on. I mean, you could run through the CCTV of every Pret he's visited in Greater London at the time of the transaction and see who he's queueing with...'

'I hope that's sarcasm.' She put her laptop down and opened it, then logged in. The screen was filled with a spreadsheet, showing countless rows of bank transactions. 'Most of Kanyif's income comes from a limited company run by his manager. Dividends and salary are paid in every month. A few expenses, which we're tying down. One transaction we've struggled with is a payment he made just under a year ago. Five grand to a business called Pennyworth Holdings.'

'That's a decent amount of money, but it's not suspicious levels.'

'I know, but I'm a dog with a bone when it comes to this kind of thing. First, there's a matching payment of five grand to one Josh Green.'

'Shit. From Kanyif?'

'Right.'

'That's... What? What the hell is that about?'

'No idea, guv.'

Fenchurch had an idea. 'Josh Green was the kind of man who bought and sold people. Young women working on the streets. Would he be stupid enough to do the transaction between bank accounts?'

Reed shrugged. 'Pennyworth Holdings is now a dormant company, but we dug into the records at Companies House.' She stepped away from the laptop with a magician's flourish. 'The sole director is one Colin Scott.'

28

Doyle drove them along Mile End Road, heading out into deepest, darkest East London. And it was dark. Almost pitch black on this stretch – the streetlights were on the blink.

Hard to imagine that Fenchurch had been in Scotland that morning, with the bright, crisp air. Maybe he should get posted up there, somewhere completely different. House prices would be a lot cheaper than in Essex, that's for sure. Then again, he'd seen the prices in St Andrews – he reckoned Lennethy's townhouse was the best part of two million quid. A village five miles away had something twice the size for four hundred grand. Very tempting.

'I was just going to sod off home, guv.'

'I get it, Ronnie.' Fenchurch clutched the oh-shit handle above the door. He must've ridden in this pool car a few times, because five little grooves were ground into the fabric on the roof. 'But Kay stayed late last night, so I couldn't ask her again.'

'You say that like *I* didn't work late neither.'

'Did you?'

'I mean, I didn't, but...'

Fenchurch looked back across the empty street, then over at Doyle. 'I can trust you, can't I?'

'Of course, guv, but I totally get it. You doubt everyone. This is sensitive stuff. But me and your dad go back a long way. Before you were even a cop.'

'Thanks, Ronnie. I appreciate this.'

'I've got your back, guv.' Doyle pulled up at the traffic lights. Up ahead glowed white under new bulbs. 'How was Scotland, guv?'

'Not bad, actually. St Andrews is nice.'

Doyle nodded slowly, like he was moving to some music. 'Played the Old Course there a few times, actually. Not the easiest, but there are tougher ones nearby. Carnoustie's a bastard if you get the winds wrong.'

'Friend of mine lives there.'

'Really? Have to give me his number, then. Could do with a bolthole up that way.'

Fenchurch watched him focusing on the lights, willing them to change. 'Didn't know you were a golfer, Ronnie.'

'Lads in the clubhouse would say I'm not, but I do alright. Eight handicap.'

'Not bad at all.'

Doyle looked around. 'You golf yourself?'

'Not got the time, Ronnie.'

'But you used to?'

'Years ago, yeah. Got down to playing off ten.'

'That's good going.'

'This was back when I was on the track to the top. More of the job seemed to happen on the fairway than in the police station. Old man used to set me up with some senior officers.'

'That how you got promoted?'

'I was pretty good at my job, Ronnie.'

'Right. Yeah. But, still?'

'The wheels being greased didn't exactly harm. Then all that stuff happened with Chloe...'

'Sorry about that, guv.' Doyle drove off. 'Just here, yeah?'

'Yeah.' Fenchurch waited for him to pull in, then got out into the rain's relentless assault. Practically horizontal – a real Scottish downpour of the Glaswegian variety. 'Not expecting much here, but you just never know, do you?'

The brutalist monolith loomed in the darkness, the rain sluicing down the angular edges of the raw concrete façade, pooling on the cracked pavement below. The building's few windows glowed dimly. The sign sputtered and flickered, casting intermittent light on them.

Tiger Blood Offices

Fenchurch winced at the name. 'This doesn't look too professional, does it?' He opened the door and led inside.

An old man sat at the desk, staring into space. If he was security, he was doing a bad job of it. Behind him were two wide single-pane windows, showing a maze of mismatched desks and threadbare dividers. Not many working in there tonight. He looked up at them. 'How can I help you, gents?' Proper old-school cockney accent.

Fenchurch showed his warrant card. 'Appreciate it's late, but we're looking to speak to someone from Pennyworth Holdings.'

'Right.' The guard stuck his tongue in his cheek. 'Stopped renting space here about six months ago.'

Fenchurch pointed through the window. 'They were in there?'

'Nah, they just used it as a mail drop thing. Like a PO Box, but we give them call answering, that kind of thing.' He thumbed behind him. 'That's what they do in that office. Pretend they're answering calls for a real business. Taking messages, all that crap.'

'Got you. Who rented it?'
'Would have to take that up with the owners, I'm afraid.'
'Have you got their details?'
'Not handy, no.'
'Are they here?'
'Sorry, nope. Based in Doha.'
Qatar. Great.

Fenchurch couldn't make this up – a lead had slipped through his grasp again. 'Does any mail still come for them?'

'Of course. Usually chuck it, but I've not got around to doing the last month's.' He reached down and picked up a pile of letters. 'Don't say I'm not good to you.' A mad cackle.

Fenchurch took it and sifted through the post. No envelopes, just glossy prints – special offers from shady lawyers and printing firms mixed with pizza flyers and mail shots from the local councillors. 'It's all just spam.' He looked around at Doyle.

But he was on the phone, looking out through the grimy windows. Fenchurch hadn't heard it ring, hadn't noticed him moving off. Then again, he was bloody knackered.

'Cheers, Lisa.' Doyle hung up and turned back round. 'Good news, guv. We've just got hold of Kanyif's phone records.' He winced. 'Bad news is who he's been speaking to.'

29

Rain lashed against the grimy windows, a relentless symphony of liquid bullets. Fenchurch stormed after Doyle through the police station's deserted office space and its rows of empty cubicles. Dimly lit, the only sound the rhythmic tapping of their footsteps on the floor. Framed accolades and certificates adorned the walls, relics of past glory when the department used to achieve things.

Along the corridor, he slowed as he reached the corner office and stopped outside. The frosted glass door bore a nameplate:

DCI Howard Savage

Fenchurch listened hard.

Two voices in there, deep and low.

The rain outside intensified and drowned them out so he couldn't hear what they were saying.

Fenchurch didn't knock – just opened the door and entered.

A grand mahogany desk dominated the room, but the leather chair was vacant and the laptop closed and sleeping.

The rain beat against the windows, casting distorted shadows across the darkened room. A sudden creak in the floorboards made him turn to the side.

Howard Savage swivelled around like he was doing something he shouldn't.

Probably because he was.

Fenchurch's dad slammed the filing cabinet door with a bit too much haste. The silver-haired charmer's crooked grin hid more secrets than he'd ever admit to. Well-worn leather jacket, faded black jeans and box-fresh white trainers. 'Simon? Ronnie? What are you doing here?'

Fenchurch smiled at Savage. 'Howard. Been a while.'

'Hasn't it just.' DCI Howard Savage was the embodiment of upper-middle-class refinement. Even at this hour, his silk tie was neatly knotted beneath his crisply pressed charcoal suit. His salt-and-pepper hair left the top of his head bare, the skin on top polished like wooden furniture. 'Wish it had been longer.'

'Bet you do.' Doyle nudged the door shut behind him, not that there was anyone to listen in. 'Hope Mary's well.' He stepped over towards them. 'Wonder what's so interesting in that filing cabinet?'

Dad grinned wide. 'Howard's collection of mucky books.'

Fenchurch couldn't help but laugh at his dad. 'Is it whisky?'

'Both of us don't drink anymore, son. Honestly, it's work.'

Fenchurch held Dad's gaze until he looked away. 'You've been keeping secrets from me, haven't you?'

'Eh? What are you talking about, son?'

'Tammy.'

Dad looked away. 'Shit.'

'You could've told me.'

'Sorry, son. It… It just never felt like the right time, you know? And you've been through so much recently.'

'Don't use me as an excuse.'

'Thing is, I was going to tell you. Then she broke it off and got married. I found it pretty painful to talk about. Having your heart broken at my age... it's *awful*.'

Fenchurch didn't want to press him too much – just needed a little buttering up, like always. 'Dad, when you retired, I expected you to actually retire. You spend more time on the job than most coppers I know.'

'Blame Howard, son. Hard to turn down some consulting work in this place.'

Fenchurch shifted his focus back to Savage. 'And what does the Trafficking and Prostitution Unit want with my old man?'

'Well, helping to investigate trafficking and prostitution.' Savage grinned, proud of himself at that. 'Your father's a good investigator. He has specialised knowledge of both the geographical area in question and the topical one. And he knows all about the motivations of our suspects and, of course, their organisational structure.'

Doyle scowled. 'What exactly are we talking about?'

'Ronnie.' Savage gave him a hefty pat on the arm. 'You're a friend, or at least I consider you to be one. As such, it pains me to say that I'm not able to share the details of our investigation.'

'Even though it's on Simon's patch?'

'I didn't say that.'

'The geographical area.' Doyle gestured to Dad. 'Me and Ian worked the East End. And only the East End.'

Savage ignored him, instead glowering at Fenchurch. 'You're just back from long-term sick leave. You should surely be focusing on that rather than the minutiae of my scope of work.'

'Should, yeah. Trouble comes when they're the same thing.'

'Go on, then.' Savage shoved his hands in his pockets. Still didn't crease those trousers, even at this hour – God knows what they were made of. 'What's this late-night visit all about?'

Fenchurch shifted so he could watch both of their reactions at the same time. 'Why has Kanyif Iqbal been calling you?'

They looked at each other and something seemed to pass between them. Fenchurch couldn't tell what, other than it was like two boys caught with their hands in the same sweet jar.

Fenchurch stepped closer to them. 'We're not leaving until you tell us what you were talking to him about.'

Dad looked at Savage, then out of the window at the pissing rain. 'Trouble is, you bloody mean that, don't you? You're a persistent sod. Wonder where you get that from?' He laughed, then his face settled into a grimace. 'If you must know, Kanyif called me up a few times in the last week or so. He told me he was looking for this girl.'

'What girl's this?'

'One he'd saved from her abuser.'

'He said that?'

'Said what?'

'That he'd saved her?'

'Yeah.'

'Okay. Did he name the abuser?'

'I'm not naming anyone, son, but that's what he was calling me about.'

'Was it Rusty Rivers?'

Dad screwed up his face. 'The singer?'

'Right.' Fenchurch fixed his glare on his father. 'You don't seem to be surprised by that name.'

Savage shook his head. 'It was him, yes. Allegedly.'

'Are you prosecuting Rivers?'

Dad pointed over to the corner. 'That's what's in the filing cabinet there.'

Savage winced.

Fenchurch couldn't decide if it was at the breaking of the news or something relating to the case. 'But you didn't charge him, did you?'

'Couldn't even approve any intel gathering, let alone haul him in for questioning.' Savage ran a hand over his smooth head. 'All Mr Iqbal gave us was rumour and supposition. And we couldn't back up any of it. People drop hints, sure, but nobody admitted to seeing things first hand. Crimestoppers tips, anonymous titbits but never enough for a warrant or to make an arrest.'

'Because he's a celebrity?'

'Those days are long gone, thankfully. Justice is doled out, no matter who your friends are.' Savage narrowed his eyes. 'The thing I find mystifying is that Kanyif was one of the few people who came to us and wanted to make a difference. Kept asking what do you need, how can I help you prove it? But the problem was, all he gave us was the same sketchy information... Until...'

Doyle laughed. 'Until what?'

'He... He took matters into his own hands. A few weeks ago, he found out about a girl being passed around like property. So he decided to put a stop to it. He posed as a buyer, saying he wanted this girl in particular. Tried to buy her to give her the freedom she deserved.'

'To *buy* her?'

'Correct.' Dad was nodding vigorously. 'Then all of a sudden, we started receiving leads on Kanyif.'

Doyle gasped. 'Was Kanyif an abuser himself?'

'Kanyif?' Dad shot him a glare. 'I'm actually insulted. That whole thing of all abusers having been abused is a myth. Yes, Kanyif acted all gangster and played up to a stereotype, but he had a heart of gold. He was acting the gangster role and tried to be cool to fit with the lifestyle that went with his music. His songs have the usual references to "bitches" and "hoes" but, in reality, he was a very enlightened man. And when he came us, we received evidence that he was abusing someone. People started chasing him. And so he fled. It's why we're here this late. The sooner we find both of them, the better.'

'Or what?'

'Or he'll do something he regrets.'

'He already has. We believe Kanyif attacked Don Avonmore AKA Rusty Rivers on Monday morning.'

'Shit.' Dad collapsed back against the cabinet. Arms folded, staring up at the ceiling. 'What? Seriously?'

'I'm not in the habit of lying or joking about this stuff, Dad. But just be glad you're not selling yourselves as an intelligence unit.'

Savage rolled his eyes. 'That's a poor joke.'

'Well spotted.' Fenchurch focused on Savage. 'Kanyif is dead.'

'What?'

'He was shot by a firearms officer yesterday afternoon. Trying to kill me.'

'This can't be right.' Savage walked over to his laptop and unlocked it, then started typing. His face went all white. 'It's true, Ian.'

Dad joined him at the machine, as though the word of a Met DCI wasn't enough. 'All he's done, all he's tried to do... it's all resulted in him dying at the hands of the cops.'

'We were too slow, Ian. He knew he couldn't live after what they said he'd done. So he chose that over anything else – he killed Rivers, then he died.'

Fenchurch saw Kanyif's face, holding the gun to his face, side on. Gangster style.

'Man, you don't get it, do you?'

He did now.

'There's a girl called Jasmine Mason.' Fenchurch couldn't look at either of them. 'She's thirteen. This might be who Kanyif was talking about.'

Savage stroked his chin, thinking it through. 'She was trafficked. He was trying to tell us where she was, but there was... Let's call it a breakdown in trust between us. It's why we've been hunting for him. For them.'

'We've been digging into Jasmine's background. Someone bought her from a man called Josh Green.'

Savage twisted his lips into a pout. 'You have evidence of this?'

'We've got something, sure. He was arrested, though.'

'We were party to that from an intel perspective. We will, of course, try to prosecute him for the charges we could level, but the usual story of lack of evidence or witnesses persists.'

'So Kanyif bought Jasmine?'

'We believe so. There was an intermediate party between him and Green.'

Fenchurch nodded. 'Does the name Colin Scott mean anything to you?'

'Should it?'

'We think it's an assumed name, but it shows up on official records for a company called Pennyworth Holdings.'

'My God.' Savage's mouth hung open. 'How the hell do you know that?'

'Because I'm good, Howard, and my team is better.' Fenchurch stepped even closer. 'Now, the problem we have is we've no idea where Jasmine is or who has her. Could be she's fine, but I doubt it. She was last seen around the time Kanyif attacked Avonmore and Thornhill. Any idea where she could've gone since then?'

'We don't know.' Savage looked at him with tears in his eyes. 'We've been looking for her, desperately. Your father fears the Machine has her.'

Those two words chilled Fenchurch's blood.

The Machine.

The people who'd kidnapped Chloe.

'But that...' His mouth was all dry. 'They can't be... Can they?'

'They're still operating, Simon.' Dad rested a hand on his arm. Just like when he was a lad, struggling with school.

'They're still doing stuff, just on a lower scale and they're a lot less brazen about it.' He gave a beatific smile. 'And the best thing is Chloe's been so helpful with it. There's a real drive in her to help stop them once and for all. So far, we've put away three people.'

'But?'

Dad's proud smile faded. 'But they don't talk. Whoever's running it now, it's locked down tighter than ever before.'

'I want to see the intel you have on them. Start with Josh Green.'

Savage walked over to the filing cabinet and hauled out a paper file. Old school. 'Like you said, Green is the lad who trafficked Jasmine. We have him trafficking eight girls from varying countries of origins, straight off the boat, pardon the phrase. These women are escaping wars and brutal regimes, and come here for a better life and trust the men who bring them here illegally. They don't know about international law pertaining to asylum or seeking refuge. And instead of dropping them at the docks, someone like Josh Green gets a hold of them. And there are also fifteen local girls who have fallen prey to him. Jasmine is but the latest in a long line. He worked for the Machine.'

Fenchurch felt like he'd been kicked in the stomach. He'd sat in a room with him. 'Seriously?'

Dad nodded. 'We spoke to a witness Kanyif had brought to our attention. She gave us proof of her own trafficking and a ton more in interviews.'

'But you don't think you can use it?'

'We were told we can't.'

Fenchurch peered into the filing cabinet. 'Can I see it for myself?'

'Nope.'

'No?'

'Because they're not here. I've got them at home.'

Fenchurch could've throttled him. 'Dad! What the hell are you playing at?'

'I know it's naughty, son, but that's some sensitive material. I can't trust anyone in the force, except for Howard here. And you, of course. And Chloe.'

Doyle laughed. 'Thanks for the vote of confidence, Ian.'

'You too, of course.'

'Okay.' Fenchurch tried to formulate a plan. 'I'm taking charge here. This secret squirrel nonsense needs to stop, okay?'

Dad scowled at him. 'Treat me like I'm five.'

'Stop acting like it.'

Savage wouldn't maintain eye contact.

'First. Dad, you're going home and finding those case files. Ronnie, can you drive him, please? Make sure we get that stuff into evidence on my case.'

'Son, I can't—'

'Dad, people are dying. Ronnie's one of my best cops, okay? You get those files into evidence and we build a case, together. Then people can stop dying. Okay?'

Dad lowered his head, like he was Fenchurch's son and he'd battered his ball off a window. 'Fine.'

Fenchurch shifted his focus to Savage. 'And, Howard, you and I are going to speak to this additional victim.'

30

The relentless rain drenched the streets of Southwark too.

Fenchurch followed Savage along the passage between two ancient buildings, now restored and turned into university offices, heading towards the student accommodation.

Savage's coat clung to his frame like a loyal partner, his polished brogues gliding with aristocratic grace.

They emerged into an open side street and Savage made a beeline for a building, its fresh brick façade weary beneath the cold drizzle. The dimly lit entrance beckoned, casting a pool of light onto the damp concrete slabs. He pushed open the heavy glass door and held it, then slipped through before Fenchurch could catch the door.

The faint hum of conversation and laughter drifted towards them, mingling with the pattering raindrops hitting the thick glass. The dampness hung heavy in the air as they ascended the gloomy stairwell.

Savage passed through a fire door and entered a long corridor, then rapped on a door halfway along. 'Kylie?'

The sound of Taylor Swift bled through the door. Most kids

these days listened to music on headphones or earbuds, but this room's occupant was old school – speakers trained at the entrance like sentries' rifles.

It slid open and a hard-faced woman stood there. Could be sixteen, could be thirty. Brown skin and corkscrew ginger curls. She glowered at Fenchurch, then it softened as she smiled at Savage. 'Howard!' South London accent. She wrapped him in a deep hug. 'How are you?'

'I'm okay, Kylie.' Savage made eye contact with Fenchurch and hopefully caught a bit of the disappointment in his eyes. 'How are you?'

'I'm good, actually. Come on in.' She broke free then raced over to cut Tay-Tay dead. Her room was small, just a single bed and a desk, with the Pac-Man bite of an en suite cut out of the space. That said, it was snug, with candles and low lighting, and she seemed happy, for a victim of trafficking. She flicked a hand towards Fenchurch. 'Who's he?'

'This is DCI Simon Fenchurch. Simon, this is Kylie Broadford.'

Fenchurch smiled at her. 'Nice to meet you.'

She tilted her head to the side. 'You don't recognise me?'

Fenchurch shrugged. 'Should I?'

'Might be just a humble Southwark Uni student now, but I was on a TV show a couple of years ago. *Straight Outta Brixton*, about teen rap stars from South London. I was Kylie Lochalsh.'

Fenchurch narrowed his eyes at her. 'As in the Kyle of Lochalsh? With your accent?'

'Right. My dad's from Skye.' She patted her hair. 'Hence being a ginger. Hence the surname, too.'

'Broadford?'

'Broadford's a wee town on the south of the island. Used to go there on holiday every year. Took *forever* to drive there. Now there's a bridge and it's a bit quicker.'

'Never been.' Fenchurch rested against the wall by the bathroom door. 'Reason we're here, Miss Broadford, is we gather you know Kanyif Iqbal.'

She looked away and sighed. 'Right.'

'Take it you know him pretty well, then?'

'And then some. They paired me up with him on the show. He was my mentor, they called it. I got to the semis, but I lost out to HT UniQorn. Total joke, man. Guy's got no talent... But they didn't want to let a mixed-race girl win, did they?'

'I thought they would?'

'Final would've been me against this Chinese girl from Blackpool. Couldn't have that, could they? No, so they let the boy win.'

'Obviously still hurts.'

'Right. It does.'

'How did you get on with him?'

'Kanyif? He was okay.'

'No aggro between you?'

'Always drama with him. I mean, he hired me to play the part of his "ho". Made me pretend I was more than a mentee to him.'

'Pretend?

Was he gay?'

'Him? No. No way, man. Kanyif just has a thing for white girls. Some girls thought he was gay, but he wasn't no batty boy.' She winced. 'That's a bad phrase, but my momma used it, you know? She was Jamaican. Didn't mean anything by it. Thing is, he talked the talk, but couldn't walk the walk. Me being on his arm was good for both of our credibility. Until it wasn't. When I lost out in the semi, I cut ties to Kanyif. Felt so ashamed.'

'How old were you?'

'Sixteen. Just turned, if you know what I mean.'

Fenchurch knew. 'Did Kanyif ever try anything inappropriate with you?'

'Hell, no. He might've been a poser, but he was a gentleman behind the scenes.'

'So he never did anything to you?'

'Nope.'

'Kylie, there's someone we need to find.' Savage showed her a photo. 'Do you recognise her?'

Kylie took her time inspecting it. 'No, sorry. Should I?'

'Her name's Jasmine. Jasmine Mason. She's thirteen.' Fenchurch kept his phone there. 'We think she's been abused by the same people as you.'

She fixed Fenchurch with a feral street-kid glare. 'Who says I was abused?'

Savage was sitting at her desk. He crossed his legs. 'Kylie, you've been incredibly open with us.'

'I told you, I was never on the game.'

'No, I get that, but—'

'And I never went with Kanyif.'

'But you had been trafficked, hadn't you?'

She looked away, shaking her head.

'And Kanyif swore to protect you, right?'

'Shut up, man.' Her voice was small, like a hopeful young teenager.

'Kylie, we know your history.' Savage stomped his foot down on the floor. 'You didn't meet him on that show. He knew you before. Met when you were fifteen.'

'He didn't do anything to me, man.'

'Not saying he did. But he did pay someone to get you off the streets.'

She shook her head. 'Ancient history, man.'

'Sure. But he had to pay them again, didn't he? Because you'd slipped back into old ways.'

'I'm clean, man. Studying at uni.'

'And you're doing incredibly well, Kylie.' Savage walked over to her. 'And we're not here to judge you. What happened to you wasn't your fault. You didn't ask for it and you didn't do it.'

'Man, you don't know what I've been through.'

'I have *some* idea, Kylie. Why don't you tell us the rest, eh?'

She shook her head again. 'After the show, I hit rock bottom. Thought I was going to make it on that. But nope, I'm nothing, just some skank bitch. So I went back to the old crew and hit the pipe. Smoked crack, man. They dosed me up. Only thing I could do to not think about what happened. They made me go back again, to where he found me. They made me... live in this dude's house. I was fourteen. Spent a year there. Smoking when I wasn't, y'know...'

Savage looked around at Fenchurch, then back at Kylie. 'I'm sorry to make you go through this again, but it's incredibly important to this case. Do you remember where this was?'

'Uh huh. Greenwich. Just opposite the park.'

'You were sexually abused there?'

She brushed a tear out of her eye. 'Some motherfucker, he... Dude abused me, man. I was there for, like, nine months. Tied up a lot. Every day, man. He'd... I... And one day, the door was open and Kanyif was there. He took me in, took me to this drug rehab place. Sorted me out. Sobered me up. Went back to my parents. They're so nice, they didn't deserve this.'

'Nobody does, Kylie. Least of all you. This man, though, did you know his name?'

'He was called Don.'

The confirmation didn't make Fenchurch feel any better. 'Were there others?'

'Right. At least one other guy... I didn't see him too well, but I think he worked on the TV show.'

'*Straight Outta Brixton?*'

'Right. I saw him lurking around there when I was on the show. He spoke to me and... Man, it's why I threw the semifinal, you know? What he said to me. Took me back to that dark place. Made me start smoking again. Then Kanyif found me again. Man, he was my superhero.'

'It was definitely your abuser?'

'Definitely. And one of them. I think he was called Colin? Colin Scott?'

31

'You know, Howard, something's bugging me.' Fenchurch leaned back against his car, arms folded. 'How you can just rock up at some girl's student flat at nine o'clock at night, without her batting an eyelid? Then get a big hug from her.'

'It's called earning their trust, Simon.' Savage stopped, caught between two cones of light, and opened his car door. 'You should try it someday.'

'You seem very close to her.'

'Because I am. I sit in meetings with these women for hours and hours over many, many days. To be honest with you, I hate it when we call them girls, but they're virtually always under eighteen, often significantly. The greatest weapon I can wield in this battle of mine is to listen to them. To let them share their stories without judgement. And after a while, they open up to me in ways you couldn't imagine. It can lead to places that help us build strong cases against their abusers.'

'Just make sure you don't cross the line, Howard.'

Savage stepped forward, looming out of the shadows, close enough for Fenchurch to smell his minty breath. 'Simon. The thing you need to get into your skull is this work is very different from yours. In murder squad, you're dealing with bodies. Forensics. Pathologists. We're dealing with live victims, not cold corpses. And the crime is their whole ordeal, not just some sharp moment where their life ends. With trafficking cases, the women involved fully expect the police to be the next abuser in a long line. Do this, do that. So in order to build trust, we have to be just the opposite. We only support them. We never place demands on them, or any conditions. We are there for them whenever they need it. We maintain a healthy distance. Establishing trust is a long game.'

'I don't trust anyone.' Fenchurch smiled at him, trying to turn his anger at this small section of the world into something a lot less volatile. 'You should try it someday.'

'Very droll.' Savage shook his head. 'I'm trying to level with you here and you...' With a deep sigh, he stormed over to his car and got in. The light flashed on and the engine ignited. He wound down his window. 'I suggest you follow me, but please call ahead!'

Fenchurch got in and started his phone before it connected to the dashboard, then the ringing burst out as the engine started. He followed Savage's car through Southwark's ancient streets, still full of menace even after all that gentrification. Pretty far from Savage's office down here, but the area was a common enough location in cases to be a big part of what passed for his patch.

And also where Fenchurch had investigated so many murders for the last twenty years of his life.

Savage's tales never quite seemed to stack up...

He had no idea what to believe about him – Savage wouldn't be the first guy in that line of work to overstep the mark with a young, vulnerable woman.

No, Fenchurch had to stop thinking like that. Savage was a good man, who'd given his whole career to solving some of the most brutal crimes London had to offer. And he'd seen it first hand, with what Savage had done for Chloe.

Fenchurch hung up and hit dial again on the same number.

He didn't like the fact that this Colin Scott kept coming up. Worse, they didn't have a handle on him. The broth was way too thin to know precisely how Kanyif Iqbal was involved with him. Or how deeply.

Still, the fact there was a financial trail there was pretty damning. While Fenchurch had seen suspect payments deposited into bank accounts to implicate innocent parties, he'd never seen an innocent party paying out to them. That wasn't standard.

Fenchurch blinked hard, almost in time with the ringing tone. He was so bloody tired from all that driving. The streetlights were blurring, but he kept laser-like focus on Savage's car up ahead.

He killed the call again. Before he could hit redial, it rang. A mobile number he didn't recognise. He hit answer.

'Fenchurch.'

'Sir, it's DI Williamson.' The north-east accent hit hard. 'Just to say, I visited Josh Green again in the Monster Mansion. Got him talking... After a fashion. No deals, nothing like that. But... He confirmed that he's part of some organisation, but that's as far as he went. If we want any more on it, that's where the deal comes in.'

'He say anything about this organisation?'

'Nope. Nothing.'

'So it's probably bollocks.'

'Usually is with these blokes. Thing is, though, he seemed scared. Like our little chat with him yesterday made him realise he wasn't just on our radar, but on someone's radar. And it meant he was in deeper trouble than he imagined.'

'Okay. I don't have any authority over that case. Can you speak to Howard Savage?'

'Who's he?'

'Trafficking and Prostitution Unit down here. Case is under his umbrella. I'll forward you his contact info.'

'Sure thing.'

'And thanks for doing that. You didn't have to speak to him again.'

'I wanted to, though. After our little chat with him yesterday, it felt like he's hiding something. Now we *know* he definitely is. And I'm a stubborn enough wanker to keep at it until he tells us exactly what. Have a good night.'

'Thanks, Chris.'

The line went dead.

Fenchurch focused on the road ahead, trying to add the information to what they already knew. The deeply cynical part of his brain made him think it was all stuff Green had heard in prison, recycled and repackaged to appeal to two desperate cops. Everything was transactional to someone like him – how much gold could he spin their doubt into?

But there was a part of him, buried much deeper, that still had hope. Hope that maybe there was something in it. That Josh Green was part of the Machine. And could help them find Jasmine.

The phone started ringing again. He answered it. 'Fenchurch.'

Sounded like a busy room. 'Inspector?' Dr Mulkalwar's voice rattled out of the speakers. 'Thought it might be you calling. Can I help?'

'Hi, I'm in Southwark just now and wondered if we'd be able speak to Mr Avonmore this evening.'

'I'm afraid that's not possible.'

Shit. 'What's happened? Did he not pull through?'

'No, Mr Avonmore discharged himself this afternoon.'

32

Savage held out a hand, pointing to the townhouse. An empty shell, devoid of any activity, the forensics officers leaving a crime scene and returning it to a home. 'Well, Simon, after you. It's your case, after all.'

Fenchurch walked over to the dark mass that was Rivers's house, then climbed the steps to the door and rattled the knocker. 'Doesn't look like anyone's here, does it?' He took out the key, opened the door and went inside. 'Hello?'

The house was silent. Probably the only things moving about were ghosts. Two fresh ones to add to the tally accrued in the couple of hundred years the place had been standing.

'Hello? Mr Avonmore? It's the police!'

No lights or tell-tale signs of anyone, just his words echoing around.

'This is a lost cause.' Fenchurch breathed out a deep sigh. 'No sign of him here.'

Savage led back outside, hands in pockets. 'So, what's the plan here?'

'I'm a bit disconcerted, to be honest with you. Him discharging himself from hospital doesn't feel good, does it?'

'You didn't think to charge him earlier?'

'With what? We had no evidence of wrongdoing, just some kind of vaguely loose allegation. Now we've got a smidgeon of evidence...' Fenchurch stared at Savage. 'Maybe if Kylie had gone on the record...'

'Simon.' Savage clenched his jaw. 'This is not at all helpful. In these cases, it's next to impossible for us to get the victims to open up for the purposes of intelligence gathering, let alone for evidence. She wasn't in the kind of place where she could talk about it. And now, with the benefit of drug rehabilitation and psychotherapy, she obviously feels strong enough to talk. I'll be paying extra close attention to make sure there's no relapse and that the impact on her studies remains minimised.'

'Any word about Avonmore's private hospital?'

'Oh, yes. Got word as we drove. My team have checked in with Mr Avonmore's preferred hospital. He hasn't signed into any of their facilities.'

'So he's just gone missing? After major surgery?'

'It would appear so.'

Fenchurch wanted to punch something. Or someone. 'An abuse ring is still operating, Howard. Powerful men like Rivers, and whoever the hell this Colin Scott actually is, are taking what they want from people and getting away with it. Meanwhile, we're not any closer to stopping the abuse. And Kanyif Iqbal decided to take matters into his own hands. Rusty fucking Rivers going to ground just makes this whole thing less and less likely to be solved. And—'

Savage's phone rang and he checked the display. 'Sorry. I hate to not take a call.'

'Could be any number of your *girls*.'

'That's not funny.' Savage scowled as he answered.

Fenchurch didn't want to just stand around listening to half a chat, so he walked off and knocked on the neighbour's door.

Neil Fields opened it, a half-smoked cigarette dangling from his lip. His shorts were almost offensively short, showing off thighs that could crush a car. Trying to stop his dog from getting out. 'Oh, hey.'

'Evening. Sorry it's so late, just wondered if you'd seen your neighbour today?'

Fields stepped away from the warmth and joined him outside. 'Don's in hospital, isn't he?'

Fenchurch shook his head. 'Discharged himself. He's not in now, but we wondered if you'd seen or heard anything this evening.'

'I heard something earlier, but didn't see anyone.'

'What do you mean you heard something?'

'I was just back from walking the hound. Heard something.' Fields shrugged. 'Could be a car on the street, plenty of them around here!'

'Okay.' Fenchurch smiled at him. 'Sorry to bother you.'

'Is Don okay?'

'His injuries were extensive and he needs constant medical attention, hence us needing to track him down.'

'Bloody hell. Look, if I hear anything else, I'll call you. I've got DI Doyle's card.'

'Thank you.' Fenchurch smiled and waited for him to slip back inside, then walked back over to their cars.

Savage was pocketing his phone. 'Just received a call from someone in County Durham constabulary asking about a deal for Josh Green.'

Fenchurch nodded. 'That's your case, right?'

'Indeed. And Mr Green is claiming to be part of the Machine. He's on your father's radar.'

'You believe it?'

'I don't know, to be honest. Your father's got some fanciful ideas. But he's also an incredible investigator. I'd say if he thinks it, then it's usually true and he's got a treasure trove of evidence to back it up.'

'Are you going to offer the deal?'

'I don't know. It's good to confirm things. Tie it all up. But...' Savage exhaled slowly. 'What's your take on it, Simon?'

'Well, we know that Josh trafficked Jasmine. And there's a financial trail showing that Kanyif potentially paid for her. And it's not the first time.'

'No.'

'He did the same for Kylie Broadford.'

'He was doing good there, Simon. Or thought he was. He took her away from some bad people.'

'How did he find you?'

'Via your father. Kanyif had somehow found him and met up with him. Then told him about this girl he'd saved. Kylie was in a very bad way.'

Fenchurch loved his dad but the daft old sod just couldn't let go. While their own family trauma was resolved, Dad wanted to save them all. And... he couldn't. One man couldn't. He swallowed down a thick lump of regret. 'When was this?'

'Over a year ago. That's when Kanyif made the payment to buy her.'

'How was she back then?'

'She was in a state. Crack addiction. We have access to a budget that lets us help these women directly. Take them to some clinics to detox and sort out the reasons they get into these situations in the first place. We provide a safe house for them to recover without fear of retribution. Used to be all the result of childhood trauma, where talk therapy worked in virtually all cases.'

Fenchurch couldn't even look at him. 'But...'

'This might give you and Mrs Fenchurch some succour, but that's old thinking. Modern-day traffickers don't prey on the naïve or the sheltered. Or the troubled. They come from all walks of life, including the best homes where there's no hint of trauma. Children like Chloe.'

Fenchurch looked up now. 'Right.'

'She's been priceless, you know. She's out of the other side of it. She helps these women see their experience doesn't have to be a dead end. How it's not their fault, but it's just the way the game is played nowadays. They make the target feel special. Gifts, cash, the newest phones, experiences. Then the worm turns. "You owe me, could you be nice to my friend, it would mean a lot to me." Then the threat of compromising photos and videos. "Play along some more or we will destroy your perfect life. How will Mummy and Daddy react? Daddy's friends at the golf club? Mummy's friends at church?" They may end up looking like street kids in the end, but they don't usually start that way now.'

'And neither Kylie nor Kanyif told you about her abuse at the hands of Rusty Rivers?'

'She alluded to it, but didn't name him. Kanyif said it was Avonmore, but the trouble is... he's had a personal beef with him for a while, so we couldn't take it as gospel without her corroboration. Or from another party. Which we sadly never got.'

'Kanyif bought the girl from a pimp. You didn't check that out?'

'Simon...Of course we did, but we didn't have the resources to do it justice. Or to get the necessary approvals. Politicians can talk all they want about how important this work is, but until they increase our budgets and pass laws that enable it to actually bloody happen, then it's just next to impossible.'

Always the case with slippery sods like Savage – the blame sat elsewhere.

'Okay, Howard, us fighting isn't going to get us anywhere. We need to find him.'

'Have some faith, Simon.'

'How? I've got to find a missing teenager who's been sexually abused. She's thirteen! Meanwhile, you're sitting on possible witnesses and letting them get away without talking to us.'

'Please don't make this my fault.'

'Fault, eh? Howard, three people are dead because of this whole thing. If you'd acted sooner or more decisively, you would've saved their lives.'

Savage looked over at the house again. 'All I can see is we've drawn a blank here.'

'But you knew about Rusty Rivers abusing Kylie, didn't you? I'm experienced enough to realise knowing and proving are two separate concepts. But in the world of policing, we *know* lots of things that we can't bring before a court. But you didn't *know* about his friend. Colin Scott.'

'I'm grateful for what you've found there.'

'Grateful? It hasn't exactly been difficult, Howard. We've managed more in twenty-four hours than you've done in years.'

Savage looked away from him. 'Listen, I've got an idea about Colin Scott. Kylie said he worked at the show, didn't she? Just so happens, the TV company are running auditions for the next season of *Straight Outta Brixton* this evening. He could be there.'

'Seems like a long shot, Howard.' Fenchurch yawned into his fist. 'And I'm *really* tired right now.'

'Rivers owns the company.'

Fenchurch felt himself frown. 'What?'

'While you were speaking to Mr Fields, I checked in with my team. The TV production company had two owners until recently. One was Rusty Rivers, via his music production business, Riverbed Songs. And the other...' Savage narrowed his eyes. 'Pennyworth Holdings.'

33

The Beagle Productions office was in a crumbling brick building that would be demolished, if it was anywhere else. Tucked away in a back street in Shoreditch, not far from the arbitrary estate agent demarcation with Hoxton, the shabby brickwork probably added to the value. Wild buddleia grew from the second-floor windows, still flaring purple in November. Rainwater soaked the walls from overflowing gutters.

The lighting in the courtyard caught the young hopefuls. Some posing in groups, all bunched together, some in their own spaces. Two lads sat on bollards, trying to look cool. Their female friends were dancing and rapping, in practice for their few moments of success. Or their attempt at it.

All hoping to be the next Kanyif Iqbal or even HT UniQorn.

Yeah, hope. The thing that tormented worse than anything else. Made these poor kids open to exploitation from powerful men.

Fenchurch got out of his car and wandered over to Savage.

'Come on.' Savage led through the courtyard, charging

between all the wannabe rappers, then inside to the waiting area.

Fenchurch followed him, but got stopped by two big lads. Even whiter than him. Tall. Broad. 'What's up, fellas?'

'Don't remember us, do you?' The one on the left leaned in. 'Arrested us for dealing Blockchain.'

Took Fenchurch a few seconds to recognise him. 'Elliot Lynch?'

'That's me. El Lynch Mob is my stage name.'

'Look, that was standard practice. You were involved in a murder case.'

Elliot stood even taller, like he could intimidate a cop with Fenchurch's experience. 'Didn't have to do that to me, man.'

Fenchurch looked him up and down. 'Your face looks like it's healed well.'

Elliot looked away, shaking his head. 'Whatevs, man.'

'You should've been prosecuted for what you did.'

'Keep thinking they'll come after me. Five years, man. Still think you'll come after me.'

'Don't make me.' Fenchurch smiled at him. 'Good luck with your rap career.' He followed Savage into the building.

Another three rappers blocked his path.

A slender man with sharp features and pale skin, eyes gleaming with intensity, wearing a sleek black suit and a fedora.

Another was dressed in a tapestry of traditional garments from around the world.

Someone else had cybernetic implants, including glowing circuitry embedded in his skin – or just wanted it to look like that.

Seeing the three of them together made Fenchurch feel like he was trapped inside a lost Michael Jackson video. He tried to shuffle past but they were stuck there.

They all turned, in unison, then screamed.

Bradley Sixsmith walked out of a door, holding it for a

young black kid. Fenchurch recognised him – HT UniQorn. He walked past and people flocked towards him as he went. Leaving Fenchurch enough room to squeeze through.

Sixsmith clocked Fenchurch and nodded at him. 'Everyone's crazy for that kid.' He shook his head at Fenchurch. 'I don't get it, but I'll take the money.' He laughed. 'How are you progressing with the case?'

'We've identified the killer.'

'So I gather. Kanyif was shot dead, wasn't he?'

'I can't comment on that matter, sir.'

'I understand. Listen, I'd love to chat, but I've got to get back to the studio. The label are pressuring me to finish mixing the single. Suspect they've heard the rumour that Kanyif died. Still not been officially announced, but they want me to get it sorted. They've booked in a top-end mastering engineer for Sunday, so they're now putting on the pressure for me to finalise the track, like *now*. Kid hasn't even finished the vocal, let alone let me mix it! So much pressure. And, of course, they've booked him on this nonsense as a guest judge.'

'Sounds a bit much.'

'It is, but you don't turn down TV. Only thing that sells anything in great volume.' Sixsmith nibbled at his thumbnail. 'But it doesn't help me. I've told them I'm taking the files to my home studio and they'll get what they get when time's up on Saturday night. So we're heading back to the studio now. Two cars picking us up. One for me, one for him. Not because of his ego, but because I can't stand the little oik.' He snorted. 'Sorry, that's unkind of me. But he doesn't know the first thing about producing a hit record. And I know the first thing and the last, plus all the things in between.'

Fenchurch stepped aside as much as the scrum would allow. 'I won't keep you.'

'No. No. Good luck.'

The crowd screamed and the additional space let Fenchurch ease through the huddle.

Savage was standing at a long desk, manned by two young people of indiscernible genders. 'I'm asking you to let me speak to the manager.'

'That's us.'

The mirror behind them caught Savage shifting his gaze between them. 'And you are?'

'I'm Rainbow.'

'And I'm Klaxon.'

Savage laughed. 'Those are your names?'

'They're the names we've chosen for ourselves.'

'We ask you to respect that.'

'Okay.' Fenchurch turned on the charm, grinning wide. 'We're looking for Don Avonmore.'

'Rusty.'

'Rivers.'

Fenchurch was getting a headache from these two. 'We know he owns this place.'

They shifted their focus to him, in the exact same movement. 'Correct.'

'Is he here?'

'No.'

'He hasn't been seen here for months.'

Fenchurch wasn't surprised – this felt like a gamble. 'What about his co-owner?'

'There isn't one.'

'Come on. We know about Colin Scott.'

'He doesn't exist.'

They knew something… 'Excuse me?'

'We've had City of London police in here asking about him. Pennyworth Holdings, correct?'

'The thing is, Mr Policeman, we helped them investigate that. It's fronts upon fronts. We don't believe he exists.'

'Rainbow is correct. Colin Scott was listed as director for Pennyworth Holdings, who co-owned this business, but we think Colin Scott is a fake name for someone.'

Fenchurch nodded. 'For Rusty Rivers, right?'

'No. Not him.'

'What about Don Avonmore?'

Rainbow rolled their eyes. 'That's Rusty Rivers.'

'Can't fool us – we're too smart for you.'

'Both of us are.'

'Sure you are.' Fenchurch smiled at them. 'Thing is, someone said they saw Colin Scott here.'

'Of course he was here.'

'Same time as Rusty Rivers.'

'It's how we know they're not the same person.'

'Told you, we're not stupid.'

'Very smart, actually.'

'You definitely seem it. Both of you.' Fenchurch shrugged. 'Can you describe him to us?'

'He looked like you.'

'Same hair, but longer.'

'And older. Much older.'

Fenchurch's phone rang. He killed it. 'Can you give us a better description?'

'We couldn't.'

'You've stretched us past breaking.'

'Happens.'

'Happens a lot.'

Fenchurch clenched his teeth. 'So Colin Scott looked a bit like me. Right?'

'Silver hair. Tall.'

'That's all we can give you.'

Fenchurch's phone rang again.

'You better take that.'

'Rainbow's right.'

Fenchurch sighed. 'Sorry.' He checked the display.

Dad Landline calling…

Another sigh. 'Back in a sec.' He walked away, shuffling past the trio of rappers. 'Dad? You okay?'

'Simon.' His voice was a thin croak. 'There's someone hammering at my bloody door!'

'Can't you get Ronnie to—'

'He ain't here.'

'What?'

'Doyle had to pop out. Ran out of milk, didn't I? He—SHIT!'

The line went dead.

34

Fenchurch skidded to a halt outside his dad's flat in Limehouse and put his Airwave radio to his mouth. 'Approaching the target destination. No sign of backup, over.'

'They're still attending a major incident in East Ham.'

'One unit was all I needed... Okay. Fine. Over and out.'

Fenchurch pocketed the radio and inspected Dad's street.

The rain-slicked tarmac reflected the glow from the streetlights. Dad's two-up two-down looked quiet. Lights off too, which was a concern, but there was no sign of anyone trying to get in, at least.

Hopefully they'd got the message and left.

Heart pounding, Fenchurch got out into the rain and raced along the uneven pavement, trying to tell himself it was all okay, that nothing had happened in his brief race down from Shoreditch. He stopped and thumped on the door. 'Dad? You okay? It's Simon.'

Nothing.

Another thump. 'Dad?'

Not good.

He tried the door – locked.

Actually...

The door being locked was a good sign – they probably hadn't got in.

Probably was doing a lot of work there.

Fenchurch reached for the rusty key in his pocket and fumbled it as he went to unlock the heavy wooden door. The anticipation clawed at him as he twisted the key, then nudged the door open. 'Dad?'

Inside, the flat was shrouded in darkness, the only lights coming from the street and the main bedroom at the back, illuminating the dingy hallway.

'Dad?' The wooden floorboards creaked in protest as Fenchurch moved through the narrow hallway, everything on high alert. 'Dad, you okay?'

Only silence in response.

He moved swiftly through the disarrayed flat, checking each room as he went – kitchen, bathroom, and spare bedroom – all empty, but none bearing the signs of a violent struggle.

The living room was a chaotic scene of overturned furniture. Shards of a broken whisky bottle glistened on the threadbare carpet.

What the hell?

'Dad?'

Fenchurch reached the open bedroom door and his heart froze in his chest.

His father lay on the rumpled bed, tied up, his grizzled face contorted in agony. The room smelled of sweat and desperation.

Fenchurch rushed to his side, trembling fingers fumbling with the knots binding him. 'Stay with me, you old bugger.'

Dad's eyes, once full of life and mischief, were now vacant and haunted.

The rain continued its assault on the windowpanes.

Fenchurch finally untied the knot. 'What's going on? What's happened?'

Dad clutched his chest, gasping for breath. His forehead was covered in sweat. His skin was concrete grey.

Fenchurch recognised enough of the signs – he was having a heart attack. 'It's okay, Dad. It's going to be okay.' He got out his Airwave. 'Foxtrot X-ray three to Control. Need urgent medical assistance at my previous location. Over.'

'Received, over.'

Dad locked eyes with him. 'Colin Scott was here.'

'What?'

'He was here!'

'How do you know?'

'Because he bloody told me!' Dad's eyes went all glassy. Like he'd gone.

Fenchurch was out of his depth here. He knew how to do it all, but panic got in the way.

The bedroom door opened and Doyle stood in the doorway, carrying a Tesco bag. 'What the fuck?'

'Do you know how to do CPR?'

'I, yeah...'

'Do it!' Fenchurch got out of the way. His hands were shaking.

Doyle raced over and started doing the chest compressions. 'What the hell happened?'

'Someone's been here.' Fenchurch couldn't watch his old man dying. 'He called me. Saying someone was outside, trying to get in. Door was locked, but...' He glowered at Doyle. 'Where the hell were you?'

Doyle was pumping Dad's chest, fast and slow. 'Brought him here, as per your instructions. Started looking for that file, but it's chaos. Went through ten stacks of papers and didn't find anything. Then he knocked over a bottle of whisky, smashed it. Your old man was desperate for a cup of tea, but the milk in the fridge was halfway to brie. It was obvious this search wasn't going to be a five-minute job, so I went out to get some milk.'

'Bloody cups of tea.' Fenchurch stood up and started checking the room. 'I told you not to leave him!'

'You know what he's like, guv! He's a belligerent old bugger.' Doyle reached over and pressed his finger against Dad's throat. 'That's... We need help, Si.'

'Ambulance is on the way.'

'Good.' Doyle went back to doing the compressions. 'Can you find some aspirin?'

'Right.' Fenchurch went into Dad's en suite. Used to be a box room, but he'd knocked through and extended it a few years after Fenchurch had moved out. He kept his pills and potions in the unit above the sink, behind the mirror that showed a tired and desperate old man. Fenchurch blanched when he realised he was looking at himself.

He opened the door and sifted through the contents. Twenty packs of paracetamol. Fifteen ibuprofen. Enough oxycodone to keep half of East London's drug dealers going for months, or to last Fenchurch a week during his recent addiction.

Hay fever pills. More hay fever pills. All the brands of indigestion tablets. Codeine...

There, two aspirin left in a packet.

Fenchurch filled the milky glass above the sink and rushed back through. 'Here.'

Doyle stopped the compressions and moved to the side.

Dad moaned about being force-fed aspirin by his son, but it was groans and not words.

He was dying.

Right in front of Fenchurch.

Someone had broken in, subdued him then tied him up...

And now he was having a heart attack.

Why? Why had they done that? To send a message to Fenchurch? To get something out of him?

Fenchurch focused on Doyle. 'Did you find the documents?'

'No.' Doyle swallowed hard. 'I shouldn't have left him. Should've grabbed all of the possible files and taken him for a cuppa in the station.'

'Damn right you should've.'

The faint sound of shattering glass echoed from the kitchen.

'Stay with him.' Fenchurch set off down the hallway, his shuffling footsteps echoing.

The realisation hit him – the assailant was still here.

He reached the end of the hallway and bolted into the kitchen.

A tall figure was silhouetted against the window at the far side. The intruder made a hasty exit through the front door.

'Stop!' Fenchurch chased after him and burst out the door into the rain-soaked streets. His coat billowed out behind him as he sprinted after the figure, the relentless rain blurring his vision. The slippery paving beneath his feet threatened to betray him, but he maintained his pursuit.

This fucker wasn't getting away.

His prey led down a side lane. He was agile, whoever he was, but Fenchurch had to hope his years of experience as a detective gave him the edge. That, and growing up around here and knowing the streets intimately.

The blue lights of an ambulance blurred past, followed by a throb of siren.

Good – professional help.

Fenchurch raced down the lane, then through a deserted square. His breath came in ragged gasps, and his muscles ached, but he pressed on, closing the gap with every stride.

The assailant's path led down to the walkway running alongside Regent's Canal.

Fenchurch reached the edge, the dark waters reflecting the stormy sky.

The figure stumbled, his foot slipping on the wet pavement as he came to a halt.

Fenchurch seized the opportunity and sprinted towards him, then lunged forward and tackled him to the ground.

He caught an elbow to the jaw and fell back onto the path, rain-soaked and mud-smeared.

The assailant stood up, gasping for breath.

Fenchurch pushed up to standing. He still couldn't make him out. 'Colin Scott?'

'Shit.' The assailant stared into the canal, teetering on the precipice. 'I should've called myself Murky Canal and played keyboards in the Reeds.'

Fenchurch recognised the voice, but he couldn't place him. 'Come on, let's have a nice cosy chat somewhere—'

The assailant set off along the towpath.

But Fenchurch had spotted the movements before they'd started. Instinct kicked in and he sprinted off, aided and abetted by his robotic knee. Five paces and he rugby-tackled the guy to the ground. No getting away this time, so he pinned him there, then forced both arms up his back. He kept his grip as he got to his feet and looked into the eyes of the man he had chased down.

Neil Fields stared up at him.

The ex-fire chief. Don Avonmore's neighbour.

Fields had been in Fenchurch's dad's flat. He'd tied him up. Interrogated him. Made him have a heart attack.

Fenchurch pinned him face down on the path's rough tarmac. 'Neil Fields, I'm arresting you for the assault and attempted murder of Ian Fenchurch.' Other charges would follow, but this was the strongest. 'You do not have to say anything, but it may harm your defence if you do not mention when questioned something which you later rely on in court.

Anything you do say may be given in evidence. Do you understand?'

'Fuck off.'

Fenchurch hauled his arm up his back. 'Do you understand?'

'Fuck you.'

Fenchurch pulled his arm up even higher and felt the bone snap.

Fields screamed, the noise tearing at Fenchurch's ears like someone was poking a knife in. 'You've broken my fucking arm!'

Fenchurch didn't let the tension slacken off. 'I'll break a lot more if you don't talk to me. Let's start with the other arm.' He knelt on his back and grabbed the left wrist. 'Who is Colin Scott?'

'Nobody.'

'But you know him. You mentioned his name.'

'I've no idea what you're talking about.'

'Why did you tie up my father?'

'I didn't!'

'I chased you from inside his fucking flat! I know exactly what you're up to. You were interrogating him to find out what we know about you and your mates.'

'No idea what you're talking about.'

'I do. You're in a group of men who abduct kids. Usually girls. Then you abuse them, kill them or just swap them between you.'

'Fuck off! I'm innocent here!'

'That group took my fucking daughter!' Fenchurch hauled the left wrist up his back, to almost the same level of tension that broke his other arm. 'How the hell did you get into this?'

'Please! That's... I'm going to pass out!'

Fenchurch gave a little thrust to show he was capable of even more tension. Then he let it slacken off. 'Talk. Now. Or I'll kill you and toss you in the canal. Say you died during the pursuit. They'll believe me. Then they'll dig into your life and your history. Find all the abuses you've perpetrated. All the ones you've covered up. Whatever legacy you think you're leaving behind will be forever tarnished. You'll be known as a child molester.'

'They'll kill me!'

Fenchurch knew Fields, or men like him. He was used to having influence because of his position.

And he also didn't know Dad had a heart attack.

As much as he wanted to kill him, the worst part was Fenchurch needed the information out of him.

'If you talk, I will smooth it over. I'll protect you.'

'If I talk, they'll track me down and kill me.'

'I'll kill you right here and now.' Fenchurch let the words hang there in the teeming rain. He let the tension go, but was ready for any movement.

Fields sat up and sighed. He was a broken man. 'I've been doing it for years. Earn good money from it. But I've *never* been involved in the stuff you're saying they do.'

'What have you done for them, then?'

'A few fires went un-investigated. Or investigations were curtailed and pointed in the wrong direction. A few dead bodies not discovered.'

'Of children?'

'God, no. People who stepped out of line or over the mark. They couldn't have you lot investigating them, so they had to do it themselves. These people were guilty. They knew it, the victims knew it. So they had to act and they had to act swiftly. My work covered over a few cases that would've hit the papers, shall we say.'

'Celebrities?'

'And politicians. Members of the judiciary. I've got information on them. You can have it all.'

Fenchurch didn't believe it existed.

'How did they snare you?'

'I was in debt. Married, with a massive mortgage. Had an affair. Wife found out. Left me. You see where I live. It's not cheap. I was ruined. But Don helped.'

'Don Avonmore?'

'Right. He gave me money. We pretended it was all royalties from an invention. But it wasn't. There was no invention. Certainly nothing I'd invented, anyway. The money came in handy. But he started asking me to do things. I said no. The next day, a letter dropped through my door. Photos of me with the girl I'd been seeing. She was a lot younger than me. I... I didn't know how young. I'd asked her, she'd said eighteen and I believed her. Her birth certificate, though... She was fifteen. They'd hooked me good and proper.'

'So you started to do corrupt things to help them?'

'I didn't have a choice.'

Words Fenchurch had heard so many times. 'Everyone has a choice, it's just the consequences they don't like. What were you doing with my dad? Were you trying to kill him?'

'No. He's a useful idiot. Sure, he knows a lot of stuff about us, but he's a bit of a crackpot. Thinks we're responsible for stuff we couldn't possibly be. Thinks we've got too much power.'

'You say "we" and not "they".'

'Sorry. It's... But he was on to us. Me, in particular. This stuff with that rapper attacking Don. Killing Adrian. When I saw you at Don's house tonight. You were only a step or two away from connecting things up. I knew something had been going on with your father and Kanyif. I needed some leverage.'

'Why him, though? Why my father?'

'We know you, Fenchurch. How you searched for your missing daughter for years. How you found her, despite how well they'd hidden her. We know your dad. How he wouldn't give up until we were stopped. Or he was.'

Fenchurch gripped his broken arm, tight enough to make him yelp. 'Were you involved in her abduction?'

Fields nodded. 'And in the cover-up. Not directly, but we… did a few things to help out.' He stared hard at Fenchurch. 'I fucked your daughter myself. She was eight. I—'

Fenchurch gripped him by the throat and squeezed hard.

This fucker.

He was going to die.

He kept squeezing and squeezing, digging his thumbs in. Fields was bucking, his eyes bulging.

Fenchurch caught a kick in the balls and stumbled forward, landing on his knees.

Something splashed.

He looked around and saw Fields in the water.

Shit.

Fenchurch dived in after him, plunging into the depths.

The icy water enveloped him, the shock of the cold coursing through his body, like he'd been electrocuted. He fought to regain his bearings, kicking strongly against the current as he scanned the darkness. He fumbled for a hold, clutching at the slick stones on the bottom. The water's pressure twisted against him, urging him to rise for air.

Through the murk, the figure of Fields floundering grew dimmer with each passing second.

Fenchurch thrust his legs and swam after him, his limbs slicing through the water, each stroke propelling him closer to his quarry.

His fingers brushed against Fields's flailing arm.

Fenchurch lunged forward again and his hand clamped onto Fields's collar with an iron grip.

Fingernails clawed at his neck.

Fenchurch was hauled under the surface and they became entwined in an underwater struggle, the cold water swirling around them in a frenzied dance.

Every instinct screamed at him to rise to the surface, to gasp for air, but Fields had his own relentless grip. It held him down, pinning him to the bottom. Time distorted underwater; every second felt like an eternity. Strong fingers dug into Fenchurch's throat, threatening to crush his windpipe. His vision started to blur, dark spots creeping into the corners of his eyes.

Fenchurch managed to reach his pocket, pulling free his keys. With the last dregs of strength, he slammed the brass Yale into the side of Fields's head.

His grip loosened momentarily, and Fenchurch capitalised on it, wrenching free and delivering a kick to his midriff. Then he drove his keys into the back of his attacker's neck.

Fields recoiled, disoriented, then went limp and tumbled away along the canal's bottom.

Fenchurch tried to follow him, but he needed to breathe. He pushed off the riverbed. He surged upwards, breaking the surface with a desperate gasp, the cold night air never tasting so sweet.

He looked around. No sign of Fields.

He needed to find him.

Fenchurch propelled himself towards the walkway at the side and dragged his soaking body up onto the wooden boards, then heaved himself up.

He looked down the canal towards the Thames, but all he saw was water.

He lay panting for a few seconds, drenched and defeated, the relentless storm beating down on him. The moonlight shimmered above, misted by the clouds.

Doyle stood over him, frowning down at him. 'Guv, are you okay?'

35

Through the open door, the hospital corridor was shrouded in an eerie darkness. The flickering overhead lights cast elongated shadows along the stained floor tiles. The constant rain drummed insistently against the frosted windows from the end of the hallway, loud even in here. The white noise seemed to absorb Fenchurch's mood.

His spare clothes hung off him – he must've lost a bit too much weight when he was off sick for all that time. Even his spare shoes felt a little too tight – how the hell had his feet grown just from getting his ten thousand steps?

Fenchurch took a deep breath and stared at his hands. Pictured them around the throat of Neil Fields.

Eyes bulging. His tongue lolling.

Then letting him go. He would've killed Fields, were it not for that swift kick to the nuts. And yet Fields had still died.

Hadn't he?

There's no way he could've survived that amount of time in the Thames.

Cargill stepped through the door. 'Don't get up.' She slammed it behind her.

Fenchurch let the breath go. 'Ma'am.'

'Chief Inspector.' She stayed standing, with her back to the door. 'We should be doing this in the station, with a lawyer or a Federation rep.'

'Doing what? I've not done anything wrong, ma'am.' Fenchurch stared her out. 'Still reeling from the attack, ma'am. Had to leave before the ambulance raced here. I can't believe someone attacked my old man.'

'And I can't believe what you did to that certain someone.'

Fenchurch had to look away. 'Do you want my version of events or are you just going to convict me based on supposition?'

'By all means.'

'I received a phone call from my father, saying someone was attempting to gain access to his flat. I was up in Shoreditch, so I drove down. Kept calling DI Ronald Doyle, who didn't answer. Called in backup, but they didn't arrive. Fearing the worst, I unlocked the door and gained access.'

'You unlocked the door?'

'Yeah. Still got a key for the place.'

'Strange, isn't it? How someone had broken in and locked the door behind them.'

'I don't know what you're implying, but I found my father, tied up on the bed. DI Doyle arrived moments later, having fetched some milk and bread from a nearby shop, then he proceeded to give my father CPR.'

'Are you saying you don't know how to?'

'Of course I know, I just wasn't in a fit state to do it. I just about managed to fetch some aspirin from a cabinet.'

'Then what happened?'

'I heard a noise. Someone was in the flat.'

'So they'd locked themselves in?'

'That's correct.'

'That just doesn't stack up for me.'

'Nor me.' Fenchurch held her gaze. He'd nothing to hide here and he wanted her to know it. 'Anyway, I didn't quite see my father's assailant, but he fled the crime scene. As the only viable suspect, I gave chase and caught up with him, at the Regent's Canal walkway. It's not far from the flat. We got into a bit of a tussle and I had to subdue him.'

'How did he die?'

'Him or me?'

'Him or you?' She laughed. 'Okay.'

'I'm serious. He almost drowned me.'

She sniffed. 'They recovered Mr Fields. A few miles down the Thames. Brought him here, but it's one of those cases where I had to speak to Mr Pratt rather than Dr Mulkalwar. Pratt's had a look at the body. You killed him, didn't you?'

'No.'

'Did you break his arm?'

'I did. Like I said, I had to subdue him. Sure you yourself have had to apply force when apprehending a murder suspect?'

She nodded. 'But he'd attempted to murder your father. And, like you just said, almost killed you.'

'That additional force was absolutely necessary. One hundred percent. He's retired, sure, but Neil Fields kept himself in shape. Really good shape.'

'Right. So that's your story?'

Fenchurch shrugged his aching shoulders. 'It's not a story, ma'am. It's the truth.'

Cargill leaned back and folded her arms, then shook her head. 'The thing I hate most is when people who work for me lie to my face.'

'I'm not lying.'

She narrowed her eyes. 'Omitting certain facts is tantamount to lying.'

'What am I omitting?'

'That you killed him.'

'I didn't. He'd supplied some information to me. I didn't torture him. He came clean on his involvement in the abduction of my daughter. He knew about it, tried to goad me. But the matter is of public record. I've met him in the last two days while investigating this case. I suspect that's given him ample opportunity to search my name and concoct a strategy in case something like this happened.'

'You don't believe him?'

'I don't want to think too hard about it, ma'am. But the people he works with, they plan for every eventuality. Myself and DCI Savage visited his neighbour's property this evening. I spoke to him. This must've alerted him to the fact we were onto something. He then tried to kill my father. Unfortunately for him, I caught him.'

'One last time. Did you try to kill him?'

'I was sorely tempted.' Fenchurch held her gaze. 'But I didn't. I'm not in the business of murdering people. No matter how bad the things they've done are.'

'Well, let's see if the facts agree with that, shall we?'

'They will.'

She shook her head again. 'You attacked him with your keys?'

'I almost drowned.' Fenchurch sat back and folded his arms. 'Listen. The Machine are—'

'The Machine?'

'My father called them that. Because they're highly efficient and fast to act, like a machine. They're a group of high-powered men who abduct and sexually abuse children. They then use their power and influence to cover it up.'

'This sounds like the sort of thing that warps people's minds on YouTube.'

'It does.'

'And it's the sort of thing that leads people to kill. Especially when they believe these people are responsible for their daughter's abduction.'

'Listen, the difference between a conspiracy theory and an actual conspiracy is one is false and the other is true. The Machine was an actual conspiracy. They were a fairly serious operation a few years ago, but the work of my father and DCI Savage put paid to it. These lot are the last vestiges of it.'

'I'm aware of this conspiracy. We had some involvement north of the border.' She straightened out her hair. 'And you think they're still operating?'

'The names might be different, but the MO is similar. They're still abducting and abusing children.'

'And Neil Fields is one of them?'

'He claimed he was responsible for the deaths of people who stepped out of line. So he's an enforcer, rather than a perpetrator.'

'Do you believe him?'

'I think the evidence is there. My father was tied up, ready for torture. That's the actions of someone in that line of work.'

'What could he possibly be torturing your father for?'

'We were closing in on the identity of one of the leading figures. Colin Scott.' Fenchurch's brain scrambled for something. 'Thing is, Don Avonmore slipped off the radar this afternoon. Discharged himself from hospital. I wasn't here, but something spooked him.'

'And we don't know where he is?'

'Nope.' Fenchurch shook his head. 'Ronnie Doyle was supposed to guard my father while they retrieved some evidence. If it wasn't for Ronnie's actions, Dad would be dead.'

Cargill breathed slowly through her nostrils. 'I'm sorry, Simon, but your father died in the ambulance.'

A tidal wave crashed over him. His heart clenched in his chest, as if a giant fist tightened around it. A cold chill ran through his body, squeezing the air from his lungs. His skin prickled, as if he was being submerged in icy water again.

The room blurred, the harsh fluorescent lights flickering like distant stars. His throat tightened and a bitter taste of despair settled in the back of his mouth. He felt a heaviness, making each breath impossibly hard.

Then his pulse quickened, drumming in his ears like a mournful dirge. His eyes welled with tears and he blinked them away, struggling to swallow a painful lump in his throat.

Fenchurch felt the world slip away from him.

He longed for just one more moment with the old bugger, one more chance to say the things left unsaid. But then they'd always be unsaid.

Cargill reached over and held his hand. 'I'm sorry, Simon.'

He could only nod.

'One last time, Simon. Did you kill Neil Fields?'

'No.'

'But he's already caused the death of one retired policeman and I doubt he'd stop there. You know that, right?'

'I didn't kill him. But I didn't save him. Not sure I could've done.'

'A likely tale.'

'Only one of us was getting out of that canal alive, ma'am, and I can tell you're disappointed it's me, but you're not surprised... Are you?'

She stared hard at him. 'Aye, I wish you'd died in that canal, Simon. I'd much rather have a suspect in custody and be rid of you!'

'That's not something you should say out loud, ma'am.'

Cargill narrowed her eyes at Fenchurch. 'I'm sure you understand that you're not on the case anymore.'

Fenchurch raised his eyebrow. 'Of course.'

'I'm ordering you to take the next two weeks on bereavement leave. Then we can discuss your future. But it won't be here.'

Someone stepped into the room, then cleared their throat. Doyle. Holding up his phone. 'Managed to get all of that recorded, Si.'

'What the fuck?' Cargill dashed over and tried to grab it, but Doyle held it just out of her reach. 'Give me that!'

'What, evidence of you saying you'd like a subordinate to have died? Sure, I'll just wipe it. It's already been emailed to ten people.' Doyle shot her a wink. 'You've been framed, ma'am.'

36

Fenchurch sat in the dimly lit living room, enveloped by grief. The flickering candle on the coffee table cast dancing shadows onto the walls, a silent tribute to the man they'd lost.

Abi's flat.

His flat.

Their flat.

Where he used to live, anyway. He hadn't been here in over a week, the last time he'd collected his son, but it felt like something had changed.

Whether Abi had moved something around or just the fact he was living in a post-Dad world, Fenchurch couldn't decide.

Chloe sat on the floor in front of him, leaning back against the coffee table, her expression a mix of sadness and determination. 'Can't believe it.'

'No.' Fenchurch brushed at his damp cheeks. 'No.'

It was all he had.

Chloe looked up at her father with wide eyes, her fingers brushing a tear from her cheek. 'You caught him, didn't you?'

Fenchurch didn't add that he'd not quite killed Neil Fields, but not far off. He just couldn't save him. 'Neil Fields is dead. He won't do hard time for what he's done to people, but he won't do it again. Or help anyone.'

'Could you have saved him?'

'Who?'

'Fields. Was it a fight to the death like it says in the report or could you have saved him?'

'You've seen the report?'

'Of course. Dad. I'm a cop.'

Fenchurch winced. Surprised, but not disappointed. 'Chip off the old block, eh?'

She shrugged her shoulders. 'Don't tell me you wouldn't.'

'True, but...' Fenchurch sighed. 'We fought. He died.'

'So you did kill him?'

'No. I tried to save him. He... It was him or me, love. I defended myself. If that resulted in him dying... I guess I'll not know until the post-mortem. Or inquest.'

Chloe took in the words. 'Good, I'm glad.' She gasped, her lower lip trembling, then she took a deep breath. Just like Fenchurch himself, she'd followed in her father's footsteps to become a police officer. 'Why did they do this to Granddad?'

Fenchurch opened his mouth to answer, then stopped. He didn't have the words. How did you tell her the people who'd been responsible for abducting her were still operating?

'Dad. You're doing that thing.'

Fenchurch frowned at Chloe. 'What thing?'

'You brush your ear when you're hiding something.'

Fenchurch hadn't even noticed. 'Do I? Shit. I didn't know that.'

Chloe leaned back against the coffee table, facing him. 'Dad, what are you hiding from me?'

'I'm not...' Fenchurch reached for his ear. Shit, she was right. And she did deserve the truth. 'This isn't easy.'

She screwed up her face at him. 'Whatever it is, just tell me.'

'Your grandfather was helping Howard Savage in an investigation.' Fenchurch watched her eyes narrow even further. 'They think the Machine are still operating.'

Chloe's lips twisted together. 'The people who took me?'

Fenchurch nodded.

'You said you'd caught them all.'

'We thought we did, love. Howard's been doing this for years. Him and Dad were confident.'

Chloe's mouth fell open. 'You *knew*?'

'No. I've been kept in the dark. I mean, I've been off work for a few months, but they didn't mention it to me, at all.'

'Why didn't they tell you?'

Fenchurch shrugged. 'I don't know.'

Chloe shook her head. 'There's got to be a reason.'

Fenchurch leaned forward. 'I promised to always be straight with you, okay?'

'So be straight with me.'

'I'm as much in the dark as you are. Your grandfather would maybe talk to me, but Howard Savage certainly won't.'

'I want to know what you know about it. And whatever wasn't part of the official record.'

'Fine, but this door can't be shut afterwards.' Fenchurch tried to unscramble his brain, but it felt like he was making a cake from cheese. 'Tonight, your granddad was heading home to fetch some evidence he'd stored there. He shouldn't have done that, but he did. And we needed it. You know what he's like – daft old sod insisted on having a cup of tea. So the cop who guarded him went to get some milk. Next thing, someone's hammering on the door. He called me, but they must've got in. I turned up and found him tied up. He was having a heart attack.'

Chloe stared into space. She looked at her father. 'So they killed him?'

'I think they were interrogating him, then they panicked when I turned up. But he panicked enough to...'

'Jesus, Dad.' Chloe stared into her lap. 'I'm working with Howard. Working with Granddad too. Surely I can do something?'

'If there's something, Howard will ask you. Okay?'

'Okay.' But she didn't look convinced.

The door opened and Abi walked in, her eyes red-rimmed from tears. 'Al's in bed now. Sorry he didn't want you to read to him, Simon.' She put the tray on the coffee table and sat down next to him. She reached out, her hand trembling, and took Fenchurch's in her own. They shared a look, a wordless acknowledgment of the pain they both felt.

Chloe shifted her focus between her parents. 'When are you going to tell him?'

Fenchurch looked to Abi, deferring the decision to her.

'I'll speak to him in the morning.' She sipped at her tea. 'It's important he gets a good night's sleep. I'll keep him off school, of course. No idea what we'll do.' She looked at Fenchurch. 'What are your plans?'

'First, I need to get some sleep. Been away a lot and... Then it's all the shitty admin, right? Arrange the funeral directors. Contact his old mates. Guess Ronnie Doyle can help with that.' The sharp tang of loss bit at his tongue. 'And I need to see his body.'

And the reality hit hard. His dad was gone. He'd never see him again, at least not alive anyway.

Chloe sipped at her tea. 'I want to help.'

'It's mind-numbing stuff, love.'

She smiled at her dad. 'It'll be practice from when you don't get away from someone trying to drown you.'

Abi scowled at him. 'What's she talking about?'

'Nothing.' Fenchurch reached for his tea. 'I got into an incident this evening. Had to jump into the canal.' He still felt the rattle of the water in his eardrums. 'It'll be fine.'

Chloe was staring at the door. 'I don't want this to sound morbid, but next year, Al will be the same age I was when they took me.'

Fenchurch swallowed down some bitter tea. 'Been playing on my mind a bit, love. Worrying that someone would do something just to mess with us.'

'I'll make sure it won't happen.' Chloe got to her feet. 'Thanks for the tea, Mum. I've got to go. Early start in the morning.'

Abi frowned at her. 'You okay there, love?'

'Sorry, I know you want to help, but I'm good at handling shit myself, Mum. I'm working with Howard tomorrow, so I'll see what he's got to say about it all.'

'Are you sure you should be working? Your father's off for—'

'They can't stop me.' Chloe's eyes hardened. 'If what Dad's saying is true and they're still operating—'

'Don't do anything stupid like your father would.'

Chloe smiled. 'I'm smarter than him.'

Fenchurch laughed. 'You are.'

Chloe leaned over and pecked them both on the cheeks. 'I love you both, okay?'

Abi kissed her back. 'And we both love you.'

'See you tomorrow.' Chloe strolled off out of the room, looking every inch the police officer. She peered into her kid brother's bedroom, then left the flat.

The door clicked shut and they were alone again.

'She's great, isn't she?' Fenchurch smiled at the door. 'After all she's been through...'

'I'd love to say we've done a great job with her, Simon, but... Those *people* who raised her... Sometimes people are who they are because of their upbringing, others in spite of it.'

'Bad people can do good things.' Fenchurch rested his cup

on the coffee table. 'And sometimes there's something that makes them do bad things...'

'It doesn't excuse what they did.'

'No.'

'And it doesn't excuse what you did.'

Here we go...

'What have I done?'

'You've got a habit of pushing things too far, haven't you? And now you're paying the price for it.'

'My father being killed is me paying the price?'

'Simon, don't try to defend yourself. You know I'm right.'

'If I push things too far... Abi, I *do* stuff. I make things happen. It's how we found Chloe. It's how we got her back. Because of me and my sheer bloody-minded singularity of focus. So, no – I don't think I pushed things too far.'

Abi just shook her head at that.

'You know I'm right.'

'Where were you tonight?'

'I was working. Drove back from Scotland.'

'You were with Ian, though?'

'Right. I saw him over at the Empress State Building.'

'That's a real place?'

'In Earls Court. Bugger to get to from this side of town.'

'But you were with him?'

'Right. What are you getting at?'

'Just trying to understand it all. Tell me it straight.'

'The deal was, Dad was to go with Ronnie Doyle to get this evidence he's got squirrelled away, while Howard and I went to speak to someone about the case.'

'Someone.'

'Another victim. Someone who went through... Not what Chloe went through, but ballpark similar. She was older when she was taken. But...'

Abi frowned. 'It's really the same people who took Chloe?'

'Possibly. I don't know. Dad and Howard think it is, but that kind of world is always very murky, love. They make things opaque for a reason – they're committing some heinous crimes.'

She nodded along with it, but her thoughts were elsewhere. 'You could've gone back to your father's flat with him instead of this Doyle character.'

'Doyle's an old mate of Dad's. Worked together just before he retired. I trust him. *Dad* trusted him. But you know Dad. He's as pushy as me – he wanted a cup of tea. He died because of a bloody cup of tea.'

'Simon, you shouldn't have been doing all that, should you? You should've been in the office, sitting on your arse. Pushing papers around. And your dad retired, what, fifteen years ago? Instead, he's still working at his age, getting involved in all of this noise. And you're jumping into the bloody canal to catch his killer? That's fucked up, Simon. Totally fucked up.'

Fenchurch sat there, sipping his tea. 'Abi, you never understood what it means to be a cop. And you never even tried.'

'You never understood what it meant to be a father or a husband.'

'Seriously?'

'Simon, you never tried to understand what it meant to be a wife to a cop. To always wonder if the phone ringing was because you'd been killed. How casually you treat jumping into a canal after a serial killer or child molester. And now you've made Chloe sign up...'

'Love, I never—'

'Don't. After Chloe was taken, you just did what your dad's been doing. Hunted for them like you—'

'I found them. I found *her*.'

'The ends justify the means, eh? Remember when we found her fucking grave? What if that was actually her in that? Eh? Would that have made all the pain worthwhile?'

She was right.

But Fenchurch didn't want to admit anything. 'I'm sorry. But I don't know how to be any different.'

'I know. And that's the whole problem. When you got yourself hooked on those painkillers, you fell apart. I was the one who had to pick up all the pieces. And you recovered, sure, but your focus was on getting back to work to do more of this carry-on, rather than fix our marriage, rather than be a father to your son.'

'Look. I'm on bereavement leave. Once that's over, I'm being transferred to God knows where. We need to have a bigger discussion about our future.'

'The one you've avoided for months?'

'My knee's been absolute agony.'

'And you wouldn't let me help, would you? I was off school for six weeks over the summer and you were so bloody stubborn. Just sat in that bloody flat, listening to the Smiths like a teenager.'

Fenchurch put the teacup down and got to his feet. 'I need to think this all through, love. I'm sorry this has been such a strain on you. You don't deserve any of this bullshit from me. Or the constant noise and pain. But we do need to come to an agreement about what our future is going to be. Either together or apart. Whatever it is, we need to decide for Al's sake as much as ours.'

'Okay.' She looked up at him through glistening eyes. 'And I am really sorry for you losing your dad. He was a good man.'

Fenchurch leaned over and kissed her cheek. 'Thank you.' He turned and left the room.

Left the flat, then thundered down the stairs, his mind like a swirling vortex full of too many thoughts. And he was absolutely exhausted. But he knew he wouldn't sleep.

The end of his marriage.

Again.

It brought him sadness like a sour taste in his mouth, mixed with bitter.

Yet beneath the surface, it was a relief. A rock had been held over his head for years, one that he feared but was unable to stop dropping onto his skull.

And she was right in a way, but wrong in so many others.

Fenchurch would miss his son, but maybe in his absence, the boy could grow up without his constant example and not continue the family tradition of policing and misery.

He could hope.

DAY 4

Thursday

37

Fenchurch's eyes slowly flickered open, his consciousness pulling him out of a restless slumber. He'd thought he wouldn't sleep and mostly hadn't. Just lay there, tossing and turning. But he'd finally drifted off. And at the worst time – no rest, but that thick-headed feeling.

The first rays of dawn peeking through his curtains, casting a pallid glow over the shabby surroundings.

And then, like a thunderclap, the events of the previous night rushed back to punch him in the guts. His chest tightened as he recalled the scene in his father's flat, then the pursuit through Limehouse and the struggle that led to Dad's assailant. And his death.

The weight of sorrow bore down on him, and he felt his heart ache with an intensity that left him breathless.

Dad was more than just a father – he was a mentor, a confidant, a source of unwavering support. He'd never judged, despite Fenchurch frequently being a bloody idiot.

But it took one to know one.

He groaned, feeling the weight of exhaustion clinging to his bones. His head pounded with a dull ache and his mouth felt like coarse sandpaper.

Couldn't even have a drink last night to toast the old sod.

Struggling to sit up, Fenchurch surveyed the familiar but dilapidated space. His old flat in the Isle of Dogs had remained unchanged over the years. He needed to change. Put it all right with Abi, once and for all, and move back there – or somewhere else.

Leigh-on-Sea seemed as good a place as any.

Fenchurch swung his legs over the edge of the bed and ran a trembling hand through his hair. His eyes darted around the room. It was like he was underwater again. Everything felt slow and blurry. He landed on a faded photograph of his parents, forever frozen in time. A wry smile on Dad's face, Mum looking like she hated being that side of the camera.

The tears welled up and Fenchurch clenched his fists, willing himself to be strong.

He dragged himself to his feet and padded through the silent flat towards the kitchen. Not even Chloe staying here anymore, just him on his Jack Jones. He poured a glass of water and sank it in one, his throat grateful for the relief. As the liquid flowed down his gullet, he couldn't escape the image of his father's eyes in his flat as the heart attack consumed him, despite Doyle's efforts.

It gnawed at his soul.

He should visit the hospital and see his body.

He needed to call the funeral director.

And there were so many other things he needed to do. So much *stuff*.

Gathering photos for the display. Then sitting and writing the eulogy.

The morning light continued to creep in, casting a pale glow on the memories that surrounded him.

Fenchurch couldn't remain lost in his grief. Stuff needed to be done. He squared his shoulders, resolving to carry the burden of his father's death with the determination that had defined his life.

Ian Fenchurch might be gone, but his legacy would live on.

Fenchurch, though... His career was over. He'd soon be pushing pencils in some stupid dead-end job at Scotland Yard or be out to pasture in Leigh-on-bloody-Sea.

The buzzer rang.

Fenchurch's blood ran cold. The clock above the sink read 06:32. Who the hell was here at this time?

He padded over to the console.

Kay Reed was waiting outside, thumbs tapping at her phone screen.

'In you come, Kay.' Fenchurch pressed the door entry button. He opened the door, then stomped through to the bedroom and threw on last night's clothes.

By the time he got into them, he realised they were from two days ago. No time to change.

Reed was walking through the door. 'How are you doing, guv?'

All he had for her was a deep shrug. 'I'll survive.'

She gave him a hug, but not too lingering – he really did stink. 'Can't imagine what you're going through.'

'Not easy, Kay. But I went through worse with Mum. She faded away to nothing. With Dad... Who am I kidding? I didn't get to say goodbye to the old bugger. At least I was there when Mum went...'

'That's the hardest part, right? Like when we lost my brother.'

Fenchurch nodded at her. It was all he had. 'Can I get you a cup of tea?'

'I'm fine. Had one before I left the station.' She stood there, fiddling with her winter coat's toggles. 'Anyway. I gather you've been put on leave?'

'Not just that. When I come back, I'll be gone. I'm being put out to pasture, Kay. Somewhere stupid in the Met or out in Essex.'

'Depends on where in Essex, right?'

'Dangerously close to Southend, I'm afraid.'

'Well, Cargill's on the warpath. She's given me your position as SIO.'

'You could've called me, Kay.'

'Yeah, I could've done, but I wanted to see you. Offer my support. I'm here because I want to help you.'

'Help? Kay, I need a psychoanalyst to unpick all the shit inside my head. Unless you've suddenly done some retraining...'

'No, of course I haven't. But I can listen.'

'I appreciate it, Kay. Sorry if I'm being all prickly. It's just...'

'Your dad's dead. I get it, guv. It's okay.'

'Right.'

'Thing is, I've been up all night going through your dad's stuff from the flat.'

'Kay, you didn't need to do that. You've got a whole team for that.'

'No, but I wanted to. *Had* to, really. Your old man's helped me out a lot over the years.' She ran a hand through her hair, fanning it out. 'Trouble is, there's nothing there, guv.'

'What?'

'The evidence you went there for. It's not there.'

'Seriously? He said he got a load of stuff from Kanyif Iqbal.'

'Nothing there, that we could find.'

'That doesn't seem right, Kay.'

'Guv, I know it's hard to accept, but it's possible his mind was going. Made him obsess about the Machine all over again, despite Chloe being recovered.'

The words gnawed at Fenchurch. His old man was a bit loopy – the whole family was – but was he that bad?

No.

'Kay, he had something. I know it. I *know* it.'

'We haven't found it.'

'Fields must've done something with it.'

'Right. And we can't just ask him.'

Wait.

Fenchurch looked hard at her. 'Kay, his dying words were "Colin Scott was here".'

'Was it Neil Fields?'

'I asked him, he denied it.'

'Yeah, and these people always tell the truth.' She rolled her eyes. 'Seriously, guv. Had you mentioned it to your dad?'

'Well, yeah. But...'

'Guv... I'm sorry. I don't know what to think, but we found nothing.'

'Nothing? At all? Seriously?'

'We've been told to move on from this.'

Fenchurch could taste vomit building up in his throat, like it was going to burn his oesophagus. 'But Dad had evidence from Kanyif. It was going to...' He was clutching at straws. He sounded desperate.

'Sorry.' Reed clamped a hand on his arm. 'Look, the only thing we've found which we can't figure out is this piece of paper.' She got out her phone and showed him a photo.

A corner of an envelope, roughly torn. Dad's unmistakable handwriting. Blue biro, reading:

$$PW = PW$$

Reed held her phone out that bit longer, in case it jogged anything in Fenchurch's battered head. 'Mean anything?'

'Nope.' Fenchurch let out a deep breath. 'Can you send me it?'

'Sure.' She turned the phone around and started tapping away.

Fenchurch reached for his charging phone and checked the message had appeared. 'Thanks for coming over, Kay. It means a lot.'

'Are you going to be okay?'

'I'll be fine. Got to contact the funeral directors today. Same one as for Mum so at least I know the drill now. Then it'll be tracking down all the old rascals he knew and worked with to let them know. Which will lead to me having to track down the precious few who've slipped off the radar, but who Dad would demand would be there. I owe it to him.'

Reed puffed up her cheeks and let the air out slowly. 'Well. Shame I can't charge Fields with his murder. I'd better get back to it.'

'Thank you, Kay.' He let her hug him again. 'See you around.'

'Yeah. Don't be a stranger.' She looked him up and down. 'And you might want to change your clothes.'

Fenchurch smiled at her. 'Always trust you to give me the cold truth.'

She gave him one last smile, then left.

Before the door had fully shut, Fenchurch was already calling someone.

'Simon?'

'Hi, Vicky. You okay?'

'Not really.' Deep breath. 'Just about to go into court in bloody Glasgow. Hate this city. It's like a song in the wrong key.'

'Right. Yeah, you mentioned that yesterday.' Fenchurch left a pause. Didn't want to seem too pushy. He was already pushy enough. 'Just wondered if you're getting anywhere with the laptop?'

'Nope.' A deep sigh. 'Thought I'd try some of the locals to check it out, but they couldn't get into it. It's sitting in my car. Was planning on dropping it off after court.'

'Hold that thought, then.'

'Why?'

38

Fenchurch stepped into the long collection area and waited, scanning the parked cars and those approaching. The fug of spent diesel hung in the air as a Toyota slid around silently, the Travis Cars logo bleeding into the gloom. Surprise to see them this far north, but time and tide waited for no man. At some point, they'd all be electric and the air would be that bit cleaner.

Might've been November, but it was a clear day in Glasgow. Bright and sunny, but absolutely freezing. Last time he'd flown into this airport, he thought he was walking into a calm police investigation. Two hours later, he'd seen two crime scenes and six bodies, someone had hit him with a hammer and then the realisation he'd be based here for weeks.

So this could be worse.

He had to keep telling himself that.

Another fresh sting of grief jabbed him under the ribs.

He saw a glimpse of his dad eating fish and chips in the pub around the corner from his flat. Teeth all hidden behind the white, brown and green mush.

A horn blared and he looked up.

Vicky was behind the wheel of a tiny little Ford thing. Probably a Ka, but he wasn't sure they still made them.

Fenchurch grabbed his overnight bag and got in the passenger side. 'Hey, thanks for meeting me.'

'Don't mention it.'

He got a good look at her. She'd applied make-up and looked like she was heading for a photo shoot, not the high court. 'You scrub up well.'

'Shut up.' She laughed, then pulled off before he'd fastened his seatbelt. 'I'd take it slowly and go through all that hiya nonsense, but the timer here is a nightmare.' She blasted up towards the exit gate, one of about ten, and stopped, her window already down. Tapping the wheel with her phone. 'Come on, come on, come on...' Then the old man in front moved off and she got to the pay barrier, then tapped her phone against the machine. The arm rose up. She sped off. 'Phew. Just in time.'

'Parking here seems like a nightmare.'

'Here and Edinburgh are disaster zones.' She pulled away and glanced over at him. 'Why are you here?'

'Aside from Edinburgh flights being full until this evening, you told me you were in Glasgow.'

'And whatever this is, you don't trust me to do it alone?'

'It's not that, Vicky.' Fenchurch sighed. 'Listen, I'm on compassionate leave. My dad died yesterday.'

'Shit, really?'

'It's a long story, but it's all part of this case. Dad had something pertinent to it. Someone broke in and took it or destroyed it.'

'Have you any idea what?'

'He claimed it was some evidence he'd received that proved a woman had been trafficked by someone. I haven't seen it, but whatever it was came from Kanyif Iqbal, so I wondered if it's on that laptop.' Fenchurch looked at his feet. 'Have you got the laptop?'

'Don't even buy me dinner or a drink first...' Vicky slalomed over the road and pulled into an industrial estate, parking outside a tiny factory. 'I've got the laptop.' She took it off the backseat and pulled the plastic case tight. The screen woke up. 'Okay, what do you want with it?'

Fenchurch reached over and typed in 'Pennyworth'.

It knocked him back, shaking the password screen.

'No joy.' He tried it in lower case. Same noise. 'Nope.' Then upper case.

The laptop unlocked.

'Bingo.' Fenchurch hated using a Mac – he had no idea how the bastard things worked. Or even if they did. 'Bloody hell.'

Vicky grabbed it. 'What are you trying to do?'

'Search for Colin Scott.'

She typed into a little box. 'There.'

A window filled with some documents. Not many, but a good enough start.

Fenchurch opened the first. Pennyworth Holdings documentation from Companies House. 'We've already got that.'

The second was a scanned document which detailed a transaction between Kanyif's real name and Pennyworth Holdings. A handwritten scrawl wrote:

'This transaction was used to purchase Kylie Broadford from Colin Scott.'

Fenchurch felt the air escape his lungs like he'd been punched. 'This is the document Dad died for.'

And it didn't give him anything. Just proved that some people purchased others like it was Ancient Rome.

He clicked on the third document. Detailed transactional record for Pennyworth Holdings.

'Holy shit.'

Fenchurch flicked through it. Nothing too detailed, but it

contained both the names of the owners. 'Half to Colin Scott, owned in the Bahamas. And half to Avonmore Holdings. That's Rusty Rivers's company.' He felt a breath slide out. 'That's a smoking gun.'

'Did you say Rusty Rivers?'

'Right. Real name is Don Avonmore, why?'

'My dad was a fan of his. Heard he got attacked?'

'He's up to his nuts in this.' Fenchurch realised he had the Machine right here. And Kanyif had. 'This shows where their money went. But it doesn't show who they are.'

'There's an email too.' Vicky grabbed the laptop off him and opened it. 'Kanyif's accountant has unpicked the ultimate ownership of the business.'

'Somehow, he's been able to do what us cops haven't.' Fenchurch nodded along with the words like they were music. 'Rivers was involved. And so were Adrian Thornhill and Rick Spangler.'

'Rick Spangler?'

'His manager. They were co-owners of the company.' Fenchurch looked out at the nearby buildings. 'But we still don't know who Colin Scott is. He's not listed.'

Vicky opened the fifth document. 'There's another asset here. A financial transaction relating to an estate in the Scottish Highlands near Loch Ness.'

'Pennyworth owns it?'

'Right. Bought it a year ago.'

'That could be where he is.' Fenchurch skimmed through the document. Not the prettiest building but it was forty or so miles from the nearest settlement. Even then, that was Inverness. 'Let's go and see it.'

'Nope.' Vicky shut the laptop lid and returned it to the back seat. 'I've gone out on enough of a limb here, Simon. This is hard evidence and I need to get it into your case file.'

39

A cold, crisp morning. Made him think he could move up this way, but then he remembered the unrelenting rain. The last few days in London had been an anomaly – up here, it rained most days, especially on the west coast. Not constantly, but enough to grind away at you.

Fenchurch couldn't even hack a winter up here. He leaned back against Vicky's Ka and folded his arms. Then he started itching to do something, so he googled Gartcosh to see exactly where he was. The other side of Glasgow from the airport. A grand building, probably less than ten years old, with Police Scotland projecting an image of proficient modernity.

He should've taken the laptop himself. Should never have trusted her.

Whoever had Jasmine was up at that house. They just had to be. And maybe Rusty Rivers would be there too.

He should've searched that laptop for Jasmine.

For his dad.

For himself. For Chloe.

For anything. For everything.

But Vicky had just shut it down and run off to teacher.

He'd been wrong to trust her. Idiot. Stupid bloody idiot.
His phone blasted out.

Unknown caller...

Could be Vicky calling from a desk phone, with something important.

He answered it. 'Fenchurch.'

'Simon.' Even Cargill's voice made his ear feel a few degrees colder.

'Good morning, ma'am. Are you calling me to wish me well? And maybe to ask if you can do anything to help with my father's funeral?' Fenchurch left a sarcastically long pause. 'That's incredibly kind of you. And unexpected. You'll be relieved to learn that I'm fine. And while I'm pressing the button to end this call now, but I'm doing it very respectfully.'

'Enough of the passive-aggressive bullshit.' Cargill left her own pause, as if daring him to actually hang up on her. 'Can I ask why you're in Scotland?'

Shit.

'I'm on business relating to my father's death. Closing stuff off.'

'Sounds like bollocks to me.'

'There's not a lot I can do back home. Funeral directors can't collect the body until Monday. One of his oldest friends lives up here and he's got phone numbers and addresses for the old team. All of them. He lives off grid on the Isle of Bute, but if I can get hold of his contacts list, then it'll save me a few days or weeks. Want to let all of them know.'

'What's his name?'

'Doubt you'd know him.'

'Right. So that's how you're playing it?'

'I'm not playing anything. My father's just died and I've

flown from London City to Glasgow so I can put his affairs to rest.'

'If you're going to Bute, why are you over here? The ferry goes from Wemyss Bay, which is about half an hour on the train from the airport.'

Fenchurch didn't have a good answer for that, so he kept his mouth shut.

Movement at the front door.

Vicky, storming towards him. She got in the car without a word.

'It's a lie, Simon, but it might help to explain why you're involved in getting into a suspect's laptop.'

Fuck.

Vicky *had* grassed.

'Ma'am... Look, I've got hold of something that the team couldn't fathom. It just so happened I was met at the airport by someone who was involved in transporting the laptop from Dundee to Glasgow.'

'Simon, Gartcosh is nowhere near the airport.'

'It's not *nowhere* near, ma'am. Ten miles or so through central Glasgow, sure, but—'

'Twenty, I believe.'

'Still, it's not like it's in Penzance, is it?'

'I still don't like this. I *hate* being lied to and it's pretty much all you've done, when you're not hiding from me.'

Fenchurch opened his door. 'Listen, I'm on compassionate leave, so I'll pick up with you next week.' He hung up, then got in the car. Waiting for the phone to ring with an order to return to London. 'So, I just had a call from my boss.'

'Cargill, right?'

'Right. She knew about—'

'Simon, you might be a cowboy, but I'm not a cowgirl. I need to make sure this whole thing's above board. That laptop is evidence in a triple homicide and in an active missing persons.'

'I get it. It's just—'

'You've done well, though. Now we're in, the lab boffins can scan the laptop and add everything to the case file. My brother's personally looking into it for me.'

'None of that makes me feel like anyone's going to head to that house to find Jasmine.'

'That's not your concern just now. Your team are professionals. If it's a valid lead, they'll follow it.'

'If that's supposed to reassure me, then—'

'I got a call from *my* boss. Thought he was checking on how my twenty minutes in court went, but no. He told me to drop you at the nearest airport and make sure you board a flight to London.'

'You can't do that.'

'The last bit? No, I can't unless I manage to blag my way through security. But I can do the rest of it. Buckle up, buster.' She started up the engine and drove off through the car park.

Fenchurch picked up his backpack and rested it on his lap. He pulled his seatbelt over and clicked it in place. 'So, that's it?'

'Like I've got any choice. I need my job to pay my mortgage. And I do actually like it.'

'I remember what that felt like.' Fenchurch started to yawn but he caught it before it took over. 'You know something, I've not always been this dark, brooding figure, haunted by my trauma. I used to laugh and make people smile. Years ago, I was destined for the top. Maybe not the *top* top. Didn't have an Oxbridge degree, political sensitivities or even the gift of the gab most had, but I was going places. Made DI in my early thirties. Probably would've ended up as assistant commissioner or maybe chief constable of a smaller force. West Mercia or Devon and Cornwall, maybe. My wife's family moved to Cornwall from London, so it'd be logical. But when those fuckers kidnapped my daughter, it wasn't just her they took. I lost myself. Stopped laughing and smiling.'

'I can see that part of you, Simon. I can still see that. But he's so buried under anger and grief.'

'Isn't he just?' Fenchurch shook his head and watched the road slip past. 'The thing that makes this all so hard, Vicky, is that these people are...' His throat closed up, involuntarily. 'They killed my dad. Who knows what they're planning next. They're not the same people who took my daughter years ago, but they're connected. I can't help but think... They might...'

'Simon, you found her. It's over.'

'We did, but they still need to pay for what they did to my dad.'

'Simon, that's not for us to do.'

'But whose job is it? And how can I trust they'll do it as well as I will?'

'You can't. But you've got a good team. You've talked about that before.' Vicky pulled up at a roundabout. Clear enough, so she entered it.

The first exit was for the M73, marked:

THE SOUTH

She drove past it and took the turning for:

(Stirling M73)

Fenchurch looked over at her. 'This isn't the way to the airport.'

'Nope.' Vicky floored it over the bridge across the motorway. 'You know what us dizzy Dundee wifies are like. We get easily lost. Besides, I hear Loch Ness is lovely this time of year.'

40

Vicky hurtled up the A82, passing over a bridge across an unmarked river. Deep into Scotland now, the landscape as distinct from London as if it was a desert. No buildings, in fact nothing much manmade, just pine trees, low clouds and tall hills.

Fenchurch could see himself living up here, far from the insane crowd. But maybe he'd get bored. Only so many books he could read and films he could watch. All those hills, though – his knee would be up to the challenge of bagging a few Munros a week.

The sign showed a left turning from the road, signposted:

Kyle of Lochalsh

Made Fenchurch wince. 'I spoke to someone called Kylie Lochalsh the other day.'

Vicky looked over at him. 'From that TV show, *Straight Outta Brixton*?'

'Right.'

'Wow.'

'You watch it?'

'Appointment telly in my house. My kids are huge fans of it. Bella was pissed off she didn't win.'

'Kylie?'

'Right. That was a wee while ago, though. What happened to her?'

'She was another victim of this ring.'

'Shite. That's awful.' Vicky slowed and indicated left. 'You need the toilet?'

'I'm not five.'

'I'm not saying you are, but *I* need to go. And we've been driving for a few hours now.' She took the turning and hurtled down the road through a tiny village that barely even existed. No signs of any businesses. 'Did you finish that sandwich?'

Fenchurch nodded. 'Did you want the other half?'

'No, just wanted to put it in the bin. This car's a rental, so I have my work cut out tidying up all the kids' rubbish, let alone yours.' She pulled into a car park outside a community hall and got out, then walked over to the ladies' toilet with her phone clamped to her ear.

Fenchurch eased himself out. That chase in Limehouse had really done a number on him. Felt like his nose had been turned inside out and he still had disgusting water stuck in his ears. He slammed the door, then walked over to the gents. He didn't really need, but something made him go. And sure enough, he needed. So he sat down and... it just collapsed out of him.

Turned out he was actually nervous.

Heading to a house in the sodding Highlands, miles off his leash as he hunted down a missing rock star and a missing girl.

On compassionate leave.

He shouldn't be doing this. But no other bugger was going to, were they?

He used the last of the toilet paper. Sodding hell. He left the cubicle and staggered into the next one. Bingo, two whole rolls. He washed his hands in soap that reminded him of his gran's house.

He caught a glimpse of himself in the mirror, distorted by glass with a diagonal crack down it. Those strained eyes, that distant look, the lines on his face. A tired man who had a ton of grief to process. Who still had a ton to process and now had another ton.

He dried his hands as he left the toilet – when would he ever find the time to start processing that?

Vicky was already outside, still on her phone. 'Cool, that's good. Better go. Bye.' She smiled at Fenchurch. 'Thought you didn't need, Mr five-year-old DCI?'

'Given what we're about to do here, my body's telling me I needed a good old clear-out.'

'Gross.' Vicky winced. 'What's your plan to find Jasmine?'

'We're not going in. I just want to gather intel, then we can go to your boss and mine with a proposed plan of attack. Big team of us, surround the place then, after we've surveil it for at least twelve hours, we go in. Assuming it's safe. I don't want to jeopardise Jasmine's safety.'

Vicky tugged at her hair. 'Are you confident she'll be there?'

'Not really, no, but I want to see if she is.' Fenchurch blew air up his face. 'Who was that on the phone?'

'Just someone with some intel on where we're going.'

'I can't quite get a read on what's going on here, Vicky. First, you're grassing me up. Now, you're as involved in this as I am. What's going on?'

'Nothing's going on. I just... I'm worried, that's all. The bureaucracy grinds far too slowly sometimes. Right now, we do need to find this girl. That's my priority, as well as yours.'

'Okay.' But Fenchurch wasn't quite convinced. 'This person. A friend of yours. Are they going to be a problem?'

'No.' She fixed him with a hard look. 'And I'm warning you

now, Simon. Your dad was killed yesterday. Truth is, you shouldn't be here. I'm only doing this on the condition you don't go over the score.'

'Like I said, we're just here to gather intel. Have a look, see what we can see.'

'But you want to make the fuckers pay, don't you?'

Fenchurch had to look away. 'Dad was a good man. When he retired, he could've sold up and buggered off to Spain. Especially after Mum died. Could've lived a life there. Golfing, drinking, walking, sunbathing. Got a packet for his house. But no, he stayed in the East End. Kept working. Not as a copper, but as a consultant with the Met's Trafficking and Prostitution Unit. And... He helped me find my daughter. And he helped other people get justice for what happened to them too. He'd have wanted us to find Jasmine and reunite her with her family. Her dad's broken by this, Vicky. Absolutely broken.'

'I get it.' Vicky stared hard at him. 'My own dad is ex-Job as well. He's had his fair share of adventures in his retirement.'

'Oh?'

'Him and a cop called Brian Bain, they...' She laughed. 'Actually, let's not get into that, eh?'

Fenchurch opened his car door and blew out a deep breath. 'Vicky, the truth is, I'm not sure what I'm going to do if I find them, but... I don't know if I can just hang back and call in backup. It might not be pretty.'

'Okay. Plan A is to do a reconnaissance job. If we see her, we report back. We wait and watch.'

'And Plan B?'

'Like I told you, Simon, I've painted outside the lines a few times. Ends justify the means and all that. I don't want to, but whatever we need to do, we will do it.'

'You're singing my song, Vicky.'

41

The sun hung low in the sky, its feeble light touching the dark waters of Loch Ness.

Vicky slowed as they neared a small settlement on the south bank, where the loch thinned into a river, ready for its journey north through Inverness before meeting the sea at the Moray Firth.

Skeletal trees lined the approach, bare branches reaching out like bony fingers.

Ivy-clad walls adorned with intricate carvings and solemn columns loomed large against the cold November afternoon. A moss-covered gate at the stone gatehouse revealed a winding gravel path leading through gardens muted by the chill of the season.

The house itself commanded attention, rising up a tall bank. Smoke whispered from chimneys. Only three lights on in the entire place.

Fenchurch pointed at the building. 'Someone's in.'

'Got it.' Vicky powered on past the house, then pulled into a small lay-by, behind another car. She tooted her horn and got one in response.

'What's going on?'

'Brought in someone to provide some local colour.' Before Fenchurch could ask any more, Vicky got out of the car and slammed the door.

Bloody hell.

The person she'd been on the phone to.

Fenchurch just wished people would be straightforward. He got out into the cold, then followed her over to the black Audi and got in the back. The heat was oppressive, burning at his cool face.

A woman sat behind the wheel. She reached around and held out a gloved hand. Olivia Blackman. 'Nice to see you again, sir.'

Fenchurch shook her hand, gripping tight to show who was in charge here. 'Why aren't you in Glasgow?'

'Our antics the other night... Boss persuaded me to take some annual leave. It'd been accruing so... My worse half is staying in Findhorn, just past Inverness, where he's researching a book. Thought I could do with a wee holiday.'

Vicky frowned. '*You* are staying at a hippie commune?'

'New Age as fuck, me. Mark's spent a lot of my life either living in or researching dark cults and evil communes.' Olivia shrugged. 'I persuaded him to spend some time documenting a positive one. Where a commune has a community. That kind of thing.' Her eyes narrowed. 'Anyway. After our stuff in Hamilton, I read up on your story. Your daughter went missing, right?'

Fenchurch held her stare. 'That's right.'

'Guessing this whole thing is personal, then?'

'Look, I appreciate the questions.' Fenchurch smiled at her. 'But we've got a job to do here.'

Vicky shot him a look. 'You said you could help?'

'Right.' Olivia passed her a novel. 'Mark's book, *Break the Chain*, it's based on when he used to live there.' She chapped at the window, pointing back in the direction of the house. 'There was a commune behind there, aye.' She reached into the console and picked up a tub of chewing gum, then offered it to them. Neither took it, so she popped a couple in and crunched them. Then slurped and chewed and spread around a minty smell. 'His parents were in a cult based in there. They lived in the lodges at the back.'

Fenchurch got a snapshot of somewhere he'd visited a few years ago. A farm on the Essex-Suffolk border. His first exposure to the Machine.

Olivia popped another tab of gum in her mouth. 'It's a whole thing, really. But he escaped with most of his sanity.' She crunched and slapped her lips together. 'But that was a long time ago. What do you need to know now?'

'We're looking for two people. A teenaged girl and an older man. We think they might be there.'

Olivia looked at Fenchurch. 'The girl who was staying with Kanyif?'

He looked away. 'Maybe.'

'Well, I can't help with those two, but I can give you an overview of the house.' Olivia flicked to the middle of the book and showed them some plans of the building, in amongst snaps of happy commune members then the subsequent burnt-out shells of their homes at the back. 'Mark had these from when he lived there and put them in the book. Twenty bedrooms inside, split over the upper two floors. Ground floor has a big hall, with four huge public rooms. You know the sort, probably seen the like on TV. Two sitting rooms, a library and a parlour. The basement has a kitchen and some rooms for the staff, as would've been. They were bedrooms when Mark lived there. Possibly the same now, but it could be a cinema or a gym or something. You know what these rich people are like.'

'Which rich person in particular?'

'Well, doesn't James McNab own it?'

Fenchurch scowled. 'The singer in the Zeroes?'

'Him.'

Fenchurch felt a punch in the gut. 'He was an alibi for one of our suspects.' He felt the knife twist in his abdomen. 'But the Machine bought that place from him.'

Olivia laughed. 'The Machine? Who calls themselves the Machine?'

'It's a codename we use, not them. But the point is, they bought it from him. It's not his home anymore.'

Olivia crunched on a fresh tab of gum. 'But it wouldn't be the first time someone sold an asset to a related party, right?'

'Good point.' Vicky looked at Fenchurch. 'You think McNab's Colin Scott?'

'Could be.' Fenchurch shrugged. 'Could be nothing to do with this at all.'

'Mark got me into a bit of bother with my boss. We turned up and asked a few questions. McNab reported us.' Olivia took off her gloves and rested them on the central console. 'What's the plan, then?'

'The plan is to identify if our targets are here.' Fenchurch leaned forward so his head was between the seats. 'There's a missing kid. She's at risk. We're just here to find out if they're here. If they are, our colleagues will help us find them.'

'Cool.'

'You've been extremely helpful, Olivia.' Fenchurch gave her a broad smile. 'You can go now.'

She swung around. 'After driving all this way, you're just telling me to fuck off?'

Fenchurch fixed her with his hardest police officer's stare. 'Drive back to Findhorn and enjoy your bowl of quinoa porridge.'

'Come on, that's—'

'*Sergeant.*'

'Okay.' Olivia scowled. 'Give me a bell if you need anything.'

'Sure.' Fenchurch took the book and snapped it shut. 'Thanks for that information. Could prove useful.'

'Before you go... I've been waiting here since Vicky called. Happened to be meeting someone nearby, so I thought I'd scout out the place for you. If there are any people in there, there aren't many. Five or six, maximum.'

Fenchurch smiled at her. 'Thank you.' He got out into the cold and waited for Vicky.

She took a while to chat to Olivia about something, then joined him. 'That wasn't very friendly.'

'I'd say I'm sorry, but...' Fenchurch watched the Audi tear off along the road. 'A bit of warning would've been appreciated.'

'Sorry.' She ran a hand through her hair. 'So, what do you think? Useful?'

'Well, if there are only five or six people in there, that's a good thing. I was expecting twenty to fifty.'

'You're intending on raiding this place, aren't you?'

'No. Like we discussed, we surveil the place. I want eyes on either Avonmore or Jasmine. Then we do it by the book. Get a few lumps down from Inverness, and probably the nearest firearms unit. Aberdeen? Perth? Your lot in Dundee? Then we watch and get a handle on what we're dealing with. Then we get in there.'

'You think Rusty Rivers is behind the Machine, don't you?'

'Him or James McNab.' Fenchurch shook his head. 'I loved the Zeroes as a teenager. Never meet your heroes, eh? Sometimes they turn out to be child molesters.' He let out a deep breath. 'Neither of them was a major player in Chloe's abduction, but they're the last men standing. Selfishly protecting their own skin. But that's not important now. We need to identify if Jasmine's there or not. Need to establish how well-staffed it is.'

'Simon, it's half past three. It's going to be pitch dark in an hour.'

'Exactly.'

'But we're not going in.'

'Didn't say we were. This is about intel gathering.' Fenchurch got out his mobile and put one of his wireless earbuds in. 'Stay on the line. I'll walk over and check out the main house, you sweep the perimeter. Okay?'

Vicky flared her nostrils. 'So I get the fun bit with all the mud?'

'It's all frozen. Besides, I get the risky bit. If the Russian I'm thinking of is involved, there's going to be guns.'

'Bloody hell.' Vicky sucked in a deep breath. 'Okay, let's do this. I've got some binoculars in my go bag in the boot. All the shite you sometimes need but forget about. And crisps. And chocolate.' She crossed the road without an offer of either, then slipped over a wall into a wooded field. She stuck an AirPod in and tapped something on her phone and his rang. 'Stay on the line at all times, okay? Anything goes wrong, we're getting out of there.'

'Deal.' Fenchurch walked off back towards the house, thinking this was the worst idea he'd ever had.

But he saw no alternative.

42

Fenchurch crouched low in the passing place opposite. A lot of old gatehouses like this would've been sold off years ago, then extended beyond buggery into private homes. This one seemed to still belong to the mansion house and the sprawling estate lurking behind it. Dark and empty, with moss and ivy clinging to weathered stone walls. Two lanterns flanked the arched entrance, their ironwork wrought with intricate detail, but their lights hadn't been lit tonight. Didn't seem like they would be.

Through the glass, the faint rays of muted daylight cast long shadows across the rough floorboards. Still just about strong enough for Fenchurch to make out nests of cobwebs draped across ancient beams. Forgotten heirlooms gathered dust on abandoned shelves. The empty hearth seemed to sigh with the memories of fires.

Yeah, nobody in there.

Fenchurch took in the big house again. Hopefully Vicky was sniffing around in the back of the field right now. He let out a deep breath. 'How are you doing, Vicky?'

'Hard to see anything, really.' Her voice was crisp and clear in his lughole. 'I'm around the back, but I can't see much. The good thing is the ground's so cold that the mud isn't wet.'

'Any signs of life?'

'Negative. But there are more lights on in the living quarters in the old house than we saw around the front.'

'Only got three here.'

'Four here. There are a bunch of outbuildings just inside the walls. No windows, so no lights.'

'Okay, so it's possible there are people in there. Any signs of movement?'

'Nope. That's it.'

'Okay. Keep looking.'

'What are you seeing?'

'Gatehouse is empty. Nobody in there.'

'So, what are you thinking?'

Fenchurch took a deep breath, trying to play it through.

His plan had been to just gather intel. See what they could see. But now he was here, the truth felt tantalisingly close. And the false logic pinged in his head – either Jasmine was here or she wasn't. It was a fifty-fifty. He knew it wasn't that simple, that one side could beat the balance of probabilities, but it was still a straightforward two-way outcome.

And he needed to know either way, meaning he had to get in there and find out.

His mouth was dry. 'Seven rooms with lights could still mean a lot of people in there. Or it could just be one person going room to room. And anything in between. Could be the day just isn't dark enough yet – but it feels close enough to dusk for any automatic lights to trigger.'

'Or for manual ones to be switched on.'

'Right.' Fenchurch felt his heart thudding in his chest. These fuckers had taken his daughter, or at least been party to it. And they had another girl. He had to act now. Knock on that door. Find out who was there. Stop them. Catch them. Bring them to justice. 'So I'm thinking there aren't a lot of people in there. Five or six, maybe?'

'Okay, agreed. But we don't know if Avonmore or Jasmine are in there.'

'No. So, I'm going to… What was it you called it earlier?'

'What, play the daft laddie?'

'Right, I'll play the daft laddie. Knock on the door, pretend I'm lost. Our car's run out of fuel or just broken down a few miles down the road. Saw the lights on, wondered if they could help. See what they say.'

'Simon…'

'Come on, Vicky. We were prepared for either nothing or everything. Either we didn't see them or we saw at least one of Avonmore or Jasmine. Right now, we're still in limbo. We haven't seen them, but we don't know if they're *not* here.'

She paused. 'Fine.' A deep sigh. 'But I'm staying here. Keep your phone on.'

'Will do.'

'Okay. Keep me updated. I'll be listening. And watching.'

'Thank you, Vicky.' Fenchurch opened the gate with a sharp creak. The light breeze brushed his face as he walked through the sprawling garden, then he climbed the mossy steps up the bank towards the house. He stopped at the top and took in the building.

Ivy tendrils curled around the stone columns framing the wooden door, which was painted a lush cream colour, the paint flecking off. The threshold bowed in the middle, the heavy stone scuffed by countless footsteps.

Still just the three lights on.

Fenchurch clenched his fists and walked towards the doorway.

'Simon.'

He stopped dead. 'What's up?'

'I can see a girl in the garden.'

'Where?'

'Your left.'

'Okay.' Fenchurch paced away from the entrance, hurrying along the front of the building, keeping his focus on each room through the glass as he passed.

Nobody inside. No lights, no fires, no signs of life.

He cleared the end of the building, where the giant stone walls carried on at a storey-and-a-half height, and stopped at wrought iron gates.

He spotted her.

Blonde hair, violet tracksuit, staring into a duck pond. She looked up and he saw her face.

It was Jasmine.

'Time to go inside. Come on.' A big man led her away towards the house. Hard to place his accent.

Fenchurch couldn't see his face. He got out of their line of sight, waiting by the wall. Heart thumping hard. 'Vicky, it's her. We need to move now.'

'Simon, this isn't what we agreed.'

'I know, Vicky, but she's *here*. We need to get her.' Fenchurch retraced his steps to the front door, then pulled the bell at the side. 'I'm doing this now.'

'Jesus Christ.'

'I'm going quiet.' Fenchurch pressed his earbud in deeper and put his phone in his top pocket, hoping it'd maintain the call.

The door opened and a tall man stood there. Broad too. Bulky. Tell-tale bulge in his jacket pocket. The man he'd just seen with Jasmine. 'Can I help you, sir?' European accent, but it could be from anywhere in the middle. Germany, Austria, Switzerland.

Fenchurch gave him a broad smile. 'Hi, mate, I need to speak to Don.' Keep it direct like that. Not Mr Avonmore or Mr Rivers. Act like they're best mates. First-name terms.

The guard looked him up and down. 'And who are you, my friend?'

'I'm part of the new security detail. Working for Yevgeny.'

He gave Fenchurch another good visual going over, then a nod. 'Come inside.'

Fenchurch followed him into the cold house. 'Supposed to be looking after Mr Avonmore until the new doctor gets here.' If there was an old one here, he'd concoct a story about a newer, better one coming in all the way from Zurich.

'I see. This way.' The guard led him down a long hallway. The ornate sconces on the walls cast a warm glow on a freshly laid rug on the parquet. The place tasted of woodsmoke. Framed paintings of hunting expeditions from over the centuries. Stags' heads mounted above two doors, both closed. 'What's your name?'

'Si.'

'As in Simon?'

'Right. Simon Fenchurch.'

'Nice to meet you Simon. My name is Leon. But it's spelled like the big cat.'

'Lion?'

'Yes, but say it like Leon.'

'Guessing you're German, if I'm not too badly mistaken.'

'Correct.' Lion led Fenchurch into the stately home's grand hallway. A spiral staircase led up two floors. Another hallway led off deep into the house. A set of stairs leading down to the basement.

Lion's gaze swept over Fenchurch, then he gestured up the staircase. 'You first.'

'Of course.' Fenchurch gripped the banister and jogged up, savouring the mobility his new knee offered. Trying to act like he belonged in there. Like he was in charge. Like he was a private security operative. 'You worked for Yevgeny long?'

'Three years, eight months.'

'That's very precise.' Fenchurch slowed as he neared the landing, then let Lion take the lead again. The first floor. Another hall, treading above the one they'd just walked along. The walls up here were even grander and the wooden floors had been recently polished.

Lion stopped outside a door. 'Here he is.'

The door opposite was open a crack. A desk in a large room – certainly not a bedroom. The faint clicking of music bled out of headphones.

'In here.' Lion jostled Fenchurch's arm.

'Sorry.' Fenchurch stepped into the room.

Don Avonmore lay on the bed, his head propped up on several pillows, the sheet tucked up to his chin. Breathing slowly. A machine next to him beeped with each pulse, fast and irregular – he was suffering an arrhythmia. Fenchurch could tell he was pretty fucked and should be in a hospital.

He smiled at Lion. 'Can you give us a minute?'

'Sure thing.'

Fenchurch closed the door, then listened to Avonmore's shallow breaths, worrying the next would be the last. He stood over him and nudged his arm. 'Don.'

Avonmore opened his eyes. 'Hello?'

'How are you doing, mate?'

Avonmore coughed. 'What's going on?' His eyes were milky. 'Are you the new doctor?'

'I work with her, yes.'

'Old one has me on some very strong painkillers. Can't really focus my eyes, Daddy. Is it Christmas?'

Fenchurch knew a thing or two about very strong painkillers... The drip leading into Avonmore's arm led to a tiny bottle of morphine. Fenchurch inspected it – even stronger stuff than what he had been on. 'I know a lot about pain.' He clamped a hand over Avonmore's mouth. His other hand grabbed his throat. 'I will kill you if I have to. Right here, right now, so don't fuck me about.' He leaned in close. 'Where is Jasmine?' He let his grip slacken enough for Avonmore to speak.

'Who?'

'Jasmine. Where are they keeping her?'

'Don't know.'

'But you know her?'

'Yes.'

Fenchurch leaned in so Avonmore could see the fury in his eyes. 'Who is Colin Scott?'

'Who?'

'The man behind this whole thing. The one who's buying and selling people. Unless that's you.'

'I don't—'

Fenchurch tightened his grip again, reminding him who was in charge. 'Who is he?'

'Bradley Sixsmith.'

Fenchurch frowned. 'The record producer?'

Avonmore nodded.

The room across the corridor... This was Sixsmith's home studio, where he was mixing that single.

Shit.

'Is he here?'

Another nod.

'Where?'

'I don't know. He... He was working on something. But he fled London. Jasmine had turned up at the studio, asking to speak to his artist. That Kanyif prick. Obviously that was a bit awkward, so he came here.'

'Where?'

'I don't know. But she's here somewhere. Please, don't hurt him. He arranged for a doctor for me. Am I going to die?'

'Yes, but not today.' Fenchurch reached over and opened the drip valve, flooding Avonmore with morphine, doubling its rate until Avonmore's eyes took on a faraway glaze. Then Fenchurch locked out the supplemental drip. He waited until Avonmore's eyes closed. His breathing slowed, but stayed steady. The heart rate didn't slow any, just the same fast skittish beat you'd hear from a drug dealer's car.

'Did you get that, Vicky?'

'Sixsmith.'

'Right. He's here. With Jasmine.'

'Have you found her?'

'Not yet.' Fenchurch charged across the room and opened the door.

Lion looked up. 'Everything okay?'

'Nope. It's not looking too rosy for Don. Someone needs to speak to Brad. He needs a doctor.'

'Mr Sixsmith is busy.'

'I get that. Just show me to his room.'

'This way.' Lion led across the hallway and opened the door.

A home studio, with the kind of mixing desk you'd see on a rock documentary, all those faders and dials. Two massive speakers, but they stood mute. All powered by a laptop hooked up to a huge display.

No sign of Sixsmith, but the music still played from the headphones.

Lion huffed out a sigh. 'I will go and fetch him.'

'Thanks.' Fenchurch waited until he'd walked away a few metres, then entered the room.

Jasmine sat on the edge of a sofa, kicking her legs. Listening to music on wired headphones and moving to the beat. In that tracksuit, with her hair in pigtails, she looked so young, like a pre-teen.

Fenchurch entered the room. 'Jasmine.'

Nothing, just nibbling her lips and moving in time to the music.

The room was freezing. The window was open a crack. Voices out there, the crunching of feet on the gravel path.

'Jasmine.'

She looked up at him, then tore her headphones out. 'Who the fuck are you?'

'I'm a friend of Kanyif.' Fenchurch walked over and peered out of the window. The side of the building. A car park. Lion walked over to a black Range Rover. Yevgeny Kordov got out of the back, smiling and hugging his employee.

Shit.

This was getting out of hand.

Fenchurch turned back to Jasmine but spoke to Vicky. 'Eyes on the prize. I'm going to grab her and leave.'

'Okay.'

'Trouble is, another obstacle has arrived. Two more guards.'

'What's your plan?'

'Can you secure the back door?'

'Will try to. I'll call in backup now.'

'Thanks.' Fenchurch turned to the girl. 'Jasmine, I'm a police officer. I'm here to escort you to safety.'

Up close, he could see the size of her pupils. Don Avonmore wasn't the only one who was on a massive dose of drugs here.

'It's all going to be okay. We'll get you back to your dad before you know it.'

Jasmine screamed.

43

The scream rattled through Vicky's eardrums. She pressed the earbud deeper in. 'Simon? Simon, are you okay?'

She waited, listening hard. Was he even there?

She stood in the woodland behind the imposing estate, her breaths shallow, her heart pounding.

Their plan was in motion, but it had gone to shit already. She was outside and Fenchurch was in that house. Guards. They'd make him, torture him. Or worse.

'Simon?'

'Vi—'

The line cut dead.

Shit.

Shit, shit, shit.

What the hell was she going to do?

She'd already called for backup – sixty seconds where he was put on hold, where anything could've happened – but they'd be coming from Inverness, the best part of an hour away.

Fenchurch was inside and at risk *now*.

Stupid twat.

He just had to go in there solo, didn't he?

She could've stopped him, insisted they didn't split up and did the reconnaissance together.

And aye, she should've dumped him at the airport. Let their bosses decide.

Fenchurch was in there, in a room facing the side. Massive creepy old place, with armed guards.

Her choice was stark – she had to wait for backup, or she had to infiltrate the mansion.

No.

She had to think it all through, see if there were any avenues she hadn't explored. Focus on the facts.

Fenchurch was inside.

Sixsmith was there.

Avonmore too.

And Jasmine, obviously.

She'd seen a guard, but no more.

How many more guards were there? How many could there be?

The only one she'd seen was the one who'd taken Jasmine inside and who'd answered the door to Fenchurch.

But someone else turned up just before. So that was two guards.

Fenchurch had mentioned Bradley Sixsmith on their drive up. Just as someone pertinent to the case, not as a suspect. And here he was. Record producer. Looked a bit seedy in person, but then they all did. Still, he was in his late sixties – she could take him.

The other two, though... They looked armed.

Okay, so that was three active participants, two likely armed. One of them a raping old bastard, with another in his hospital bed.

And Jasmine, who had screamed the place down when Fenchurch found her.

So they'd know about him, be in there in a flash.

Aye, she just had to get in there, didn't she?

'Okay...' Her breath misted the air. Getting cold now in the dusk. She looked down at what she was wearing. Dark trousers tucked into ankle-length boots. Floaty top. All black. At least she'd put on make-up for court that morning. She puffed out her hair.

Sod it, this could work.

She opened the gate and set off through the gardens. The scent of damp earth and moss lingered in the air – the walls helped the ground thaw in here. A few stone steps led down to a gravel path that wound its way through a secluded garden. Much less grandiose than the front, but the back entrance was a sturdy door framed by rough-hewn stone. A lantern hung over the doorway, casting a soft glow.

A guard stood there, a hulking presence, his muscles rippling beneath a tailored suit.

He'd told Fenchurch his name. Lion, wasn't it?

Shit.

Well, here goes...

Vicky approached him with a soft pout, her eyes shimmering with feigned vulnerability. Made her heels click softly on the pathway. 'Excuse me?'

Lion looked over at her, hand going to his jacket. Aye, he was armed. 'What are you doing here?'

'Sorry, I might be lost, but I'm supposed to meet Mr Sixsmith here. He told me to come through the back and ask for Lion, one of his best men. I'm not quite sure—'

Lion scrutinised her with a sceptical gaze. 'Who sent you?'

'Brad himself.' Vicky lowered her gaze, feigning hesitation. 'He said he needed a bit of... company tonight.'

'He already has—'

'*Adult* company.' Vicky brushed a hand through her hair.

'Look, I'm just trying to make a living, okay? I don't ask you questions, so please show me a bit of respect, eh?'

Lion's brow furrowed, but he couldn't quite mask the flicker of doubt in his eyes.

Vicky offered him a coy smile, her voice dripping with allure. 'Honey, Mr Sixsmith's waiting...'

Lion hesitated, his nostrils flaring like he'd caught a scent he couldn't quite place. And didn't like. He glanced at the mansion, then back at Vicky. 'Wait here.' He turned and walked away a few paces, then spoke into an earpiece. A few sharp glances back her way.

Vicky's heart raced as she waited, her act of desperation hanging by a thread.

Lion walked back, head bowed, casually flicking his hand inside. 'Follow me.'

She followed Lion through a lavish hallway, making her heels click on the polished floors. The flickering candlelight cast shadows on the ornate wallpaper. Through a door into a grand entranceway.

'Wow, this is quite some place.'

'We go up.' Lion ascended the staircase.

Vicky's heart quickened as she followed. The gravity of this stupid gamble was tugging down at her. Maintaining her cover and avoiding arousing suspicion was much easier thought than done.

Lion stopped outside a heavy wooden door at the end of a corridor. His hand hovered near the doorknob, then he opened the door. 'After you.'

Vicky stepped into the room, her heart still racing. 'Thank you.'

'Mr Sixsmith will be along soon. Make yourself comfortable.' He walked back the way they'd come.

Vicky took in the room, an opulent chamber with three

windows. The centrepiece was a bed with intricately carved wooden details, dressed in silk-embroidered linens.

She shuddered to think what had happened on that.

Sheer curtains flapped at the window, hiding a private balcony through a set of French doors. Plush seating and an elegant bistro table. Even from here, she could see the breathtaking panorama of rolling hills and trees hiding Loch Ness.

The en suite bathroom was like a spa. Gleaming mosaic tiles on the floor and walls. A freestanding bathtub with polished chrome fixtures. Soft, fluffy towels and designer toiletries artfully arranged on a heated towel rack.

The final door was to a walk-in wardrobe, filled with designer clothes and accessories. Suits in six different colours. Shirts in four colours with a rack of matching ties. A display of watches glistened. More cufflinks than she had earrings.

'Excuse me.' Lion was back. Hand in his suit jacket pocket, like he had already gone for his gun. 'What did you say your name was?'

44

Fenchurch was way past being sick of people pointing guns at him.

Yevgeny Kordov was the latest one, training a Glock pistol at him. Not for the first time, either. 'Fenchurch, Fenchurch, Fenchurch... You again, ah?'

Fenchurch stared past the barrel of the gun into the man's eyes. 'Where have you taken Jasmine?'

'She not here, my friend.'

'You know her name. And I know she's here. Because I bloody saw her with my own eyes. Outside and in this room.' Fenchurch waved around the space. 'Is this her room? Where you're keeping her? Or just where she's being raped?'

'My friend. Listen to me. She was *not* here. She does *not* have a room here. There is no Jasmine that I know of.'

'So, who called out for help?'

Kordov leaned his head back. 'Are you alone, Mr Detective Chief Inspector?'

'Of course not.'

'I do not believe you, my friend. Nobody else is stupid

enough to do this. I do not think this is official police business, is it?'

Fenchurch held his gaze, long and hard. 'Answer me this – do you get to abuse her too?'

'Excuse me?'

'I know what Sixsmith and Avonmore get up to with her. She's thirteen, Yevgeny. It's wrong on every level. But why are you helping them? Can't just be money – a man with your skills must be in demand everywhere. Do they let you have a go?'

'What?'

'Is that your thing? You like them really young?'

'Be quiet.'

'Is that what gets you off? Young girls like that?'

'Shut your face!'

'Do you get them all drugged up on something so they don't remember?'

'Shut up!'

'Or so they just don't resist. She's *thirteen*, you animal.'

'That is not happening.'

'It is. I know it is. We've got evidence of it. If you don't know what's been going on, then you're a fucking idiot.' Fenchurch saw he was getting somewhere. Maybe the big palooka genuinely had no idea what his paymasters were doing. 'Bradley Sixsmith and Don Avonmore, AKA Rusty Rivers, AKA the man in the hospital bed through there, are both serial abusers of children. Girls in their teens. They pay the people who have trafficked them to own them. Five grand a skull. Absolute bargain for them, right? But what happens to the kids after? Do they kill them? Do *you*?'

'Shut up, my friend.' But Kordov wasn't so sure now, those words were laced with doubt.

'They pay *you* to protect them. That makes you complicit in that abuse. Are you happy with that?'

'I am not complicit in anything, my friend.'

The door opened again and Bradley Sixsmith waltzed in. 'Ah. DCI Fenchurch.' His hair wasn't slicked back now and was allowed to curl out naturally. Navy trousers and a tight V-neck sweater, bare skin underneath. His chest was as bald as a baby's bum. 'What brings you here, mate?'

'Looking for a couple of people.'

'Oh yeah?' Sixsmith sat on a chair and crunched into a giant Granny Smith apple. The juice ran down his chin and he wiped it clear. 'Long way to travel, isn't it? London officer like you. Must be, what, five hundred miles from home? Maybe six? Must be important.' Another bite of the apple. 'Who are you looking for that's so urgent?'

'Not looking anymore, Colin.'

'Colin?' Sixsmith laughed. 'Name's Bradley. Not Brad. Bradley.'

'Doesn't matter. I've found them. Don Avonmore is along the corridor, opposite your home studio. Is that so you can keep a close eye on your partner in child abuse?'

Sixsmith took another crunching bite of his apple.

'He looks fucked, Colin. Like he should be in a hospital.' Fenchurch waved his hands around the room, trying to own the space. 'If you ask me, this is a nice house you've got here, but it doesn't look like much of a hospital.'

Sixsmith finished chewing with a slurp. 'It's not.'

'But Mr Avonmore clearly needs to be in one. Someone cut off a bollock and did a bit of advanced butchery on his innards. Not sure he'll survive too long in here.'

'He's getting excellent medical attention. The finest care.'

'From who?'

'That's not your concern. You should be more worried about what's going to happen to you.'

Fenchurch laughed it off, but his heart was pumping like an intercity train's engine. 'Who was the girl in here?'

Sixsmith shrugged. 'Don't know what you mean.'

'Oh you do. Jasmine, her name is. Jasmine Mason. Canning Town girl. Strange to find her here, a stone's throw from Inverness. Like you said about me, it's a long way to travel. Especially at her age. Being thirteen.'

Sixsmith shook his head. 'You're imagining things.'

'She was right here, Bradley. This is her room or it's the room you abuse her in, right? And you know she's thirteen, don't you?' Fenchurch focused on Kordov. 'It means whichever one of you fuckers is having sex with her, you're all committing a crime. A very serious one. And I'm guessing it's definitely you and Avonmore, Bradley. Right? And this creep here? I bet he's done it too.'

Kordov snarled. 'We should not listen to this *svoloch*.'

Fenchurch smiled at him. 'I don't know that word, but I'm guessing it's Russian for "man who does not abuse girls". Right?'

'Yevgeny, it's important we listen to him.' Sixsmith crunched into his apple again. 'I want to hear what he's got to say. What the Metropolitan Police think they have on me.' He chewed hard, then slurped. 'Thing is, at least as far as I was aware, Mr Fenchurch has been investigating the assault of Don by that talent vacuum, Kanyif Iqbal. It doesn't explain why's he here, sneaking around my home.'

'Reason I'm here is to rescue Jasmine. The girl you're abusing.'

'Oh, you superhero.' Sixsmith laughed. 'You've no idea what's happening, do you?'

'I do. You're a beast. A nonce. A stoat. A child molester.'

Sixsmith bit down to the core of his apple. 'I will level with you, seeing as how you've gone to so much effort to travel all the way here. Only reason Jasmine is here is to find out what she's told you lot.'

'We haven't spoken to her.'

'*You* might not have, Fenchurch, but we know she was speaking to the police. Her and Kanyif were talking.'

'None of that's on the record. I don't believe it actually happened.'

'Right. Sure.'

'Where is she now?'

Sixsmith laughed. 'Like we keep telling you, she's not here.'

'That because you're finished with her? Had your fun, then passed her to Yevgeny here. Maybe even let Lion have his fun. Now she's satisfied your disgusting urges, you're going to kill her, aren't you? Same with Avonmore. Clean up your act.'

Sixsmith ate his apple core, then licked his fingers. 'The only person who is going to die here is you. The beauty of owning this property is there's absolutely fuck all around for miles and miles, in whatever direction you go. Yevgeny here can find one of many lonely moors or woods where we can dump your body and it will never be found.'

Those were the words Fenchurch had used many times over the years. Hearing them turned back on himself... He swallowed hard. 'Let me walk away and I promise I won't come after you. You can escape to wherever you want. You won't be hunted down.'

'Why should I believe you?'

'The only reason I know your name is because of Don Avonmore. Well, that and you swanning in here like a Bond villain to lay out your devious plan.'

Sixsmith laughed. 'We could've been friends, Fenchurch. In some other life.'

'One where you didn't molest children?'

A dark look passed over Sixsmith. 'Your offer doesn't make any sense, Fenchurch. We're in my domain, not yours. I can already do what I want without having to escape. If I kill you, then I don't have to worry about you finding me.' He wiped his fingers on his trousers. 'Does anyone know you're here?'

'They do. I was on a phone call. I've told them everything. And they heard it all. We've got six cars and a couple of meat wagons on the way here.'

When your nuts are in a vice, oversell the cavalry.

Kordov laughed. 'That's bullshit.'

Fenchurch smiled at him. 'They'll be here very soon.'

'Yevgeny, get into his phone, please.'

Kordov held the mobile up to Fenchurch's face. Then frowned at it. 'It's not unlocking.'

'I turned that feature off, you daft bastard. You'll have to use the passcode to get in.'

'What is passcode?'

'It's Kordov is a nonce.'

'Shut up.'

'But you are one.' Fenchurch focused on Sixsmith. 'Let me go. Run away. Escape. You'll never be heard from again. I'll walk to Inverness. By the time I get there, you'll be in the air. Sure you've got enough money hidden away in Pennyworth Holdings to—'

'My, you have done your homework.' Sixsmith clapped his hands. 'Impressive stuff. But I bet none of it traces back to me. Because it doesn't.'

'It will, somewhere. I've got a mate in the City of London Police who is digging deep into you now. They can find anything. Hell, even Kanyif Iqbal had found stuff. And the financial records I've seen are pretty damning. Like how you bought this place. How you've paid for the lives of trafficked young women.'

'That's all bullshit. He had nothing on me and neither do you. If Kanyif did, do you think my testicles would still be attached to my body?'

'Backup will be here very soon.'

Sixsmith sighed. 'Yevgeny, please check on that.'

'Sure thing.' Kordov pressed his earpiece in and left the room.

'That backup thing is absolute tosh, isn't it?' Sixsmith glowered at him. 'You're on compassionate leave, aren't you?'

'You seem to know a lot about me.'

'You know what my favourite song of all time is? You're probably thinking it's something by the Beatles, maybe Floyd, or Fleetwood Mac or someone. No, it's "Know Your Enemy" by Rage Against The Machine. I love the music and vocal delivery in that and have used it as a template for some rock productions. But it's also a watchword of mine. We've kept a close eye on you for years, Fenchurch. Obviously after what happened to your daughter. Congratulations on finding her.'

Fenchurch felt the blood drumming in his ears. 'Keep her out of this.'

'I intend to. I hope you appreciate us leaving you both alone.' Sixsmith looked out of the window. 'Thing is, Mr Fenchurch, you and your father have a habit of being a bit too bloody nosy for my liking.'

'Is that why you got Fields to kill him?'

'We weren't going to. Just wanted to know what he knew. But he had a weak heart, didn't he? A broken one. Shame.'

'If you don't escape tonight, I will hunt you down and kill you with my bare hands. Believe me, I know places I can bury bodies and nobody will find them. And I will do it.'

'Sure.' Sixsmith laughed. 'I believe you.'

Kordov walked back in and whispered in Sixsmith's ear, 'I cannot get hold of Lion.'

'Can you please go and check?'

Kordov nodded, then hurried out of the room.

Sixsmith stared at Fenchurch. 'Are you alone?'

'Of course not. Told you I have an army of cops on their way here right now. And three firearms-trained officers inside the building. Leave while you still have the chance. Maybe you'll miss the convoy of cars.'

'No.' Sixsmith reached into the cupboard and pulled out a guitar. A Gibson Les Paul, the thick wooden body catching the light. 'Speaking of knowing where to dispose of a body, I know a perfect spot out in the wilds about forty miles west of here. Away from Loch Ness, down a long glen, by a river. Beautiful spot up there, absolutely teeming with wildlife. Red squirrels, Scottish wildcats, pine martens. Even eagles. Nobody's really allowed to visit, so you'll just rot away in your grave.'

'Go. Just go. And don't look back.' Fenchurch waved over at the door. 'You can leave now before it's too late. You don't have to do this. It'll only make things worse for you.'

'No, no, no. I'm a very busy man. I can't be running off. I've got to finalise the mix of that UniQorn single by Saturday. And I'd normally want to take my time with you, but if backup is coming, then time is of the essence, is it not?'

'Let me go.'

'Oh, God no.' Sixsmith held up his guitar and stared at the thick body. 'On a golf course, do you only have to say "fore" when you hit your ball into someone, or does it still count if you hit them with a golf club? And what about a guitar?' He raised the guitar over his shoulder, ready to swing.

45

Vicky darted along the dimly lit hallway, turning her neck to check behind her.

Lion was pursuing her through the mansion with the ruthless determination of his namesake big cat.

Her breaths came ragged as she navigated the winding staircase, desperation fuelling her every step as she climbed.

Was this the right way to go? She had no idea.

Lion was closing on her.

She pushed through a door and bombed down another corridor. But she was running towards a dead end.

A door at the end of a corridor.

She twisted the handle. Locked.

Lion's massive form closed in on her.

Vicky's heart was a metronome of terror. She tried to twist around him, but he grabbed her by the throat, lifting her clean off her feet. He pressed her against the wall as the fingers of his other hand tightened around her throat.

Vicky was a survivor, a cop with nerves of steel. She wasn't going to die, not here and not like this. She girded herself and lashed out, cracking her bare toes into his bollocks.

He grunted and tightened his grip.

Another kick, missing.

But he let go.

She dropped to the floor and his massive frame towered over her.

She scuttled forward, trying to squeeze past but he trapped her with his giant arm and pinned her against a different wall now.

She reached down and fumbled at her belt, gargling as his grip tightened around her throat. She saw black. Stars winked into existence, clouding her vision. Everything went blurry.

She managed to release the buckle, then tugged the belt through the loops. It flopped onto the floor. She reached down, tracing her fingers along the carpet. There. She lunged at Lion, wrapping the leather strap around his neck.

'What?' He let go.

She used the moment of confusion and jumped forward, pulling with every ounce of strength she possessed, both hands gripping the belt around his throat and hauling his bigger body onto her back.

Legs kicking into her.

Fingers scratching at her.

His struggles stopped.

Vicky let go and he slumped onto the floor. Her hands trembled from the struggle, the leather cutting into her flesh like wire into cheese.

She rose to her feet, gasping for air.

Stupid. So fucking stupid.

She felt for his pulse. Alive, but barely.

She didn't want to have killed again, that was for sure. Nobody could blame her – he was going to murder her, was most of the way there.

She pulled off her socks and balled them up, then stuffed them into his mouth. She kicked down on his face.

Night night.

Vicky gulped in a deep breath.

But her respite was brief.

She needed to get out of here. She needed to find Fenchurch. But she needed to escape.

How many more of these bastards were there?

Wait.

Lion was armed.

She reached into his jacket and found his holster. And the handgun. She wasn't firearms trained, but she knew enough from her dad to think she'd be able to shoot something, if she had to. Just point, aim for centre mass and pull the trigger. Don't jerk, don't snatch at it, just keep it steady.

Right?

Most of the time, guns were a deterrent. A threat. People backed away when they saw one.

She held the pistol, her finger off the trigger, pointing down the side of the weapon. It wouldn't go off by accident and shoot her own leg.

Vicky took another deep breath and rubbed at her throat.

Okay. Let's do this.

She turned to walk down the corridor and another figure emerged from the shadows.

He stepped into the dim light, his face a mask of cold determination. She recognised him from Fenchurch's photographs – Yevgeny Kordov.

His eyes bulged.

Kordov reached for his weapon.

The gunshot echoed through the stately home.

Kordov crumpled to the ground, with a loud scream. Blood poured out of his bloody knee.

Vicky stood there, trembling, her heart still racing.

She'd pulled it by accident. She'd kneecapped him.

Whatever words he cursed her with were in Russian.

Her response came in Dundonian. 'You better put direct pressure on that wound or you're going to bleed out.' She reached down to pick up his spilled gun. 'Stay there.' She pointed the gun at his head. 'Or I will kill you.' She grabbed the barrel of his gun, much bigger than Lion's, and clubbed him on the temple.

He collapsed back in a heap, eyes closed.

But Kordov's wasn't the only scream she heard…

Sounded like Fenchurch.

46

Fenchurch was sure he heard a gunshot. Came from somewhere else in the house. Shit, he hoped Vicky hadn't...

No.

Don't even think about it.

It stalled Sixsmith's swing, shifted his attention to the door. He twisted his lips, then gave a casual shrug and stepped forward.

Fenchurch shut his eyes, bracing himself.

The metallic whoosh of the guitar cut through the air, striking Fenchurch's nose.

Blood sprayed almost as fast as the pain.

His face felt like it'd been dowsed in acid.

Sixsmith swung again, hitting Fenchurch's outstretched arm with a wet thud.

Pain shot through him like a lightning bolt, clawing up his arm, through his chest, up to his skull.

Fenchurch gritted his teeth to stifle a cry, but it burst out anyway.

The impact sent shockwaves of agony radiating from the point of impact. His arm went numb, like it had fallen off.

Fenchurch staggered backward, clutching his injured arm as searing pain coursed through him. He crashed against the wall, then toppled onto the floor and landed on his knees. His vision blurred with the sheer intensity of the pain.

'Might need to restring this.' Sixsmith was inspecting the end of the guitar. 'Hurts, doesn't it?'

'Fuck off.'

'I wish I could savour this moment, but I've really got to be quick.' Sixsmith thumbed behind him. 'Yevgeny's probably found your friend.'

'I don't have any accomplices.'

'Bullshit. A female cop. Lion found her.'

'Ask yourself where he is.'

'I'm guessing that shot was her death.' Sixsmith hefted the guitar above his head, like Adrian Thornhill in the one Rusty Rivers and the Reeds concert Fenchurch had been to. 'Guessing you're a par five, after all.' He swung the guitar back behind his shoulder.

A gun pressed into his neck from behind. 'Drop it.'

The guitar bounced as it hit the floor.

'Move.' Vicky pushed him against the wall. 'On your knees.' She braced the gun in both hands like she was on a TV show. 'Now!'

'Please.' Sixsmith raised his hands, then went down on both knees, facing the wall. 'This isn't what it looks like.'

'No? Because I see my friend covered in blood and you holding a guitar covered in his blood.'

'Let me go.'

'Is that what you heard from Jasmine?'

'Who are you talking about?'

Vicky cracked him on the back of the head with the gun and he tumbled forward. 'You know who I'm talking about.'

Fenchurch got to his feet and grabbed the guitar with both hands. He placed it under Sixsmith's chin, then rested his new knee against the back of his skull. He pulled the club back, digging the neck into his throat. 'How do you like this? Eh? Gibson make some pretty strong guitars, don't they?'

'Please! Let me go!' Sixsmith's voice was a gurgle. 'I can pay you!'

'It always comes down to money with you fuckers. You took my daughter. Kidnapped her off the street. I missed the best part of her life growing up. I lost *myself*. I lost my wife. And you've taken so many others too. People suffer because of your selfish greed.'

'Please. Let me go. I'll—' Gurgle. '—make you rich!'

'No.' Fenchurch hauled the fretboard back against his throat. Tempting to just end him right there. 'Your only hope here is you tell me the truth. And that our backup arrives in time. Otherwise I'm going to fucking kill you.' He slackened off the grip.

Sixsmith moaned and gurgled. 'I was involved. I...'

'I know you were involved. How did you start?'

'It's not easy. You just get roped in to something. It started out so innocently. And before you know it, they know every-thing about you. *Everything*. Absolutely everything.'

'You're in charge, though. You could just stop it, couldn't you?'

'I inherited this position.'

Fenchurch tugged hard against this throat. 'Someone I worked with who got involved talked about being coerced into it. Same as you. But the thing is, there's nobody left to coerce you. It's just you. A man who likes abducting kids. Sorry, that's wrong. You buy them from street dealers and pimps. Means you think you're one step removed, but it's just the same, isn't it? It doesn't change your guilt, does it? And you can say you were coerced into it, but you keep doing it to people. Don't you?'

'You don't understand.'

'No. I don't. And there'd be something wrong with me if I did. Because understanding why you fuck children would mean I'd be inside your head. And that's a fucking cesspit.'

'I know the men who took your kid. They're all dead. All of them. Two died in prison.'

'Just supposed to take your word for it?'

'Please....' Sixsmith gasped. 'This conviction won't stick.'

'No. You're probably right.' Fenchurch let him go and hefted the guitar in both hands. Like when he used to play, before all of this shit he'd been through. When he'd been normal. When he had a future. He wielded the guitar behind his head.

The dim light flickered blue, casting eerie shadows across Sixsmith.

Fenchurch swung the guitar and drove it into Sixsmith's ribs with an unmusical clang.

Sixsmith screamed out.

The crunch sickened Fenchurch. His hands stung with the reverberation. He swung again. Again and again, each blow resonating as it connected. His breaths came quick and ragged.

With each impact, Sixsmith's form crumpled further, his face contorted in agony. Three of the strings had snapped, dangling free. His jumper had turned scarlet. Blood spread all over the floor, his handprints like those of a child's painting at nursery.

Fenchurch's heart beat in time with his strikes, playing out of tune and out of key. Each one blow pulled him closer to justice.

'Stop.' Vicky grabbed his arm. 'Don't kill him. Please. You don't want to do that.'

The room fell into silence, broken only by the harsh sound of Fenchurch's laboured breaths and the dying sounds of the broken guitar. 'I do. Trust me, I really fucking do.'

'Simon. You don't. Stop it.'

Fenchurch pressed his shoe onto the throat of the gurgling mess at his feet, then swung the guitar back. 'He's behind what happened to my family all those years ago.'

'I know. But he'll face justice. He has no power left to go after anyone's kids, least of all yours. Leave him like that.'

Fenchurch clenched the guitar like a club, his hands still resonating from the repeated brutal acts. 'I should kill him, Vicky. I'll go to jail for this, so why not just go through with it.'

Blue lights flashed outside.

Vicky peered past Fenchurch. 'Backup's here.'

'Shit.' Fenchurch swung the guitar back again. 'Better do this now.'

Vicky pointed the gun at him. 'Stop.'

'Vicky. Please.'

'No. You're not a killer.'

'What about Fields?'

'You told me that was unavoidable. You even jumped into a minging river to try to save him.'

'A canal.'

'Same difference.' Vicky pulled her finger away from the trigger. 'I'm going to help you explain this, but we're doing it by the book. We'll spend the next week explaining what we did and why, but saving a young girl justifies a whole pile of colouring outside the lines. Sometimes, the ends do justify the means. Avonmore and Sixsmith will go down for a conspiracy to commit human trafficking. Both Kordov and Lion have illegal firearms. They all go down.'

Fenchurch stared at her with the frenzy of a killer. 'Why are you doing this?'

'I'm paying this forward, Simon. Someone else helped me a while back. Don't go to jail for these people. Just don't. That's how they win.' Vicky handcuffed Sixsmith's left wrist, then secured him to the immovable bedpost. She held out a hand. 'Come on.'

Fenchurch took it and felt like a child. He dropped the guitar with a tuneless crash, then followed her out into the corridor. His body was a confusion of pain. Felt like his jaw was broken. And his arm…

They turned the corner and two men lay there, one struggling to move, the other completely out of it.

'What did you do?'

'What I had to.' Vicky stopped outside another door. 'Can you hear that?'

Sounded like whimpering.

Fenchurch eased the door open. The same room he'd been taken to earlier – Don Avonmore lay on the bed. Rusty Rivers, breathing his last, judging by the chaos on the machine next to him.

Jasmine was cowering on the floor. The source of the whimpering.

Fenchurch kept his distance. 'It's okay.'

But the sight of Fenchurch must've been something to behold, because she pushed back against the wall, twisting her head to one side, then the other. Like she was eight or nine.

A sharp elbow nudged him out of the way, then he was pushed backwards.

'I'm Vicky.' She crouched low and reached out a hand. 'I'm a cop. My friend here is too. We've sorted out the men who did this to you. We're going to take you away from this, okay?'

Jasmine looked at her through suspicious eyes, head turned to the side.

'Jasmine, we know what's happened to you. Okay? We're going to keep you safe.'

Jasmine shook her head.

'It's okay. The men who are doing this to you are gone. Trust me.' Vicky held out a hand. 'Okay?'

'Okay.' Jasmine finally reached out to meet her hand and let

Vicky help her to her feet. She looked much younger than thirteen.

Fenchurch pointed at Avonmore. 'Do you know him?'

Jasmine nodded.

'Did he do something to you?'

She nodded again.

'Okay.' Vicky rested her hands on her hips. 'There are police officers outside. We'll get you to them, okay? Then men like him can never do this to you again. Okay?'

'Okay.' Jasmine took one last look at Avonmore. 'He said he killed Kanyif.'

'That's not true.'

'Kanyif's alive?'

Fenchurch kept her gaze. 'I'm afraid not. But Kanyif was doing everything he could to help you.'

Jasmine stared back at him through teary eyes. 'Okay.'

Vicky leaned into Fenchurch. 'I need to inform the army of cops what happened before they end up on the wrong end of this. You stay here.'

'Sure.'

Vicky led her out of the room. 'Come on, let's get you somewhere safe.'

Leaving Fenchurch alone with a child abuser. 'You need to be in hospital, Don. You're dying.'

Avonmore looked up at him. 'Please. Help me.'

'I mean, I can delay medical help getting here. Put you in the same grave as your friends.'

'Please! Kill me!'

47

Fenchurch parked his car behind a big work van. His engine's low growl faded into the silence of the tree-lined street. Leafy but not particularly nice.

Last time Fenchurch had been in Inverness, he'd arrested an amateur boxer for supplying steroids to an East End gym. Long way to run. Best part of twenty years ago, with him as a fresh-faced DC on the way up.

Before all of that shit happened.

The house's brick façade bore the scars of the years gone by in each crack. Bay windows protruded out, but didn't quite match the brickwork. The garden lay dormant, its flower boxes relics of summer. A low fence wrapped around the property, guarding it from the street. Behind those curtains, a life unfolded.

Fenchurch got out of the car. The night was still, save for the distant hum of city life. The cold air bit through his coat and he felt every inch of the five hundred odd miles from home. He passed the car, opened the gate and walked up the path. Did his best police officer knock.

Music played inside, some smooth soul or something.

The door clicked open and Cargill peered out. 'Simon. I didn't expect you to come here.'

'No, well, you shouldn't have sent me this address.'

'I'd rather do this tomorrow.'

'And I'd rather do it now. You flew up, then?'

'Managed to catch the last flight to Inverness, aye.' She thumbed behind her. 'This is my wife's sister's place. Would rather not do this here, but seeing as how you're here... You're not coming in.' She disappeared inside, then came back out with a padded jacket. 'How are you doing?'

'Really?' Fenchurch let out a breath, misting in the air. 'Getting too old for this crap.'

She scowled at him. 'How old are you?'

'You know how old I am.'

'Forty-eight, right?'

'Right.'

'Same age as me.' She gave a wistful smile. 'First, there are a few things to cover off. DI Nelson in the City Police dug into some of the paperwork related to them buying that home from James McNab. He's entirely innocent, but they were trying to frame him. Howard Savage spoke to him this evening. He said he'd heard all the rumours about Rivers and Thornhill. Even came forward, but he couldn't get anyone to go on the record, so he had to settle for the tried and trusted technique of persuading people to keep a distance. And he heard about what happened to Kylie Lochalsh. Told people. Again, nobody did anything. He tried, but it fell on deaf ears.'

Fenchurch swallowed hard. 'The Machine?'

'The Machine.' She fixed him with a hard stare. 'Have you got closure now?'

Fenchurch looked away, then back at her. He could still hear the clanging of the Les Paul. 'I think I have.' He shook his head. 'Thing I keep going back to is Fields. Hard to accept that... he was working with child molesters to... People like Sixsmith.

There are so many things he covered up. So many people who didn't get justice for their own traumas.'

'Just be glad he's dead, Simon... He'd only be in prison with them now.' She clamped a hand on his shoulder, smiling wide. 'Listen, I like the results but your methods leave a lot to be desired. Especially as they were borderline criminal.'

He raised his eyebrows. 'That's charming.'

'That's policing, Simon. I could poke around in this and I'm very confident I'd be able to pull at some of the threads from this case and open a massive can of worms. Not just with you but with your Scottish girlfriend too.'

'My girlfriend?'

'DI Vicky Dodds. I know her reputation. Thing is, Simon, it's not just you here. There are a lot of connected careers here. It'd harm a few people. Now, if you could take the transfer to Essex, then we could call the whole thing a draw…'

EPILOGUE
TWO WEEKS LATER

The cold wind whispered through the skeletal branches of ancient oaks lining the perimeter of Tower Hamlets Cemetery Park.

Fenchurch stood there, in his brand new police uniform, the fabric clinging to his form, cooled by the chill of the day. Bright blue skies, without a single cloud.

Dad would've loved that.

Chloe stood beside him with stoic resolve, her young face shadowed by the weight of the occasion. His own daughter, so long an unanswered question, but now a constable in her own right. And a permanent fixture in his life and career.

Through his stifled tears, he recognised a few friendly faces. Tammy, in floods of tears.

Michelle Grove, staring into space – even though she'd been cleared of any wrongdoing in the murder of Kanyif Iqbal, the fact it was her bullet still hit hard.

A rumpled collection of old men, in various stages of health, balance and grief – some stoic, some a tearful mess, others not sure where they were, or why.

Kay Reed. Howard Savage. Julian Loftus. The bulbous mass

of Jason Bell, now reduced to a fraction of his previous weight.

And Vicky Dodds, in her own uniform, giving him a tight nod.

No Cargill.

Typical.

On the other side of the crowd of mourners, Abi stood resolute. Her eyes glistened with unshed tears and met Fenchurch's. A silent understanding passed between them. Al clung to her side, tall for his age – Dad would've joked about it being from Fenchurch blood flowing through his veins.

At the side lay the final resting place of Ian Fenchurch. His father, his mentor, the old rogue with a heart of gold. The headstone was worn by time, bearing Mum's name and now his, in fresh etching. The dates marked their full journeys through life.

The mourners gathered around, their heads bowed in a collective moment of reflection. As the ceremony had unfolded inside, the words washed over Fenchurch in a cold, unrelenting wave, like being back in the canal again. The eulogies had told of a life well-lived, of a man who had worn the badge of honour, just as he did now.

Fenchurch regretted his eulogy already. As much as he'd practised it, what came out... An outburst, maybe, but his father had been taken too soon.

The hard fact was it was mostly by Dad's own failure to call it quits when the band was no longer playing his tune. There was a time for everything, and Dad's time as a police officer had passed long before his interest in being one had evaporated.

A common feeling among the Fenchurch men. Perhaps height wasn't the only genetic trait. Or they were just raised that way.

The scent of damp earth and fallen leaves mingled with the metallic tang of his uniform. Even in death, life's relentless march continued.

As the mourners spread apart, Fenchurch couldn't help but

feel the weight of his father's absence, the emptiness of a world forever changed.

For the first time in his life, Fenchurch was apart from the old rascal. He'd been born to him, been raised by him, been helped through his career by him.

And now...

Now he was gone.

Seventy-three was no age. Not nowadays.

Fenchurch looked up and Abi had already left.

Another part of his life was ending.

Howard Savage waved at Fenchurch, then walked off, head bowed.

'Guv.' Jon Nelson appeared, his suit a few shades lighter than his skin.

Holding hands with DS Lisa Bridge. 'Sir.'

'Jon. Lisa. Thanks for coming.'

'Your old man was a lovely guy.' Nelson gave him a kind smile. 'He didn't deserve that.'

'I know. It's... Such a futile death.' Fenchurch smiled at Nelson. 'How are you doing in the City?'

'Well. I thought my career was over, but thanks to you, I've got the opportunity to restart. Turns out I'm decent at it too. We've got our work cut out with that stuff you passed to us.'

'You're a good guy, Jon.' Fenchurch smiled at Bridge. 'You've got a good man there.'

'I know.' She smiled, then her gaze darted to the side. She tugged at Nelson's hand and they walked off.

Fenchurch thought he saw her absently pat her belly. Well, well.

'Simon.' Superintendent Julian Loftus replaced them. Full uniform, cap in hand, the sun bouncing off his shining head. 'I'm truly sorry for your loss.'

'Thank you, sir. It's...' Fenchurch tasted that bitter regret. 'I... I don't know what to say.'

Loftus screwed up his face. 'Was it truly the Machine?'

'What was left of them. And now there's nothing. They're gone, sir.'

'Good, well.' Loftus shook his head. 'How are you bearing up?'

'Well, I've got some closure on what happened here, but... losing Dad... it's made me focus. All through my ordeal, it's hope that kept me going. Through what happened with Chloe.' Fenchurch looked over and saw her chatting to Reed and Bridge. 'And after all that, I just hope I can make a difference before my time runs out. Just like Dad did.'

'I gather pastures new beckon?'

'That's right.'

'And you've got some irons in the fire?'

'I'm not a detective anymore, sir. I'm leaving for a new life in Leigh-on-Sea, yeah. Station commander. I'll see my boy on alternative weekends and I'll work out the financial details with my wife. But it'll be a chance for me to get involved in a community. A new start. Neighbourly disputes. Some drugs. An assault or two. Small crimes, but crimes that make a difference to people when you solve them. And crimes you can actually solve.'

'Sounds like bliss.' Loftus nodded slowly. 'I've been handed a new assignment. One I can't discuss as it's rather...'

'Murky?'

'Yes, quite. Thing is, Simon, I may need someone with your skill to navigate the turbid waters ahead. Obviously you're a bit of devil yourself but you've worked well with me over the years. While you did your bull in a china shop impression, I was the steadying hand on the tiller.'

'I'm not sure, sir.'

'No. No, I get it. But you go out to Essex, live this new life. Just remember that I may have need to call on you for matters of national importance.'

AFTERWORD

Well, that's that.

Huge thanks to James Mackay for the development editing, to John Rickards for the copy editing and Julia Gibbs for proofing. And to Fiona Cummins for listening to me talk about this book over fish and chips – I had a little cry when I realised I wanted Fenchurch to have a happy ending. Or as happy as I could make it.

Fenchurch was the first project I started working on as a full-time writer almost literally ten years ago, at the time you're mostly likely reading this. 4th January 2014. I sat down for a week between contracts to see if I could write full-time or if I would just bugger about on the internet all day. While I'm not entirely innocent of the latter, forty books in ten years shows I can and do get the work done. And I won't dwell on the fact that those early cuts of the outline featured Fenchurch investigating a Jack the Ripper copycat who happened to be a vampire... So Fenchurch marks both the beginning and end of my first decade as professional writer. Bizarre to meet that milestone, despite my health travails over the last few years.

London is a city that's close to my heart. I worked in the City for a few years, staying in Fenchurch's patch and getting to know the various locations I've written about in these ten novels. Having been involved with publishing for the ten years since I have become completely unemployable, it's impossible to not spend a lot of time in the city every year and so my fondness has only grown. At some point, I'll have to return to writing about London, won't I?

And so, this is the last book for old Fenchy, at least for now. Fenchurch has been my most successful series, at least until the Marshall books, and as much as I've had fun tormenting the old sod, I feel like he can't go through much more. And I honestly get a feeling of dread about having to put him through that again – and myself. So it's time for him to have that well-earned time in the pasture, chewing slowly on the grass and watching the trains pass in the distance, safe in the knowledge I could come back at any time and make his life an absolute misery all over again. Or I could just leave him solving silly (and not so silly) crimes in Leigh-on-Sea.

If you want to dig a big deeper into some of the relationships in this book, there are five Vicky Dodds books set in Dundee and Tayside, including a guest appearance from a certain sparrow-eating cockney DCI in the fifth, and DS Olivia Blackman co-stars in Lost Cause, a standalone psychological thriller I released in 2022. And my recent focus has been on the DI Rob Marshall books, with four novels published this year (and a prequel novella late last) with another three to come in 2024 – I hope you enjoy them.

Please let me know how you get on with this, either by posting a review on Amazon or by emailing ed@edjames.co.uk – I try to reply to every single one (even those that complain about swearing and blasphemy but don't seem to mind murder, rape or child abuse).

Anyway, thanks for reading these books – it really means a lot and I hope you keep reading my work.

Ed James
The Scottish Borders, November 2023

ABOUT THE AUTHOR

Ed James is a Scottish author who writes crime fiction novels across multiple series and in multiple locations.

His latest series is set in the Scottish Borders, where Ed now lives, starring **DI Rob Marshall** – a criminal profiler turned detective, investigating serial murders in a beautiful landscape.

Set four hundred miles south on the gritty streets of East London, his bestselling **DI Fenchurch** series features a cop with little to lose and a kidnapped daughter to find..

His **Police Scotland** books are fronted by multiple detectives based in Edinburgh, including **Scott Cullen**, a young Edinburgh Detective investigating crimes from the bottom rung of the career ladder he's desperate to climb, and **Craig Hunter**, a detective shoved back into uniform who struggles to overcome his PTSD from his time in the army.

Putting Dundee on the tartan noir map, the **DS Vicky Dodds** books feature a driven female detective struggling to combine her complex home life with a heavy caseload.

Formerly an IT project manager, Ed filled his weekly commute to London by writing on planes, trains and automobiles. He now writes full-time and lives in the Scottish Borders with a menagerie of rescued animals.

Connect with Ed online:
Amazon Author page
Website

ED JAMES READERS CLUB

Available now for members of my Readers Club is FALSE START, a prequel ebook to my first new series in six years.

Sign up for FREE and get access to exclusive content and keep up-to-speed with all of my releases on a monthly basis.
https://geni.us/EJM1FS

Printed in Great Britain
by Amazon